Freeuse to Forever After

An Age Gap Erotic Romance Series

Freeuse Halloween
Freeuse Thanksgiving
Freeuse Christmas
Freeuse Valentine
Freeuse St. Patrick's

April Cross
&
Matt Lake

TWISTED ROSE
+PUBLISHING+

Contents

PREFACE

This story is dual point of view with April Cross writing Willow and Matt Lake writing Mike.

Enjoy the experience of two distinct voices telling the story while both authors bring their own writing style and creativity to give the characters life.

Freeuse Halloween

Freeuse to Forever After Book 1

April Cross | Matt Lake

CHAPTER 1

MIKE

I pick up the cape from the bed and clip it around my neck with the gold chain. Looking in the mirror, I smile at how good my costume looks on me. Even the little flash of gray in my hair fits in with my vampire outfit. The gray matches my eyes; at my age, everything seems to be turning gray.

I had considered going for something more modern; a Freddy, or a Jason—something like that. But at heart I'm more old-fashioned, and a vampire says 'classic and stylish' to me.

Checking my watch, I see I still have an hour until the start of the party. More than enough time to finish up and drive over there. Cherry's Halloween party is always the highlight of the year, not just because of the amazing costumes and the great atmosphere, but also because it's a freeuse sex party.

Everyone invited to it has a choice. If they want to be used in any way, they wear a green ribbon tied to their wrist. If they want to be used but not have anal, they wear a red ribbon. This lets the other guests know they're available for any sexual encounter. No ribbon? Then they are the ones that are going to be watching or doing the using. I'm very much in the "doing the using" category.

For the last three years, I've been going to these parties, and I've had a fantastic time at each of them. There always seem to be at least a few women who go for my brand of domming, and a few times, it's led to more adventures after the event. It's exhilarating to find someone that gets off on being used just as much as I crave being in control. The parties are a safe and easy way to find like-minded people.

I'm single now; it's been about ten years since my wife died. We married in our late teens and were together for twenty years before she passed away suddenly from a heart condition. We had a good life together. Neither of us wanted children and instead, we concentrated on having fun together. And we had plenty of that before I lost her.

She had always said that I should find someone else if something happened to her, but by then I had been out of the dating scene for so long that it no longer felt like a thing I wanted to do. People my age were mostly married, and no younger person would want to settle down with someone as old as me, so I decided that staying single was the way to go.

I made peace with the fact that my wife was the one love of my life. I won't be getting married again, and it's just as unlikely that I'll ever have a long-term relationship. I'm more than happy to fool around and have sex. And I think my wife would have approved of that. When we were married, we would go to swingers' clubs or pick up a third for a threesome, and my wife used to love watching me use a pretty young thing. I have to admit, I also enjoyed seeing her with other women, so it worked out for both of us. Who knows, maybe she's up there looking down at me when I'm at the parties, happy that I'm still getting some.

I grab some packets of lube and a few condoms and head out of the house. They usually have stuff at the party, but like consent, it's always best to make sure. In the past, Cherry has gotten excited about the party and forgotten little things. And when I say excited, I mean horny as she fucked some lucky guy, forgetting her party planner duties. At least this year, she said she's hired helpers to make things run smoother.

As soon as I'm outside, I hear someone say my name, and look toward the voice. I see Nancy, my next-door neighbor, getting out of her car. She has this cute/awkward vibe going on and I smile as I notice she has her jacket caught in the car door. She lets out a little yelp as she tries to turn, and the jacket pulls her back. Somehow, she manages to get tangled up in her clothing and can't seem to work out how to get unstuck.

We've been joking and toying with each other since she moved in a year ago, but I know it'll never go anywhere. With the age gap between us, it's unlikely to work out. Even as a casual thing, I don't want to risk us breaking up and having awkward conversations as we pass each other. So we just keep on flirting and making each other a little breathless. I have jerked off a few nights thinking about her, imagining her under me and moaning as I growl into her ear that I'm going to use her. I wonder if she's done the same.

So clumsy, I think as I watch her struggle, but somehow it makes her even more adorable.

I jog over and assist her, opening the door and helping her pull free. We end up pressed up close to each other and I get a smell of her perfume, something flowery and light. My eyes close for a second as I breathe it in and I can feel my cock hardening at her nearness.

"Thank you kindly," she laughs and gives me a soft kiss on my cheek before stepping back.

"Always a gentleman, not always a gentle man," I joke, giving her an exaggerated wink.

We stand there for a moment, looking at each other, and then I remember where I'm going.

She flashes me a smile and as I walk over to my car; she's definitely checking me out. "Looking good, Mike. You make one sexy vampire."

"You're looking pretty good yourself," I reply, and I mean it. She's in her mid twenties, fit and beautiful in a classic blonde way.

"Don't scare any virgins," she says sternly and starts walking to her house, but she looks back over her shoulder and gives me a little wave and smile.

"Who, innocent old me? As if."

I watch her ass swaying in her tight jeans, then shake my head and focus. Such a shame it wouldn't work out. She would make a lovely sub to play with.

I smile as I get in my car and think to myself that anyone I hook up with tonight has little chance of being a virgin.

Chapter 2

WILLOW

I stare at the two Halloween costume choices laid out on my bed and huff at my best friend, Alice, on the phone.

"If this party is a freeuse party and I'm going to fuck a bunch of guys, why do I even need a costume?"

Alice's soft laugh doesn't help my anxiety, and the butterflies in my stomach swirl faster. Am I overthinking this?

She replies, "Because it's festive. Just pick one. What're your choices?"

I study the options. "Sexy black cat or a sexy policewoman. You were right. All the other costumes were either too weird or out of my price range."

This is what I get for last-minute online shopping. It was slim pickings to get a costume delivered before today. My hands tremble from nervousness and I fight the urge to call off going to the party. This is a horrible idea.

Alice urges me, "Willow, just pick one!"

Grabbing the cop outfit, I sigh. "I think the cop. I'll look like a desperate, horny woman in uniform. That'll tempt people to fuck me."

She snorts. "It's called freeuse. You don't need to tempt them."

She has a good point. My nervousness eases a little and my core tightens with lust as I daydream about how it'll feel to have a cock sliding inside me. How many men are going to fuck me tonight? I stare critically at the tight blue shorts with the fake belt. Why didn't I choose a costume with easy access? Someone'll have to pull my shorts down to fuck me.

I swallow, my throat suddenly dry. I glance at the mirror hanging on the back of my closet and try to imagine what the guys at the party will think when they see me. I'm attractive—I know I am, but I also know looks aren't everything. I've got a list of issues a mile long, and five months of therapy have barely scratched the surface. No one is going to want to date me – not that I'm looking for a relationship – but I think I'm fuckable... or at least, I hope so.

Shit, why did I decide to do this? Oh yeah, I know exactly why I'm doing this. Today is my 25th birthday and I'm a virgin. I feel like the freak of all my friends and I continually lie to them about my sex life. Who in the hell is still a virgin at 25?

I was dating Oliver-the-Asshole for seven years, and no one would believe we didn't have actual P-in-V sex. Sure, lots of oral sex, but Oliver had a problem...specifically, a premature ejaculation problem. Whenever his cock touched my pussy, he instantly came. I tried to kindly suggest that maybe he should talk to a doctor, but he shut the door on those conversations quickly.

But I was blinded by love, and it's not like I was going to toss him out of my life for his problem. He tried to satisfy me in other ways, even though that never worked either. It got to where it seemed as if he was trying to win by making me orgasm, and the pressure made it even less enjoyable for me. It was pleasurable, but since he couldn't just accept that I liked sex for the connection, I learned how to fake an orgasm. I just don't understand what the big deal is about sex.

It's been six months since Oliver-the-Asswipe left me, and it's time to become a super slut so that someday I don't look back and regret my 20s. What better way to do it than at a freeuse party?

Alice whines again. "Willow! We both need to leave to make it there in time before the trick-or-treaters swarm the streets."

I sigh because she's right. I'd feel better if we were going together. But since we're using a ride-sharing app and live across town from each other, we're meeting up at the party. My phone alerts me that the driver is close. Eep! I better get a move on.

I grab my costume off the bed. "Okay, Alice. See you at the party. I'll be the sexy cop wearing the tiniest pair of shorts known to man."

She laughs. "Oh, trust me, the shorts will come right off once you get in the house. Now go, go, go! See you soon!"

She hangs up and I shimmy into my ass-hugging shorts over a pair of sexy red panties. The shorts are so tiny, they show off my butt cheeks. But they're stretchy, and my ass is one of my best features. I quickly toss on the fake uniform top. It makes my tits look fabulous, though you can see a bit of the red lace of my bra. It only adds to my slutty vibe. Once I get the fake belt on, I look surprisingly cute. I just hope no one expects me to act like I'm in charge tonight.

With only seconds to spare, I twist my long brown hair into a severe topknot—I'm a no-nonsense cop, after all—and slip on black combat boots. My phone pings that the car is right outside my apartment, and I hurry out the door as I shove my phone in a small clutch purse.

When I climb into the backseat, the driver smiles politely and pretends he doesn't notice my bare legs. Shit, these shorts are so tight, I probably have a camel toe. My stomach flutters from a mix of apprehension and excitement as the driver makes a few attempts at small talk. When I'm not chatty back, he falls silent.

Can I really do this? A low hum of desire makes me squirm in the seat. Even though my mind is thinking I'm crazy, my pussy is ready to board the slut bus and buy the t-shirt. I've been wet for days thinking just about the party. Who gives themselves up for anyone to use for their first time?

I mean, it's not like I haven't had fingers up there, but the real problem is that I can't orgasm. Oliver-the-Douche tried, and nothing happened other than a few pleasant moments. I thought maybe it was him, but even when I was alone, I always ended up thinking about my to-do list, or my college assignments. I read online that some women just can't, and eventually I gave up trying.

That's why tonight is perfect. The goal isn't to orgasm – hell, are the guys even going to try to make the women orgasm? I can lose my virginity without overthinking everything, and without the expectation that it's going to be mind-blowing. Plus, I'd really like to know what an actual cock feels like.

If my parents weren't such assholes, I could have talked to my mom about this. They had me late in life and they never wanted a child. I was an accident when my mom was 41. Whenever I did something wrong as a kid, my mom would grumble and say she should have made other choices before I was born. My therapist and I are still unpacking that.

So yeah...my childhood was fucked up. It's probably why I stayed with Oliver-the-Asshat for way too long. He's the first person who loved me. Or I thought he did, until he cheated on me and was able to have sex with another woman. He then blamed me for his years of sexual dysfunction. I doubt my magical pussy made him come so quickly, but I guess if a bunch of guys lose it before fucking me tonight, I'll know if I have a mystical vag. Talk about a superpower no one wants. I can't orgasm AND no guy can fuck me.

I snort, and the driver gives me a questioning look in the rearview mirror. I smile sweetly at him before peering out the window at the passing houses—or rather, mansions. Shit, this neighborhood is swanky. It makes my studio apartment in a shady part of town seem like a real dump, but it's all I can afford right now. I'm not exactly making the big bucks at my job as a barista, and I try not to dwell on the social services degree I'm not using—or the student loan that came with it.

When we pull up at the address, the street is crowded with cars. A rush of adrenaline makes me almost giddy. I hope Alice is already here. She's the only person I'll know tonight. I need moral support, or my mind might win the battle against my pussy and make me run away.

Even as I have that thought, I know it isn't true. I've been working up to this day for weeks and nothing will stop me from my ultimate plan to be a complete slut for my 25th birthday. The fact that people are going to use me is why I'm here. I don't want to think or make any decisions. I want someone to just bend me over and take me.

The driver tells me the cost of the fare, and I pay on my phone before getting out. The smell of wood smoke coming from a nearby fireplace greets me, and the sounds of laughter in the distance helps to remind me that tonight is all about good times and pleasure.

Halloween is my favorite holiday. People get to dress up in crazy costumes and eat tons of candy. It sucked as a birthday because everyone usually had plans, but it's not like I had friends anyway. Alice has been my only friend since elementary school.

My phone beeps with a message.

Alice

> Hey, so my ride got in a fender bender and I'm going to be late. Everyone is fine, but I can't leave yet.

Don't go too crazy without me, but if you're busy when I get there, I won't bug you. See you soon!

Oh fuck. I quickly text back.

Willow

Thanks bitch. I mean, see you soon!

Oh god, can I do this alone? I only hesitate for a moment. Well, it's not like I planned to stick close to her while fucking other people. That would just be weird. We made an agreement to ditch each other as soon as we checked in.

Yep, I can do this. I square my shoulders, stand as tall as my 5 foot 3 inch frame allows, and strut towards the front door. Time to put out and take some cock.

It's showtime.

CHAPTER 3

MIKE

When I get to the party, things are already in full swing. After signing in and flirting with the hottie named Bianca at the reception area, I head inside. After my encounter with my neighbor, Nancy, my cock's decided it's very much time for me to find someone to play with. I quickly find one of my favorites, a woman named Lita that I met at the party last year. We had used one of the private rooms upstairs, and after edging her for an hour, she begged me to fuck her. Eventually, I gave her exactly what she wanted. I hoped she would be here.

Tonight, she's wearing a cute French maid outfit that's all lacy and revealing, but more importantly, she has a green ribbon on her wrist. I make my way across the room and hope that no one gets to her before me. I have to admit, I'm not much of a sharer. If I'm with someone, then I want all their attention on me, or at least, to be the center of their focus. I think it's the Dom inside me, wanting to take control and be the only one in charge.

Thankfully, she's still on her own when I reach her.

"Oh, I thought you might be here," she says, leaning forward so that I get an eyeful of her cleavage, tightly wrapped up in her dress.

"And I was hoping to make you moan for me again. I seem to remember you were quite loud last time."

She almost blushes. People told us afterwards that she was shouting so loud when she came that they could hear her in the next room. I'm rather proud that it was my name she was calling out.

"Shall we get one of the bedrooms?" she asks.

I lean in so that my lips are right next to her ear. "This time it's going to be out in the open. I want everyone to see what a good little slut you can be. And for them to see what I do to you."

"Oh, are you going to bite me and drink my blood?" she playfully gasps as I take her hand and lead her out of the crowded room.

People are already fucking, and others are standing around watching. I want to go out to the corridor where it's less crowded, but we can still be seen.

"I think you know exactly what I'm going to do," I growl.

"I really was hoping you would be here tonight. You were rough and commanding and knew I could take it. A lot of the guys here are sweet, but think I'm made of china. You know you can have your way with me and I won't break. My boundaries haven't changed."

She's right. I like my sex rough. Last time, we talked about limits, so I already know what she's up for. Just because someone consents to you using them, it doesn't mean you shouldn't check that your idea of rough is the same as what they're thinking. Luckily, Lita and I are very compatible in that regard.

I grab her and flip her to face the wall, my leg slipping between hers and making her spread them. Holding her skirt, I pull it up and see that she's not wearing anything underneath. All the easier for me. I give her ass a sharp spank, getting a yelp of happiness in reply.

"Oh, fuck yes. Do it again. Leave a mark."

I slap her once more, this time hard enough to leave a hand-shaped red mark on her skin.

"Ask for it," I say, my mouth next to her ear as I push her back to the wall. The moan that escapes her lips seems to send a tremor through her body.

"Please fuck me like the naughty slut I am. Hard and deep."

I pull the zipper down on my pants and take out my cock, pausing for a moment to slip a condom on. Rubbing my cock against her pussy, I get another moan from her. It would be fun to tease her a little more, but I really want to be inside her. So instead, I slide my cock up and down her wet folds and then push deep into her.

"Oh FUCK!" she moans out loud, drawing a look from a zombie girl walking past. The zombie smiles at us and gives us a little clap before walking away. She's cute, and wearing a green ribbon. I might have to look for her later. I wonder if Lita is into women? Now is not the time to ask.

I thrust in and out of her, and she pushes back onto me with equal force as she spreads her arms out on the wall. I have no intention of coming with her; this is just a warmup. But I do intend to make her orgasm so hard that when she goes home later, it will be me she's thinking about when she's touching herself and reminiscing about the party.

Grabbing her hips, I hammer into her, harder and faster, almost lifting her off the ground with the force. I slow down, drawing it out, teasing her with the change of speed, keeping her needy.

She looks back over her shoulder at me, panting hard. "Can I turn around? I want to see you as you fuck me."

I slide out of her and stroke my cock as she turns, and push her back to the wall. Lifting her leg, I sink back into her pussy, filling her up. I need this as much as she does. I need to feel someone under my control and gasping at my touch.

Down the corridor I hear a door opening. No doubt another guest checking in.

Lita's eyes roll into the back of her head and her body starts to shake again. Wrapping my hands around her, I lift her up and fuck her hard, pounding into her as she's pinned to the wall.

With a howl, she comes, but something distracts me.

From down the corridor, I hear a gasp and I look over.

Standing in the archway down near reception is a woman dressed as a cop. She looks like she is in her early 20s and she has that wide-eyed innocent look that drives me wild. Her uniform is tight across her chest and her shorts look like they're one size too small. Even from here, I can see she's biting her lip like she's nervous. She's utterly gorgeous and I know that before the end of the night, I must have her.

CHAPTER 4

WILLOW

Once I get closer to the front door, my confidence vanishes, and I almost turn and run. The massive three-story, white wood and stone mansion seems ominous, but the sounds of laughter and talking from inside soothe me. There's a sign hanging over the doorbell that says 'Cum Inside for Pleasure,' and I snicker.

The entryway is huge, and there's a woman seated at a card table. Behind her is a wall of storage lockers. This is odd.

She gives me a wide smile. "Hi, I'm Bianca! Are you joining us for our freeuse Halloween party? Can I get your name?"

The guest list is why I felt safe coming to this party. Supposedly everyone has been vetted, and it's invite only, so you have to know someone else here or the hostess. I tell her my name and she scans the list.

"Right...Willow...it says here you want to be a freeuse guest. Is that still your choice?"

I can feel my face flush and I almost trip over my words. "Y—yes."

She gestures towards two baskets on the table. One has red ribbons and the other has green ribbons. "Which do you want—green or red? The green ribbon means anything goes. The red ribbon is if you don't want anal. I'll tie the ribbon to your wrist so it's clearly visible."

I nearly choke. Oh fuck, anal? I didn't even consider that. Why didn't Alice warn me? My entire body lights up as I imagine having all three of my holes filled at once, and then shake my head to clear it.

"Red, please."

She smiles softly as she affixes the ribbon around my wrist. I stare down at it, suddenly feeling like a complete slut. Dammit, I wish Alice was here so she could assure me I'm not crazy—but then I'd have to admit to her that I'm a virgin. She thinks I fucked Oliver-the-Dipshit years ago.

"Do you want me to lock your purse up for you?"

Oh, I guess that's what the lockers are for. "Yes, please."

I hand over my purse with my phone in it. She turns and puts my purse in a locker and writes something on her guest list. "Okay, you're in locker 69—how lucky for you! When you're ready to leave, just come back and I'll get your purse out."

"Um, thank you."

Dang, this place is slick. I shouldn't be surprised, Alice said the lady has been throwing holiday parties like this for several years, so she probably has this all planned out and streamlined now. Can you imagine being rich enough to have elaborate freeuse parties multiple times a year?

Bianca's voice is cheerful. "You're welcome. If you have any questions or want to stop being a freeuse guest, just take the ribbon off and no one will touch you."

My hands tremble and my knees suddenly feel weak. "Okay, thanks."

She gestures for me to go through an archway behind her. Holy fuck, this is actually happening. I'm about to know what a cock feels like. Oh god, what if no one wants to fuck me?

There's only one way to find out. It's time to channel my slutty cop persona and find someone who wants to frisk me instead of the other way around.

The sounds of laughter, music, and voices get louder as I make my way past the check-in. It opens up to a hallway, and I almost trip over my boots and gasp.

What the hell? There's a vampire fucking a French maid right in front of me—and she's howling like she just had the best orgasm of her life.

I lock eyes with the vampire and my internal temperature rises ten degrees as my brain buzzes. He's every woman's fantasy of a sexy, older vampire. Like in the movies and books, when you imagine some guy who has lived for a thousand years and knows exactly how to please a woman? That's this guy. He's easily in his mid 40s with a chiseled jaw and salt and pepper hair.

An aura of dominance surrounds him as his intense gaze holds me hostage. My pussy clenches and I can feel myself growing wetter. The way he pumps in and out of the French maid mesmerizes me. I want him to pull out of her and take me right here.

The woman in the French maid costume moans as she comes down from her high and she sounds so delighted that it snaps me out of my spell. Oh shit, I'm just standing here staring like a freaking pervert. Though, they're the ones who chose this location in the middle of a potentially busy hallway, but still...I should give them some privacy.

I finally tear my eyes from the vampire, and step to the side and keep moving deeper into the house. The noises of laughter, mixed with moaning, grow louder and there are some spooky Halloween decorations, but my main focus is finding someone who wants to have sex with me. But first, I need a beverage. Watching two people fucking was thirsty work.

An archway leads to a large, open-concept living space filled with people mingling and having a grand ole time. In the far corner, there's a bar set up with two bartenders with a large variety of options.

One bartender spots me, and we exchange smiles as I head her direction. Her tight black and red corset hugs her curves, making her waist appear tiny and her boobs extravagant. She's gorgeous.

"Hi there! Would you like a drink? No alcohol tonight, but I make the finest mocktails this side of the train station."

Since the train station is on the outskirts of town, I'm not sure how impressive that is, but I laugh anyway. "I'll take anything! Just give me something festive and sweet."

"Coming right up."

Within a minute, she's sliding a drink in front of me. "This is my version of a Cherry Bomb. Happy Halloween!"

She even garnished it with a cherry and a fake plastic Halloween bat. It smells like a cherry Coke, so I taste it and nod approvingly. "Perfect. Thank you."

I barely wet my throat before someone takes the drink from my hand and puts pressure on my shoulders, forcing me to kneel. Oooooh, fuck.

I don't get time to look at who it is, and as I sink to my knees, I encounter a hard cock and a pair of massive balls. The guy is naked from the waist down, so I don't think it's the vampire, plus chances are he's still busy with his lusty maid.

The guy taps his dick on my cheek. I blink, not expecting a cock to be tossed in my face like this—though I probably should have been. I open my mouth to object, but all I get out is a, "Hey, wha–!" before the mystery man slides his cock deep into my mouth and the tip of it touches the back of my throat.

Oliver-the-Pencil-Dick got plenty of blowjobs from me, and my mouth closes around his cock automatically. I start sucking him, sliding my tongue along the underside of his shaft, which makes him groan. Holy fuck, I just walked in the door and I've already got a cock in my mouth. It makes me feel sexy and submissive.

"Good, slutty cop. Take it all," he encourages, and I relax my throat so he can drive in deeper.

I bob my head as he grasps my bun with his hand and thrusts into my mouth vigorously. Oh wow, this is better than I thought it would be. His pre-cum tastes tangy. It's weird to have an anonymous guy's cock in my throat.

"Ohhhhhhh, suck it. Such a pretty mouth. Do you like being used like a filthy slut?"

When he asks the question, my chest tightens briefly from surprise and confusion, and then my thoughts clear and I feel my body relax. No one has ever called me a filthy slut before, but it resonates deep in my soul and I realize the truth. Yes, I do like being used.

I came here tonight because I want to feel this way. I wasted too many years with Oliver-the-Douche-Nozzle, and it's time for me to take control of my life...by surrendering for a night of pleasure.

I try to answer, but with his cock in my mouth, all that comes out is a happy gurgle and a tiny nod. Placing my hands on the man's hips, I hold myself steady while he plows into my mouth. His cock thickens, and I flick my tongue and hollow out my cheeks to bring him more pleasure.

"Ohhhhhhh, the slut really does enjoy being used, huh? Do you want a taste of my cum?"

No answer is necessary and a moment later, he hisses in pleasure and spurts of warm cum hit the back of my throat. I swallow it greedily. His thigh muscles quiver and his grip tightens on my bun. His movements become erratic until he completely stills, pulling back to slide his length out of my mouth.

Cum and saliva run down my chin and I try to wipe it up with my hand while another voice behind me says, "It's my turn to fuck the pretty slut's mouth."

I turn to the guy who spoke, and I encounter another dick lined up with my face – this one is attached to a fairly realistic Viking. Next to the Viking is a priest with his robe open and his cock out. Holy shit, it's a queue of dicks for me to suck. What have I gotten myself into?

The Viking pulls my hair loose from my bun and runs his fingers through the strands, loosening them to fall in soft waves to my shoulders. He tips my head back, and I peer up at his smirk. I have to hold in my giggle. These guys might think I'm a freeuse slut tonight, but in reality, I'm the one using them. Everyone who shoves their cock in me is giving me what I need and what I've never had before—the freedom to be a complete whore.

My drenched pussy throbs for attention, but I shove my desire aside to focus on my role for the night – I'm a cum dumpster for people to unload in. I flutter my eyelashes up at the Viking, ready to take my next dick.

He cups my chin with his thumb and index finger and guides me forward to the tip of his cock. As his shaft slides past my lips and I taste his unique flavor of pre-cum, my brain sinks further into submission. He holds the sides of my head and stands still, rocking me, and forcing me on and off his cock slowly. The longer he fucks my mouth, the fuzzier my mind gets. Before all thoughts switch off and I become the ultimate fucktoy, I have a fleeting thought that I hope the sexy, older vampire finds me. I'm curious what a vampire's cum tastes like.

CHAPTER 5

MIKE

Lita puts her hand on my face, turning me to look at her and breaking my eye contact with the cop girl.

"Fuck, that was good," she sighs, before kissing me hard. My cock is still inside her and I'm gently rocking, sending shivers of pleasure through her body as my cock fills her up. I can feel her pussy clenching me and for a moment I think about just fucking her, slamming into her until I explode.

But now I have someone else who I want to fill with my cum.

I lower Lita back down and help her steady herself. I can see the orgasm has taken it out of her and know she needs a little aftercare.

"Stay here a moment," I say as I slide from her, removing the condom and tucking myself away.

She nods and leans against the wall, eyes shut and a happy, spaced-out look on her face.

I walk down the corridor to reception and grab one of the many bottles of water they provide for the guests, then take it back to Lita. Cracking the lid, I hold the bottle to her mouth.

"I never drink... water," she says in a deep voice.

I recognize that she's referencing the old Bela Lugosi Dracula movie where he said the same thing about wine.

"You do tonight."

She takes the bottle and knocks it back, drinking about a third of it in one long gulp.

"I'm okay," she says, standing up straight and smoothing down her outfit. "You should go find that pretty young cop you had your eyes on. If you don't, someone else will."

"Are you sure you're okay?" I ask.

A burly guy in a hockey mask walks up to us and, without saying anything, lifts her up over his shoulder, and starts walking towards the stairs.

"I think I'm going to be fine," she calls back to me. "Looks like I've already found my next playmate. Go get her, and don't worry about me."

She's right, I want to find the cop girl. Something about her resonated inside me as soon as we locked eyes. I could tell she was going to be very popular at the party and I had a sudden urge to claim her for myself.

The house is pretty full, guests arriving all the time and spreading out through the rooms. She could be anywhere by now, so my only choice is searching the rooms one by one.

I walk into the living space at the front of the house and try to push my way through the crowd. A couple are fucking on the couch just inside and I recognize the woman as Cherry, our host. Her body is painted red, and she's wearing demon horns. She catches my eye as I pass and she flashes me a smile before pulling down the head of the man she is riding, pressing it to her breasts as she bucks up and down on him.

Cherry has a thing about being watched and always knows how to create a spectacle to get people gathered around. Unfortunately, that just makes it harder for me to get through the room.

I remember seeing a bar earlier, so I head in that direction, figuring that maybe she had gone to get a drink. As I get near, there's a small circle of people watching something, and I push my way over to see.

The cop girl is on her knees, getting her mouth fucked by a Viking. Since I last saw her, she has taken her hair down, framing her face. It makes her look even sexier and my cock throbs in anticipation of using her.

The Viking has his hands on the side of her face and is rocking her back and forth on his cock. I can see her eyes and recognize that faraway look in them. She's a sub, dazed from the feeling of submission and eager to please.

I almost growl with need.

"Oh fuck," says the Viking as he thrusts into her mouth. One hand moves from her face to the top of her head and I can tell he's about to come. The girl keeps bobbing her head, lost in her own pleasure. When he explodes in her mouth, she savors his cock and cleans it with her tongue, her hand coming up to milk the last drops out onto her outstretched tongue.

Behind the Viking, there's a guy dressed as a priest. Maybe he's supposed to be Rasputin? He's stroking his cock and I can see he's planning to take the Viking's place. I step forward out of the crowd as soon as the Viking moves away. Sliding between the girl and the priest, I pull her up from the floor.

"Hey man, it's my turn. You can't just..."

I turn to him with an icy, penetrating stare. "There are no turns. If you want something, you take it. And I want her. So unless you want to take her from me...?"

He pales and backs away, pulling his robes over his cock. I'm sure he'll find someone else to fuck, but it's not going to be my cop girl.

I turn back to her and see that she's coming back around, blinking as she looks at me.

"Oh, it's you," she gasps.

I crouch down and grab her shorts, pulling them to the floor. Her little red panties follow.

Standing back up, I look at the people gathered and see the excited expectancy on their faces.

"I know some of you were hoping to use her, but I'm sure she won't mind showing what a wet little slut she is."

I feel her slip one arm around my waist and hold on to my side.

"Are you going to be a good sub?" I ask her.

When she nods, I sense nervousness in her. She may be at a freeuse party, but I have a feeling that she's not very experienced. She seems to be a natural submissive and I'm looking forward to bringing that out more.

I command, "Spread your legs so that everyone can see your pussy."

Her eyes go wide, but she obeys, spreading her legs for the gathered crowd.

"Good girl."

I slip my hand between her legs and dip my fingers into her wetness. She's soaked and I think how easy it will be to fuck her. But not now. First, I'm going to put on a show. My fingers brush her clit and she lets out a low moan, closing her mouth to try to keep it in. She tries even harder when I rub in a circular motion.

"Oh no, none of that," I say. "Mouth open so all the ladies and gentlemen can hear how much you like being used. Look at how many of them are touching while watching you. I bet that turns you on, all these people getting to see what a good slut you are."

She mumbles something, and I give her pussy a little slap. "Use your words."

Her head falls back and I can see she has closed her eyes. I have an overwhelming desire to kiss her, but my dom side is far too busy enjoying showing her off.

"So good," she moans. "Want to be a good obedient slut, have people watch."

I move my fingers faster on her clit in little tight circles. From the noises she's making and how hard her legs are shaking, I know she's loving everything I'm doing. But I don't want her to come yet. I have all night to play with her and this is all about getting her feeling even more submissive and owned.

I hear a groan and look over. The priest has his eyes firmly fixed on us, but a woman in a pixie outfit has her hand in his robes, stroking vigorously. Her other hand is squeezing her own breast, and she seems as enchanted with our display as the priest is.

"Now then, be a good little toy," I say, "and show the ladies and gentlemen what a slutty little freeuse toy you are. Maybe if you're good, some of them might even come while watching you."

I give her pussy another slap and her low moaning changes to a loud cry.

"Oh fuck. Oh fuck yes," she shouts, grinding herself on my hand, trying to give herself more pleasure. I'm still not ready for her to come, so I pull my hand away.

From the corner of my eye, I see the priest coming in the pixie's hand as my cop girl falls into my embrace. I scoop her up into my arms, and the crowd parts for us as I carry her across the room. Someone has already claimed the pixie, and she gets down on her knees to take on everyone who wants her. As much fun as it is to watch people play, I want some privacy so I can ravish this enchanting woman who is now all mine.

There are private rooms for people to use upstairs, so I grab her discarded clothes and carry her up there. I close the door behind me with my foot and the thickness of the wood drowns out the sounds from the party. We're alone now, just the two of us.

I lay her down on the center of the bed and then walk to the end. Her eyes follow me as I pull off my costume, and I smirk at how her eyes widen again as I take out my cock and stroke it to its full size.

"You know what I am going to do to you?" I ask.

Her voice is quiet. "You're going to fuck me."

"Do you consent to me fucking you?"

She nods.

"I need to hear you say it."

She pushes herself up onto her elbows, and her eyes go to my cock.

"Please fuck me. I want to feel your cock inside me."

There is a desperation in her voice that makes my cock pulse and bounce in the air, getting a giggle from her.

"Take your top off," I tell her as I bend down and take a new condom from my trousers and roll it down my shaft.

She complies quickly, eager to get ready for me. Underneath her top, she is wearing a red bra and I stop her before she removes it.

"Leave it on for now."

I crawl onto the bed on top of her, kissing her softly. Her mouth opens for me and her hands come up to hold my face.

I break the kiss and slide my hands over her wrists, pinning her down to the bed. I press the tip of my cock to her pussy and I am just about to thrust into her when she gasps.

"Wait! I have to tell you something first."

CHAPTER 6

WILLOW

The vampire pauses, the head of his cock hovering right at the brink of pushing in. His eyes hold me hostage and there's lust and need reflected back at me. I desperately want him to fuck me, but what if it hurts? I debate for two seconds about what to say. It's now or never.

I hope to hell this doesn't screw everything up and make him stop. After the show he made me put on in front of everyone else and how quickly he turned me into his obedient toy, I want him to be my first. It's beyond ridiculous how turned on I am.

I close my eyes, summon my courage, then look straight at him, murmuring, "I've never had sex before."

The change in him is immediate. He stills as if he's in shock, and his eyes go dark with desire. "Really?"

My clit throbs, and I try to rub my body against him. "Yeah. Don't freak out. I have the red ribbon and I'm here because I want this. Please fuck me...please?"

I'm practically begging at the end, and I rock my hips, trying to nudge his cock inside me, but he doesn't thrust in. Shit, this is a disaster. Why did I tell him? He's going to leave me horny and unsatisfied.

I swallow my disappointment. "It's okay. I'll leave—"

"Shhh, be still," he growls, his voice full of raw power.

I snap my mouth shut, powerless to resist him as pleasure pulses through my veins. Ohhh god, I think he's going to fuck me. Lust burns in my brain and all I want him to do is take me and do whatever he wants to me.

Wild, raw need passes between us, and the vampire lets go of my wrists. My bra has a front-hook, and he quickly opens it. My bare tits bounce free, my nipples hardening in the cool air, and a satisfied hum vibrates from his chest.

"I'm really the first?"

"Yes," I whisper as I slide my hands down to cup my breasts, squeezing them enticingly.

He turns primal as he leans forward and swirls his tongue around each nipple before giving each one a gentle bite that sends electric bolts straight to my core. Oh shit, this is new. I didn't know I'd like a little pain, and I moan loudly. I might die of shame tomorrow for how much of a slut I am, but not tonight...Right now, I'm free to do whatever I want, and it's like the floodgates of desire are wide open.

His voice is harsh. "Don't move."

My body vibrates with desire at the command, and I moan in compliance as he continues.

"I'm still going to fuck you, but we're taking things nice and slow so you get used to how it feels. If something hurts or you get uncomfortable, you'll say 'yellow' for me to slow down, or 'red' for me to stop completely. Do you understand?"

"Yes, sir," I breathlessly respond as his domineering presence makes my insides twist up deliciously.

"Oh, I like you calling me sir. But I'm not your Sir, babygirl—not yet."

"Yes, sir. Sorry, sir." I wince as I hear myself use the word. I can't help it: something about him makes me want to obey.

My hands are shaking with need, and I hold the undersides of my tits for him again. His fingers lightly squeeze my nipples, which only fuels my hunger to have his cock inside me. I have no clue if this is a normal conversation for the first time, but it feels right to submit to his dominance and the sexual tension crackles between us.

"Tell me why someone as delectable as you hasn't had sex before."

The tone of his voice isn't harsh or demanding—just curious, with an underlying current of passion that I crave. I sigh and stare up at him as he hovers over me, holding himself up on one elbow. I can still feel the tip of his cock at my entrance, but he's not moving it yet.

Shit, I might as well tell him the truth. "My long-term boyfriend had premature ejaculation issues, and..." I pause for a split second and force myself to continue. "...And I can't orgasm, so no one else will want me. I just need you to fuck me so I know what it feels like, please? I just want to know."

He doesn't say anything as his hand slips up under my neck and his lips crush against mine. I wrap my arms around him and slide my tongue in his mouth, hungrily returning his kisses. It's a crazy, raw connection to experience with someone who's essentially a stranger—and the opposite of how I usually am with men—but I've been fantasizing about this party for weeks. I want to be possessed and fucked by someone. Nothing else matters except fulfilling this need burning deep inside me.

When he pulls away, he strokes my hair gently, gazing down at me softly. "I want to know what you think will make you orgasm."

Blushing furiously, I stammer. "I...I don't know. I gave up trying."

He raises an eyebrow and I'm drawn into the depths of his gorgeous gray eyes. Spilling my intimate details to this guy is strangely erotic. My heartbeat thuds in my ears, and my eyes widen as the tip of his cock slips inside me, stretching me. There's no pain like I expected, just an exquisite pleasure. He sinks in slowly, filling me up bit by bit. I moan and toss my head, needing him to be all the way inside me.

When I tilt my hips up and try to make him press in deeper, he shakes his head. "Remember what I said about letting your body get used to how it feels, babygirl. If I had known this was your first time, I wouldn't have teased you in the kitchen. But you seemed so wet and eager."

"I am," I insist, reaching out for him, but he resists me and pins both of my wrists down by my sides. Mewling in frustration, I look at him and silently plead for him to fuck me. I'm aching to feel his entire length and for him to get lost in me.

He's inside my pussy, but not nearly all the way, and I wiggle my hips impatiently. "I need to feel you deeper."

He leans down for a searing kiss before thrusting the last few inches into me. I let out a loud gasp as I feel him bottom out. He's so huge that I feel stretched wide to my max.

"It's okay if you don't come tonight, babygirl. But I want you to enjoy this either way," he rumbles as he moves my hands above my head and crosses my wrists so he can pin them down with one hand and explore my body with the other.

I moan when he kisses my throat and massages my tit, rubbing his palm over my nipple, then running his fingertips along my stomach and sliding down to circle my clit.

"Oh god," I whimper, lost as pleasure floods through my body.

He starts fucking me slowly, rolling his hips in a leisurely fashion that's almost torture.

"Pleasure doesn't have to be about coming," he murmurs as he bites at the sensitive skin on my neck. "Sometimes it's about opening yourself up to the experience in the moment, and just feeling every sensation and emotion."

The room spins as tendrils of bliss ripple through me. I thought he was going to fuck me savagely and just take what he wanted from me. But instead, he's focused on my pleasure as his fingers circle my clit relentlessly.

I need more. More speed and force. "Please... faster."

"You don't get to decide how fast I fuck you," he groans, and I can tell he's in his element while driving me wild.

I lose track of time as he tenderly strokes my clit in a rhythmic motion, all the while continuing the gentle fucking, taking me to dizzying heights and then pulling me back down. An unfamiliar pressure builds inside me, and I whimper as I put my feet flat on the bed and try to meet his thrusts to force him in harder.

"Faster! More!" I cry out, my pussy walls contracting around his thick cock as my vision blurs from delight.

"Beg for it like you're the filthiest slut you can imagine." His fingers tighten on my wrists. "Then I'll give you more."

I'm delirious with pleasure and his words set me on fire. A pathway in my brain lights up and suddenly I'm noticing every tiny detail: the warmth of his body, his cock throbbing inside me, and his powerful grip on my wrists. I need this man to do whatever he wants to me. The realization makes the edges of the world go fuzzy, and I feel myself sinking down into a place I've never been before.

I wanted to be a freeuse slut for people to use for my first time.

I am the filthiest slut I can imagine.

Words burst out of me faster than I can think. "Please, sir...harder...fa ster...I need you to fill me up with your cum...make me yours...make me scream..."

The vampire's cock thickens, and my words trigger something in him. His thrusts become punishing as he pumps in and out of me in hard, vigorous strokes that light up every nerve ending in my body. My breath comes in quick gasps as I focus on the pleasure and I arch my back up off the bed as he grinds against me with each downward stroke. The vampire releases my hands and leans over me, pounding into me with abandon.

A keening wail erupts from my lungs as he fucks me, and I grab the back of his neck and hold on for dear life. The unfamiliar pressure bursts inside me, and I'm suddenly flying high. I scream out as ecstasy explodes like fireworks across my body. Every muscle tenses and I buck up as his cock brings wave after wave of sheer rapture crashing through me.

I never want this moment to end.

My orgasm triggers his climax and he pounds into me faster, grunting as his muscles tighten, then spills his load. He keeps fucking me, as tiny aftershocks of bliss ripple from my fingertips to my toes.

When he finally stops, he's panting as his forehead rests on mine while his chest heaves from exertion. The vampire stares down at me in amazement. "That was so unbelievably sexy. I loved watching you come."

He rolls to my side and I'm frozen in place. What just happened? The pleasure I just experienced was life altering. It's like my body and mind switched on, illuminating something I never knew existed.

When I shiver, the vampire pulls me on top of him. My breasts flatten against his chest as I melt. I'm floating on a cloud of happiness, and now is not the time to question anything. I've got the rest of my life to think about tonight.

Chapter 7

MIKE

She rests her head on my chest, and I slip a hand down to cup her ass. I can feel heat radiating from her and her little murmurs seem like she's content, but fuzzy. She's got to be feeling over stimulated and out of it.

"Just rest. You're all right. Catch your breath, just breathe slowly. All you need to do right now is snuggle up and relax. I'll keep you safe."

I always make sure to give aftercare, but I'm not usually this gentle. But in this case, aftercare is very much needed. She's been through a lot and I'm the only person she has to make sure she's ok.

"Oh god, that was..."

She doesn't finish the sentence and instead squeezes me, wrapping herself tightly around me. I stroke her hair and hold her, giving her the time that she needs so she can think clearly.

"We need to get some water inside you," I say. "You're going to be dehydrated."

She nods, but doesn't move. Her head on my chest makes it look like she's listening to my heartbeat.

Suddenly, she lifts her head. "I need to use the bathroom."

Without waiting for me to answer, she hops off the bed and scampers over to a door, pulling it open and revealing a walk-in closet. I'm far too busy looking at her cute ass, so it takes me a minute to realize she opened the wrong door.

"It's the one next to it."

She looks back at me, an embarrassed smile on her face, then pulls the other door open and disappears inside.

It's fair to say that tonight has not gone the way I had planned. I was expecting some domming and rough fucking.

I was not expecting to take someone's virginity.

It's all a bit much to take in. I need to think about this, process it. All I know is that I'm glad that I was her first.

The door opens, and just her head pops out. "Got water. Be out in a second."

She disappears again and I chuckle. Her youthful exuberance is intoxicating. I wonder how old she actually is. Mid twenties, or younger?

There is something about her. At one moment, innocent seeming, then the next full of passion and lust. And there's something soft and loving about her. It makes my rough dom side roar and my softer side want to hold and protect her.

This is an unfamiliar feeling for me.

She appears again, wrapped in a towel, and runs over to the bed, launching herself onto it and snuggling up to me.

"Thank you," she says, kissing my neck and then resting her head on my chest.

"You're very welcome. And thank you for letting me be your first."

We lay on the bed not saying anything, just enjoying the feeling of each other. It can't last, but it feels intimate and right.

"I know you probably want to get back to the party," she says. "But can we cuddle for a bit more? I'm not ready to leave just yet. It's been overwhelming. In a good way."

I lean down and kiss the top of her head.

"As long as you need."

We cuddle together for a bit, and I marvel at how she fits perfectly against me.

She finally sits up and looks at me. "Let's go back to the party. I want to see what everyone else is doing. And I should probably find Alice to let her know I'm well taken care of."

I don't know who Alice is, but if it's her friend, then we should probably make sure she's not panicking.

We start getting dressed and end up a giggling mess. She trips while pulling up her shorts and falls into me, knocking us both onto the bed.

"If you wanted round two, you should have just said," I laugh.

"Mmmm, it's tempting." She reaches down and squeezes my cock. "Oh, you're hard already?"

One thing I've always been grateful for is how quickly I recover.

"Always hard, always ready."

She laughs and drops her head down and kisses the tip.

"Well, you'll just have to wait. Maybe next time."

Next time? Now that sounds promising. For a moment, I consider taking her and showing her what freeuse is really about. But she's had an eventful night already, so I decide to not overwhelm her.

Eventually, we're both dressed, and I help twist her hair back up into a bun. It was something I used to do for my wife and for a moment, it's like old times. I noticed it before while we were having sex, but her hair smells gorgeous. Something sweet, like cotton candy? Whatever it is, I like it.

"Ready to go back out?" I ask.

She nods and takes my hand, and I realize she still has the red ribbon on her wrist.

As soon as we step outside, a nude couple runs past us. The party is in full swing now and people are having sex all over the place.

"Oh wow. I thought it was wild earlier, but this…"

I lean in and kiss her neck. "I'm sure they all got worked up after seeing you being a good slut earlier."

She turns and snorts, putting her hand up to cover her face. It's so adorable that I want to pull her back into the bedroom and fuck her again. As we walk to the stairs, a guy dressed in a werewolf outfit comes out of a side room and puts his hand on her arm, trying to take her away from me.

"Oh. Oh no, sorry." She pulls the end of the ribbon and it falls down to the floor, a little red trail of material that means she's no longer freeuse. "I forgot it was still on," she says to him.

He nods his head, shrugs, and walks off down the corridor in search of new prey.

She turns, cuddles against me, and bats her eyelashes adorably. "There's only one guy for me tonight."

How did I manage to get so lucky as to end up with this intriguing woman?

Chapter 8

WILLOW

My heart races as I entwine my arm with his, feeling the warmth of his skin. Being this close to him makes me feel protected. There are so many people having sex in the main part of the house that it's difficult to take in all the debauchery. We pass the priest from earlier, who's sitting on one of the couches with his robe open, a couple of women taking turns sucking him off as a small audience watches. I'm fascinated, and as much as I'd love to stay and observe, I want to find Alice.

As we wander the downstairs, several people glance at my wrist to check for a ribbon—not just men. Whenever I notice a woman looking, I blush and hide my face against the vampire. I don't know why I assumed only men would use women. Tonight could have turned out very differently...

Hey, wait...I don't even know his name. Do I want to know? I could just always think of him as the mysterious older guy who gave me an amazing night of pleasure. Mmmm, and what a night it's been. My pussy buzzes as I think about fucking him all night. Oh no, I want a name to put to the experience when I'm daydreaming about it years from now.

The party is loud and I tug on his arm to get his attention and try to speak up over the noise. "So what's your name?"

He kisses my neck before answering. "Mike, but I'm afraid there's a catch."

"Oh?"

His breath tickles, and a shiver of delight runs through me as his eyes, once again, mesmerize me. His lips curl up mischievously. "You'll have to give me yours."

I laugh. "I'm Willow. It's nice to meet you, Mike."

"Pretty name." He pulls me into a hug.

I'm stunned at the unexpected affection, and a little awkward at first. When I finally relax, I give in to the sense of calm that comes from being in his embrace. It feels wonderful, like he can shelter me from the craziness going on all over the place. We didn't discuss him not fucking other people, and just because I took my ribbon off doesn't mean he isn't free to find someone else to play with. But somehow, I know he's only interested in me right now. That could just be the sex talking, but at least for right now, I feel special.

The entire downstairs is wild, free-for-all fucking. I now understand just how nuts my plan of coming here to lose my virginity really was. God, I got so lucky.

When he squeezes my ass, I giggle and push at him. "Hey, I need to find Alice."

"Sure. Is she a friend?"

"Yeah. I just want to make sure she's okay."

He helps me search for Alice and as we pass a doorway, I catch a glimpse of her. She's on a couch, leaning back, her mouth hanging open. Her eyes are half shut while her tits bounce as a guy dressed up as a pirate thrusts into her. Oh yeah, she's fine.

When Mike notices I've paused to look at the couple on the couch, he asks, "Is that her?"

"Yep. I'd say she's enjoying herself."

He hums in agreement and puts his arm across my shoulders, leading me away. "Let's go find something to eat."

I'm not really hungry, but I don't disagree and we make our way to the kitchen. Once we're in there, I spot a plate of goodies on a table and get distracted. "Oooh, cupcakes!"

Grabbing a vanilla one with white frosting and orange sprinkles, I hold it up for him. "Want one?"

He arches his eyebrow and takes a chocolate one off the plate. "I'm not really into anything vanilla."

I flush from the innuendo and stick my tongue out at him playfully. He reaches up to tuck a loose strand of my hair behind my ear. It's an oddly familiar gesture, and my skin tingles wherever he touches me.

While I munch on my cupcake, I take a better look at him. He has the most gorgeous piercing gray eyes. His broad shoulders are inviting and his firm build is incredibly sexy. Being close to him makes me giddy, and I keep thinking I should pinch myself to make sure this isn't all a dream. He's the perfect guy for my first time. How is this real?

Should I ask for his phone number? My stomach tightens with indecision. He's older, and he probably won't want to talk to me again. I bite my lip, fighting the urge to ask him.

I'm so engrossed in my own thoughts, I'm surprised when he smears chocolate frosting on my lips. He licks the remaining icing off his finger and winks. "Oops, guess I better clean that off."

I grin at his teasing, but when he presses his mouth to mine, my legs go weak. His kiss tastes like chocolatey goodness and my mind blanks from desire.

We exchange slow, heated kisses, surrounded by a bunch of strangers going at it, oblivious to the fact we're here. It's oddly romantic, and when he slides his hands to my ass, I forget about everything as I encircle his neck with my arms and pull him closer.

Just as his tongue is deep in my mouth, something jostles my shoulder and breaks us apart. A young woman, about my age, bends over the island, a guy slamming into her from behind while she texts on her phone.

I giggle at the interruption, and her phone reminds me. I seize the moment. "Want to exchange phone numbers?"

"Definitely. But my phone is in the lockers."

"Mine too."

He takes my hand, and we navigate through the crowded rooms to the entryway. I give Bianca my name, and I'm barely mature enough not to snicker when I say I'm locker 69.

When Mike whispers in my ear, "We should have tried 69," my entire body zings alive. I'm about to be brave and suggest we do that if we meet up another time, but Bianca interrupts me.

"Here's your phone."

Damn her. She gets Mike's phone out, and we exchange numbers. When we're done, I shift from foot to foot, suddenly feeling uncertain of what I'm doing. I should go in case he wants to fuck someone else. He didn't sign up to babysit me all night.

My anxiety gets the better of me, and I quickly make up an excuse. "I've got to get going. I'm house sitting. Thanks for the lovely time."

Before I can move, he pulls me to him for a deep, toe-curling kiss. I'm reeling when we separate.

He grins and kisses my nose. "No, thank *you*."

A lump forms in my throat, and I don't want to leave. Oh God, I need to get out of here before I make a fool of myself. I blow him a kiss and give him my cutest, "Goodbye," and hightail it outside.

I sneak around the side of the house, so it looks like I'm gone. Leaning against the siding, I request a pickup from the rideshare app and reminisce about the mind-blowing sex. By the time my driver arrives, my nipples are hard and aching and I can feel wetness between my legs.

God, why can't guys my age fuck like that?

CHAPTER 9

MIKE

I pull the car up in front of my house and sit for a moment.

What an unexpected night.

I rarely ever give out my number to anyone at a freeuse party unless they're experienced and nearer my age. I still don't know exactly how old she really is.

But this time, it felt right.

Who knows if anything more will happen? After all, she's way too young for me, so it's not like she would want to date or anything. But having some more playtime, teaching her how to be a good sub? I can see that happening. Better me teaching her than someone who's not so caring and gentle. The world is full of bad doms and an innocent like her could get hurt.

I'm not going to let it go to my head, though. I don't want a relationship; at least, nothing lasting.

While all that is true, I have to admit that I also really want to fuck her again. To see her eyes roll into the back of her head as I pound into her and make her come for me.

Yeah, I can see the two of us getting together in the future.

I get out of the car and notice the blinds twitching in Nancy's darkened window. Then I see the light go on so her silhouette appears. She's taking her top off and I can see the shape of her breast projected onto the blind. I wonder if she's been waiting for me to return home just so she can up the flirting with this?

I know she's watching, so I make a beating heart shape with my hands, letting her know I saw her.

Unfortunately for her, there's only one person on my mind as I let myself into the house.

I head straight for the shower, stripping off and letting the warm water spray over my body. My head seems to clear and for a moment, I don't think of anything except how good the warmth feels.

As I get out of the shower, I notice that there's a message on my phone. My heart leaps as I think it might be Willow, but instead, it's just someone from work.

I throw the phone down on the counter as I towel off, surprised at how disappointed I am.

Usually I would leave it a few days before calling. But she just had a hell of a night. I took her virginity, the least I can do is check in on her.

I finish cleaning up and head through to the bedroom and lay down on the bed, looking up at the ceiling.

Just thinking about Willow gets me hard, and I wonder what she's doing right now. Is she lying in bed thinking about me?

I wrap my hand around my cock and I gently stroke, remembering her silky heat as I thrust into her. Maybe I'll just get myself off, clear my mind, and go to sleep.

Instead, I grab my phone and find her number.

I'm the first person she's had sex with. It's only right I send her a quick message to check she's okay.

I hit send and lie back on the bed. I don't expect her to text back straight away. She might not text back at all. Almost instantly, I feel tired. So I close my eyes, wait for sleep, and wonder what tomorrow will bring.

Chapter 10

WILLOW

By the time I let myself into my apartment, I'm exhausted. It's been one hell of a night. After locking the door behind me, I quickly text Alice to let her know I made it home safely and asked her to do the same whenever she's done fucking the pirate. I giggle, imagining her reading the message and blushing because she'll know I saw her.

I pull off my costume and climb into the shower. As I soap up my body, I'm extra sensitive everywhere—even my breasts feel bigger. Normally I don't pay attention to my body in the shower, but tonight I explore my curves as if it's the first time I've ever touched myself for pleasure. My body feels more alive and every nerve ending is sensitive.

I run my fingers between my legs, and they come away glistening with slick, clear fluid. My skin is hot, and I imagine it's Mike's hands caressing me everywhere as the warm water cascades over me. I slip one finger inside my pussy and gasp. Even my finger pressing into me feels different after having his enormous cock in me.

When I recall how gentle Mike was, tears threaten to spill from my eyes. As fabulous as the sex was, his aftercare meant more. It made me feel like a person rather than just a freeuse slut. I didn't know that was exactly what I needed for my first time until tonight. He even made sure I drank water, and he cared about how I felt afterward. Is this how older men are, or is he just a good guy?

When I settle into bed, I'm still turned on. I pick up my phone, hoping to see a message from him, but I know I'm being silly. Hell, he's probably still at the party fucking other women. I turn my phone on silent and set it facedown on my nightstand to avoid the temptation of looking at it.

I'm still hot and bothered from my shower, and when I turn the lights off, I slide my hand between my legs. My fingers trace my sensitive skin and when I brush against my clit, I moan and imagine Mike is with me.

The memory of being held down, his fingers on my clit as he thrust into me, has my pulse racing. My body responds and I raise my hips to meet my fingers as I add in a second hand to finger fuck myself while stroking my clit. The thought of how much I loved being under his control, submitting to him, makes me moan and my body shudders as I push myself toward the edge.

I imagine him whispering dirty words into my ear and telling me to be a good girl and come for him. My toes curl as I slam my fingers inside me and when my orgasm hits, I cry out and arch my back as waves of pleasure ripple through me.

Holy fuck. I just made myself come.

I collapse onto my pillow, breathing heavily as my thoughts drift. My body feels lighter and I close my eyes, so relaxed now that I can tell I'm going to fall asleep easily.

Yep. Best birthday ever.

Freeuse Thanksgiving

Freeuse to Forever After Book 2

April Cross | Matt Lake

CHAPTER 1

WILLOW

The moment I wake up, I immediately feel a delicious soreness between my legs. As I roll onto my back and stare at the crack in my ceiling, memories of the freeuse Halloween party last night flash through my brain. I can't stop grinning. It was the best fucking experience of my life. Literally. I even came! Twice! I had no idea how much I would enjoy submitting to someone. Mike was a gentle but assertive dom, and he made me feel safe while also turning me on beyond belief. I still can't believe my luck. Who knew I'd meet Mr. Right at a freeuse party?

Hmm, stop right there, Willow. He's not Mr. Right. He was Mr. Right-For-The-Night. I can't get ahead of myself, although I hope he messages me again. Oh shit, what if he doesn't? What if I was just a fun piece of ass he used, and then after I left the party, he went back in and found someone he liked better?

Ugh.

My thoughts whirl as I grab my phone to check the time. I squint at the bright screen, trying to focus. It's almost noon on November first. My

Halloween birthday is over. I'm 25, and no longer a virgin. Hey, that's what I'll do...I'll message him and thank him for giving me a wonderful birthday. I never actually told him last night that he was my birthday present to myself.

Oooh, I've got text messages! Shit, I need to relax. It's probably just Alice. Butterflies swirl in my stomach as I swipe open my messages.

There *is* a text from Alice—which I temporarily ignore because there's also one from Mike. I squeal and bolt upright to a sitting position.

Mike

> Just checking you got home safely and you're not too sore. Text me if you need anything.

After I read it at least ten times trying to evaluate it, I take a breath to steady my nerves. It's a little formal, but he actually messaged me and didn't string me along for days, so that's exciting. Hmm...need anything...like his wonderful cock pounding me into the mattress again? My pussy hums and I giggle at myself. Yeah, I need that.

Shit, now I have to reply, but what do I say? I definitely want to let him know how incredible last night was, but I don't want to sound thirsty, like "can we do that again today?"

I debate what to say, then my brain takes over and my fingers fly on the keypad. Before I can question myself, I hit "send," and give myself a mental pat on the back. What I said was perfect. I was witty and engaging.

Willow

> I'm wonderfully sore in the most delightful way. Had a fantastic night. I'm definitely a fan of freeuse!

Almost the instant I set my phone aside, it pings. Eep! I jump out of bed – with only a slight wince at my soreness – and skip to my tiny joke-of-a-kitchen to make coffee while I compose myself.

This is going well. I just need to be myself. That's all I have to offer, anyway. If he doesn't like it, oh well, that's his loss. It's taken a lot of therapy to give myself this pep talk.

I'm not looking to marry the guy, but I wouldn't say no to some more sex. My single-cup coffee maker chugs away while I read the next text from Mike.

Mike

> I had an excellent time as well. If you'd like to continue exploring, I'm happy to help. I enjoy toying with obedient little freeuse sluts.

Oh fuck. All thoughts drain from my head. Toying with obedient sluts? Was I a "toy," or was I a willing participant? I daydream about him spanking me, calling me a slut, and making me beg for his cock. Heat builds in my core and my clit pulses as I squeeze my legs together, imagining him holding me down, his massive cock pounding into me while I'm completely powerless. Yep, I'm a willing participant... who enjoys being a toy.

Coffee forgotten, I perch on a kitchen chair and type out another message.

Willow

> I'm always up for being a toy, or other kinds of play. Would like to spend time with you again, if that's agreeable?

Ugh, did I sound too formal? I chew on my thumbnail as I stare at the three little dots that show he's typing a response.

Mike

> Perfectly agreeable.

He sends me two smiling emojis and my body floods with relief, not just because he seemed to like my overly proper-sounding text, but because it means I get to be with him again. I've only just met the guy, and he's already got me in a dither over a simple text.

Oh shit, Alice! I quickly check Alice's message and she confirms she got home fine, and jokes that the pirate rocked her world. He was definitely rocking the couch when I saw them together.

I spend most of the day messaging back and forth with Alice in between texting Mike. I keep hoping he'll invite me over for a hard fucking tonight, but he doesn't. My apartment is too shitty, and I don't want to invite him over here, but I might if I get desperate enough.

After flirting most of the day, I'm wound up like a clockwork toy. Dammit, now that I've had a little taste of pleasure, my body wants more. Why doesn't he invite me over? If anything, it feels like he's keeping his distance.

Eventually, it's dinner time and my stomach rumbles. Shit, we've been texting all day. I need to put the phone away and get something to eat. On the way to my fridge, I suddenly remember that I'm supposed to be a responsible adult and I had errands to run today. I sigh in disappointment. Adulting sucks. Mike is like the new shiny toy catching my attention. and the high I get every time I get a message from him is addictive.

As much as I don't want to, after dinner I reluctantly get ready and go out to drop some mail at the post office and I need groceries from the store. I keep checking my phone to see if he's responded to my last message. Nothing. Ugh.

When I check for the tenth time, I force myself to turn the sound off and shove my phone in my purse. Oh shit, I really am getting obsessed. All the dude did was give me two orgasms.

Mmm, but it was good. REALLY good.

Fuck. I shake my head to clear it. Nope, this is stupid and I refuse to get my hopes up and make him into something he's not. I went to the party to lose my virginity on my terms, with no one expecting me to orgasm. There's probably tons of guys like him out there, so what makes me think this is different—just because we had sex and then I discovered I can orgasm?

I shove aside the little voice in my head that tells me I'm wrong, and there's something special about Mike. I just want some more sex, dammit. I wonder what freeuse looks like outside of a party? Can just two people do freeuse? I daydream about Mike fucking me over a dining table full of food as I finish my errands.

Mike finally replies to me and we flirt over text until bedtime. He's entertaining, and I can tell he probably enjoys a good joke and sexually teasing in person. He's not what I'd expect from an older guy.

I wonder what his story is.

CHAPTER 2

MIKE

I put my phone next to me and lie back on the bed, wondering where this is going.

I've spent pretty much all day texting with Willow, getting to know her a little better, but mainly flirting. Considering how much younger than me she is, I'm surprised that we talk so easily. I keep telling myself that maybe this is a bad idea. She's far too young for me and I have no interest in having a relationship, but then she sends me a message that makes me smile and I type back.

What I really want to do is invite her over so I can fuck her again. I'm pretty sure that if I asked, she would say yes. But I'm also sure that it's not a good idea for either of us. At the past Halloween parties, if I give my number to someone, I usually leave it a couple of days to let them know that I'm interested in sex and not seem too keen, but that's it. There's no expectation for any more than that. I've already broken that rule with Willow and I worry that if I invite her over, she's going to think it's more than it is.

I think I'm going to play it cool for a bit. I've offered to teach her more about freeuse and kink, and I hope she takes me up on that. But no rushing into it, because as good as it was, it's still just going to be some fun sex.

Closing my eyes, I decide to hold off with the texting. Maybe for a day or two.

***

Well, all of my plans went out of the window.

It's been a week since the Halloween party and we've been texting each other pretty much every day. I really tried to play it cool, but something about her seems to weaken my resolve.

In a way, it's a good thing. Thanksgiving is coming up, and that was one of the holidays I enjoyed the most with my wife, and it brings back memories of her. I don't have any other family, so being alone at Thanksgiving always feels haunted by the ghost of celebrations past. As usual, I plan to hunker down at home, watch terrible TV shows, and think about reading all the books on my shelf that, realistically, I will never get around to reading. So talking to Willow has been a pleasant distraction from that looming on the horizon.

Our texting is still flirty, but there seems to be an edge to it now. I think both of us want to take it further, but neither of us is making the first move.

It's still early in the morning, and I get out of bed and head to the kitchen. Pancakes may not be the healthiest thing to start the day with, but on the weekend, it's my treat for being good during the working week.

I'd just finished making them and I'm sliding them onto my plate when my phone buzzes. It's Willow.

Morning! I woke up early, so I thought I'd check in with you. If you're even awake. Do people as old as you even sleep?

I smile as I type back. She found out yesterday just how much older I am and has been bringing it up jokingly ever since.

Less of the cheekiness, young lady, or I will put you over my knee.

There is a pause and then I see her replying.

Is that a promise?

I rest against the counter and think about putting her over my knee, dragging her panties off and spanking her ass.

Are you still in bed?

There is no pause.

Yeah. Want to join me?

Someone's feeling frisky today. Time to turn that to my advantage.

Remove your covers and spread your legs. I'm going to give you some instructions.

This time the reply is a little slower, like I caught her by surprise.

Oh, okay. Done.

I carry the pancakes to the bedroom and set the plate on the nightstand. I have a feeling they're going to go cold before I have time to eat them.

Mike

> Slip your hand up over your breasts. I want you to close your eyes for 30 seconds and think of me removing your panties and putting you over my knee. And while you do that, rub your nipples.

My cock is stirring as I think about her lying in bed, doing what I tell her. The whole thing about being a dom is control. Let's see how she is at taking commands.

My phone beeps.

Willow

> Done. I feel a little fuzzy.

That's a good sign. I love it when a sub gets all fuzzy headed and obedient.

Mike

> Place one hand between your legs and finger yourself. Think of my firm grip on your ass, ready to spank you for being rude about my age.

This time it takes a while for her to reply.

Willow

> Done. Got distracted rubbing.

Mike

> Good girl. What were you thinking of?

She hesitates, and I'm not surprised. Even though she went to a freeuse party to lose her virginity, I sense that she's still a little shy. Hopefully, I can get her to come out of her shell, but that's going to take time.

I was thinking of being across your lap with one of your hands on my shoulder, pinning me. The other was caressing my ass in a circle, giving me gentle pats, ready to spank me.

I'm about to reply when I see the three dots and know she's writing something else.

Can I keep touching myself?

That makes me smile. She really does have the makings of a good sub.

Keep rubbing. Put one finger on your clit and make little circles. Imagine it's me doing it. Close your eyes and let your thoughts drift. I want you to think of nothing else except how good it feels. Understand?

She's so fuzzy that she's not even typing full words. Which is just how I want her. I really want to stroke my cock, but as hard as I am, I want to maintain some control. So instead, I squeeze myself through my jeans.

How does it feel?

So good. My body feels all heavy, like I'm sinking into the bed. Trouble thinking. Just want to keep touching.

Mike

> Good girl. Keep on touching. That's all you need to do. Reread my words and touch yourself.

I leave her for a few minutes, letting her sink into it. I imagine her lying there, eyes shut, hand between her legs, lost in it.

Mike

> Willow …

Willow

> ?

What I'm about to do is a little cruel, but it's also going to drive her wild. And be better for her in the long run.

Mike

> I want you to stop touching and wake yourself up. Playtime is over.

Willow

> WHAT? NO. I want to keep touching.

Maybe she's going to be a bratty sub. That's going to make things fun.

Mike

> How do you feel right now?

Willow

> Needy.

I couldn't have planned it better if I'd tried.

Mike

> And that's how I want you to feel whenever you think about me.

Willow

> Oh.

I pick up my plate of pancakes and start eating them. She might go back to touching, she might not. But now that I've put the thought in her head, she'll always think about being horny when she talks to me. And that's what I wanted.

Willow

You got me all turned on. Now I'm going to be distracted all day. You better be around to talk to me.

Mike

I will be.

Willow

Good. Now if I can't come, I'm going to go find some food.

I look at my phone as a picture comes through, her lips pushed up against the screen.

Willow

Talk to you later!

She's funny, sexy, and adorable. And I wonder if I'm allowing her to get too close. But for now, she makes me smile, and that's all I can ask for.

Chapter 3

WILLOW

My alarm blasts me awake from a delicious dream of Mike fucking me while I have another guy's cock in my mouth. Groaning, I pick up my phone and blink the sleep from my eyes so I can check my messages. It's the first thing I do every morning since Mike and I started flirting constantly. But I'm getting impatient. I want to fuck him again. Bad.

It's been over two weeks of texts and it's the longest sexual flirting I've done with anyone since Oscar-the-Slimeball cheated on me – AND I haven't even tried to orgasm all this time. I'm afraid I'll be too in my head again. I keep hoping he'll invite me over for a fuck, so I've just been keeping myself on edge. Why isn't he inviting me over?

I've been worried that he'll get bored with me since he's so much older, but he doesn't seem to be, and we had some enjoyable sexting that didn't end with any release. I think it's time to make a move. Hell, if he rejects me, then at least I'll know he isn't interested in anything more than sexy flirting.

I roll out of bed and get up to take a shower before work. I don't dislike my job, and being a barista has its enjoyable moments. My coworkers are great, but it feels like I've taken a step back in life. Before I broke up with Oliver-the-Douche, I had a job offer to be a resident services coordinator at an assisted-living facility. But before I accepted the offer, my then-boyfriend, Oliver, played hide the salami with a woman he met at a bar and everything went to shit.

After I dug myself out of the hole I was in, two months had passed and all I felt mentally capable of doing was barista work because it's what I did for years. During college, I worked at a local coffee shop and my old boss jumped at the chance to have me back. Now I've lost my confidence, and I don't know what the hell I want to do with my life. I'm not sure I can handle the stress of social work. Look at what happened when my boyfriend cheated on me. Just another thing my therapist and I are working on.

It's Thanksgiving next week and the coffee shop is busy. There's been a line for pumpkin spice lattes that extends halfway to the door most of the morning. When there's a pause, I grab a washcloth and clean the counter, lost in thought and counting down the hours until closing. I might head over to Alice's and see if she can help me figure out what to do about Mike. I need the perfect way to get him to fuck me again—preferably before Thanksgiving, because I'm spending the long weekend over at my parents' house like I do every year. My parents are kind of assholes, and I don't want to go. But it's free food, and I rarely see them, so it always feels like it's the right thing to do.

When my shift is over, there's a voice message from my mother asking me to call her, and I snicker at the perfect timing. Right when I'm thinking of going over there, she wants to talk. I'm assuming it's to discuss details about me cooking something for Thanksgiving, so I dial her as soon as I get to the bus stop. It's windy and dark, and I wrap my coat around me tighter as the phone rings on her end.

When she picks up, I greet her in my best fake-cheerful voice. "Hi Mom!"

She doesn't sound enthused. "Willow, hello."

Wow, her tone's weird, but it might be a bad connection. There's a dead silence, so I prompt her. "Uh, you wanted me to call?"

"Yes. I was wondering if you would house sit over Thanksgiving. Your father and I booked a long weekend at a romantic resort."

My mouth pops open, but she keeps talking.

"We need to get out of town and relax, but someone has to feed the fish and bring in some packages I ordered."

So we're not doing dinner like usual? I'm confused and a little hurt. It's not like I want to go, but I also don't want to sit at home all alone on Thanksgiving.

My thoughts are a jumble, but if I'm not having Thanksgiving with them, I might as well house sit. Their place is bigger and a lot nicer than my shitty apartment. I sigh and suck it up. "Sure, Mom. I can do that."

"Excellent. I'm sure we can trust you with the house while we're gone."

What the hell, of course she can trust me! What am I, five?

I'm about to gripe at her, but she continues. "I'll send you our travel plans by email. Talk to you later."

She hangs up the phone, and I pull it from my ear and stare at it. Well, shit, now I really *do* need to fuck Mike as soon as possible. Being his mindless toy will make me forget about my asshole parents so maybe I can enjoy my frozen pizza on Thanksgiving – the fuck if I'm cooking anything elaborate just for myself.

The bus arrives, and as I get on, I stew about Thanksgiving. Who wants to spend it alone? I'm an introvert, but I enjoy having something to do on holidays. I wonder what Alice is doing. Maybe I can tag along with her.

Wait...

A burst of excitement makes my heart skip. I've got the perfect plan. My hands are shaking as I type a message to Mike.

Willow

> Want to house sit with me at my parents' house over Thanksgiving and have freeuse of me?

There, sent. No taking it back now.

Oh God, he saw my message. Those three dots are a good sign, right? It's not a quick "no." I have to close my eyes and take deep breaths. I'm so wound up that when I hear my phone ding, I nearly drop it trying to open the message.

Mike

> Sounds tempting. Are you ready to be a good little freeuse slut again for me?

Hell to the fuck yes! I do a little dance in my seat right there on the bus. I'll have a couple of days with him. I feel like I've won the lottery, and now I have something to look forward to.

We spend the rest of my bus ride texting to hash out the details of the freeuse agreement. For the days we're at my parents' house, I'm his toy to use unless I say my safeword, which he makes me choose; I tell him it's the word 'lime,' because a woman on the bus is wearing a lime colored t-shirt.

By the time I'm in bed later, it's hard to fall asleep. My entire body feels like it's crawling with electricity and I desperately want to touch myself and see if I can come on my own again, but I also want to hold out. It's just one more week. I can make it, right?

***

I get to my parents' house the day before Thanksgiving, just in time for them to head to the airport for their romantic getaway. They left me some money to buy groceries, so I borrow their car to go shopping. I snatch up one of the last pumpkin pies in the deli and hunt for the smallest fresh turkey I can find. No frozen pizza for me!

I plan to plop a container of pre-made mashed potatoes into a casserole dish and pretend I made them. Even the canned gravy can be spruced up with some real turkey flavoring. Mike won't know that it came from a can—or that's my hope. Hell, I'm not even sure I can cook a turkey. I looked up online how to do it and it doesn't seem too difficult. Shit, I better get some frozen pizzas after all, in case this turns into a disaster.

When I wake up Thanksgiving morning, I'm in the guest bedroom of my parents' house. I could say it's my old bedroom, but when I moved out, they gutted it and re-did everything. Nothing of my old self is left, and it's bland with no personality. Now it's just a spacious room decorated in light blue, with a queen-sized bed and plush beige carpet.

A glance at the clock spurs me to get up. I don't have enough time to lounge around all day. I want to spend a little extra time on getting ready, and then I have plenty to do in the kitchen. After my shower, I blow dry my hair and keep the styling to a minimum so it'll be extra silky. I go light on my makeup as well. I want a natural look.

Once I'm done, I put on my sexiest black bra and panties, and a silky red dress that nips at the waist and has a full skirt that ends at the knees. I want to be comfortable, but also make him want to fuck me. It's not every day I get to have a freeuse fuck fest with the hottest guy I've met in forever.

Giving myself a final critical look in the mirror, I decide to put my hair in a ponytail. Once that's done, I look perfect. Smoothing out the imaginary wrinkles in my dress, I imagine Mike bending me over the table and pinning me to it so I'm unable to do anything but submit to him. He'll lift my skirt, move my panties to the side, and fuck me hard. A wave of desire rushes over me and I close my eyes as I feel my nipples ache. Fuck, I wish he was here already.

I shove the thought away. I need to be patient. He'll be here soon enough, and we'll have a nice dinner, and then he'll ravish me. Before I leave the bedroom, I put on a pair of black ballet flats. I'd love to wear some fuck-me high heels, but I'm a sensible girl and I'm not going to be in the kitchen wearing those safety hazards.

Shit, I hope I can come again. What if that was a fluke? I should have tried again on my own, but if that hadn't worked, then tonight could be terrible. How much I'm wound up over the thought of having sex again and worrying about my orgasm tells me I need to chill out. It's less likely to happen if I don't relax. If I don't orgasm this weekend, it won't be the end of the world.

But I hope I do.

As I walk through the house, I imagine all the ways Mike could fuck me – the couch in the living room, the floor in front of the fireplace, bent over the table....

Okay, I need to focus. I'm overheating, so I step out onto the back porch to cool off before starting the turkey. It's cold outside, so I only stay a minute before I'm back inside and tying an apron around my waist to keep my dress clean.

When the turkey is in the oven, I unlock the front door and text Mike that he can let himself in when he gets here. If he's anything like me, he'll still knock or ring the doorbell. It's weird to just waltz into a stranger's house.

Two hours later, I've got all the food in baking dishes and prepped, and the empty packages buried deep in the trash and recycling so no one will accidentally see the empty gravy can. I'm jittery from anticipation, so I dig around in the pantry and find a can of olives and some pickles. I'm prepping a relish tray when I sense someone behind me.

Looking over my shoulder, I spot Mike and my pussy contracts in pure, unadulterated lust. I stare at the object of my wet dreams—Mr. Perfect Dom—standing there, all broad shouldered and muscular. It might be because I'm turned on, but he's sexier than I remembered from Halloween. He's wearing blue jeans that hug his muscular thighs, and a dark green shirt that sets off his eyes.

I barely have time to smile at him before he's right behind me, pushing my shoulder to the counter. Ohhh, wow. We're doing this now? When he trails his fingers up the skirt of my dress and strokes my pussy through my panties, all my thoughts evaporate as my nerve endings hum to life. Mmm, yeah, right now is perfect.

Before I can gather my thoughts, he yanks my panties down, and I step out of them and widen my stance. The feel of his hand on my skin is electric and I'm instantly wet. When his fingers slip into my slick folds, I gasp and rise onto my toes. Pleasure ripples from my core and I fight the urge to grind against his hand.

This is going to be a fabulous Thanksgiving.

CHAPTER 4

MIKE

I'm not waiting around. She invited me over for freeuse and that's what she's going to get. Food is a nice little extra, but it can go cold if it has to. I've been wanting to fuck her for days, and I'm taking her now. If she really wants to be a good slut, she'll be ready for it. She has a safeword, so she can stop it in an instant whenever she wants.

The oven makes a buzzing sound, startling her. For a moment it seems like she's going to move towards it, but I brush my middle finger gently over her clit and she pauses.

"The food..." she says, but I give her pussy a gentle smack.

"Can wait. My pleasure comes first."

"Yes, whatever you want."

Putting my hand on the back of her head, I gently push it forward.

I growl into her ear. "Head back down on the counter and keep it there. You can get the food in a few minutes, but for now, you're my slutty little fucktoy, and I get to use you whenever I want. And I want to use you now, understand?"

She nods her head slightly and mumbles a yes. I have a feeling she's going to be a very obedient sub for me over the next few days. I might even let her call me Sir.

I unzip my pants and she tries to peek back at me, but instead she gets a spank on the ass.

"No, keep looking forward. You don't need to see it. I'm going to be fucking you with it soon enough."

My cock springs free, and I slap it gently against her pussy. I want her to feel how hard it is, a little preview of what she has coming. And I know that me doing this will also make her feel slutty because she's letting a guy do whatever perverted thing he wants to do to her.

"The food smells great," I say as I position myself behind her, my hand slipping over her ass.

"Thank you... oh FUCK."

My fingers sink deep into her pussy. She's soaking wet and ready for me.

"Tell me what food you have."

Her voice wobbles as she tries to tell me, but my fingers pistoning in and out of her pussy seem to distract her. "Turkey. Gravy. Mashed potatoes. Umm. Can't think."

Before I left my house earlier, I grabbed a handful of condoms. Then, thinking of what I had in mind, I took a few more. I don't plan to do much more this Thanksgiving besides eat and fuck. While she's talking, I get a condom out of my jeans pocket and stop fingerfucking her long enough to slip one on and rub the tip of my cock against her pussy.

"I can see more food. What else is there?"

"Relish tray..."

Grabbing her hips, I thrust forward and sink deep inside her. She's so tight and warm that I nearly groan, but I turn it into a growl that makes her shiver.

"Good girl. Is there pie? There better be pie."

I thrust in and out of her, slow and steady, and she groans while her legs tremble. "Yes. Pie. Pumpkin and cream – whipped cream."

I resist making a crude joke and instead concentrate on how good she feels wrapped around me.

Reaching forward, I place my hand on her throat. I'm not going to choke her—she's far too inexperienced for that—but having my hand there will make her feel controlled.

"You're mine for the next few days. Whenever I want you, however I want you. Understand?"

She groans a, "Fuck" and thrusts herself back against me.

"I said, do you understand?"

She tries to nod. "Yes. Yours to use whenever you want."

"Good. Now be a good freeuse toy. I'm going to use your pussy nice and hard and you're going to spread yourself for me. I want you to imagine you're being watched, just like you were when you gave those guys blowjobs. Don't forget, I know what a slut you can be."

I have a feeling that some light degradation will work on her, and from her sighs and moans, I can tell I'm right. She shifts under me, her head on the counter, and I speed up my thrusts.

"What do you want?" I ask.

"Fuck me. Want you to come. Use me like the slut I am."

Slapping her ass, I speed up, giving it to her a little rougher, but not too bad.

She gasps, "Oh, fuck... yeah. Like that. You don't need to be gentle."

For a second, I wonder if she could take me at my roughest, a leash in my hand and a collar on her neck. When I picture it, she has the most gorgeous look of ecstasy on her face. Maybe she could take it. But not now, not today.

It's been a few days since I masturbated, and I know that when I orgasm, I'm going to come hard. The tightness of her pussy and the sound of her moans are going to make it quick, but we have all weekend, so I'm not worried about blowing my load too soon. There will be plenty of time for more pleasure later.

"Ask for it."

She grabs at the counter, trying to steady herself as I slam into her, but she doesn't respond.

"Willow, I said ask for it."

She glances over her shoulder, and she looks gorgeous. Her face is red and her ponytail is disheveled, but what stands out is the need in her eyes.

"Please. Come in me."

I groan and let loose, emptying myself. My fingers tighten their hold on her hips and I thrust so hard that I nearly lift her off her feet. She lets out a satisfied groan and I continue to pound into her, letting her feel every throb.

After a few seconds, I pull back, giving her ass a slap.

"Good. Now let's see about getting this food served up. I'm starving."

***

After I use her, it takes a little while for her to be able to think again. After all, we only really met once before and then here I was, fucking her over the counter. But when I start getting the food ready and taking it to the table, she jumps into action and we get it all served up. Luckily, the turkey didn't burn even though we left it in the oven too long while we were fucking.

We chat about a variety of things over dinner—pretty normal conversation after I railed her against the counter. After dinner, I lean back in my chair and let out a content groan. I can't remember the last time I had such a good meal. Willow looks just as happy, and is beaming across the table at me, pleased to see I enjoyed it so much.

"That was SO good. You're one hell of a cook."

She does one of her cute little giggles that is so adorable it makes my cock twitch. "Oh, it was nothing."

I tell her to stay there and relax while I take everything back to the kitchen. She deserves a break, but I also want her to stay at the table for my own reasons.

When I come back, I sit down again. "Come here," I say.

Willow snaps to attention. She is already learning what my dom voice is and reacting to it.

She gets up and walks around the table, standing in front of me.

"Sit on the edge."

She hops up onto the surface, her legs swinging in the air. I stretch out and wrap my hands around her ankles and rest her feet on the edges of my chair.

"I'm going to lift your skirt and look at your pussy. Because for the next day or so, it's mine."

She nods her head and bites her lower lip. She's giving off nervous energy but also looks excited.

Taking the hem of her skirt, I lift it until I can see her pussy. She's shaved recently and I almost want to snap a picture of it. It looks so fucking cute.

But instead, I reach out and take her hand. "I want you to touch yourself while I watch. Put your fingers on your clit and rub little circles. Can you do that for me?"

"Yes," she says in a quiet voice.

I guide her hand to her pussy. For a moment she does nothing, and then she starts to play with herself.

I look up at her and I make sure she makes eye contact with me. This is all about control and submission. I don't need to see the movement of her fingers. I want to evaluate how she's reacting.

Willow holds my gaze for a few seconds before her eyelids flicker.

"Good?" I ask her.

"Yeah, so good."

Reaching out, I slip my fingers into her folds, getting them wet. Then I raise them to her lips. Without a word, she takes them in her mouth and sucks them clean.

"Good fucktoy. Keep rubbing, doing what you're told. Because that's what you really want: someone to take control of you, tell you what to do and to fuck you mindless."

She nods her head as my fingers slip from her mouth. "Are you going to fuck me?"

"No. Not yet. I have other plans."

Tightening my grip on her ankles, I lift her legs up, tipping her backwards onto the table. Before she can react, I sink to my knees and let her legs rest on my back as my tongue slides through her folds.

My fingers slip inside her and curl up, getting a groan from her. Gently kissing around the outside of her pussy, I tease her, keeping her on edge. Then my mouth rests on her and my tongue flicks over her clit.

It's like a bolt of electricity going through her, the table rattling as she arches her back and presses her legs down on me, guiding me forward.

"Oh, fuck yes. Don't stop, please don't stop."

I massage the inside wall of her pussy in just the right spot to make her legs tremble as I suck on her clit. The plan for this weekend was for us both to have fun, but not put any pressure on her to come. But I know the signs. She's only moments away.

"Do you want to come for me?" I growl into her pussy.

"Yes, fuck yes."

My thumb brushes over her clit and she grabs the table to keep from sliding away.

"Then come for me."

She howls and digs her feet into my back, and I'm grateful she's not wearing heels. Her orgasm is hard and fast and I hold her until she stops shaking. Reaching up, I slide my hands over her breasts and gently squeeze, giving her a last taste of control before I slip her towards me, taking her in my arms and kissing her.

The trembling is not surprising. She just came hard and no doubt her head is a muddle. Wrapping her up and lifting her onto my lap, I sit and let her rest until she wants to speak.

"That was SO good," she laughs as she nuzzles her head against me. "Who knew you had a talented mouth as well as a big cock?"

"You have not even seen the start of my talents."

I notice her nipples are showing through her dress, and I growl at the thought of sucking on them, maybe even coming over them. As soon as she hears the growl, she snuggles in tighter.

"Where is your bedroom?" I ask.

"Upstairs, second door on the left."

I stand up, taking her with me, cradled in my arms. She feels as light as a feather and smiles up at me as I carry her.

"You know what I'm going to do to you?" I ask, taking the stairs two at a time.

"Anything you want, all night long."

"You're damn right I am. I'm going to use that sweet mouth of yours and fuck your throat, then if you beg well enough, I'll pound your cunt so hard you'll be sore for days."

"I can beg. I can beg really good."

I give the door a kick, and it swings open and we go inside. With a backward heel, the door shuts behind us, and we don't leave the room for the next 12 hours.

CHAPTER 5

WILLOW

I groan as I wake up. Oh man, what a night. I don't even know how many times I came. Was it four? No, I think I lost count at four. I should have been fucking an older man all along—to hell with guys my age. They don't know what they're doing.

As I lie there, my brain kicks in. Mike is still asleep next to me, and I don't want to wake him. He deserves the best sleep after rocking my world last night. I climb out of bed and tiptoe into the adjoining bathroom. After I turn the shower on, I quickly brush my teeth while the water is heating up.

The mirror reveals the flush on my cheeks and the sparkle in my eyes. I look happy. Hell, have I ever looked this content before? I've got two more days of freeuse before my parents get back. But first, this slut needs a shower.

Stepping under the water, I tilt my head back and let the warmth cascade over me. There's no point in rushing. Today can be a lazy day. And besides, I want to get as clean as possible before Mike gets me all dirty again.

Suddenly, the shower door opens and I turn as he joins me. There's a wicked smile on his face, and I resist the urge to jump on him. I'm his fucktoy for the next couple of days. If he wants to fuck me, he will.

He forces me up against the wall of the shower, brushing his hand along my stomach and between my legs to caress my pussy while the other hand plays with my nipple.

"You're still mine."

I nod my head, his words making my heart race.

"Be a good toy and bend over."

He removes his hands so I can turn around. I put my palms flat on the wall and slant forward, presenting my ass to him. I'm curious about what he's going to do. When he uses a finger to rub my asshole, I jolt in surprise and moan from the unexpected dirty pleasure. Ohhhh, do I want this?

My mind fogs, and the more he touches me, the more desperate I get. He slides a finger into my ass, and I imagine it's his cock instead. It feels different, but not painful. When he begins to fingerfuck me, my pussy flutters, and I wish I had both holes filled at the same time.

What is this guy doing to me? When he removes his fingers, he slaps my ass, and I yelp.

"Good slut. Now soap me up."

I stand, eager to comply with his request. Holding back a smile, I squirt body wash into my hand. I can give just as good as I take.

Lathering the soap on his chest, I glide my hands over his muscled torso, inching slowly towards his cock. I love how his muscles contract when I touch him, and his already-hard cock pulses at my gentle caresses.

I lower a hand to cup his balls. Getting him nice and clean is the least I can do for the owner of the cock that made me come so many times. If only I could convince him to keep me, I'd do this every single day.

My hands still. What the fuck did I just think?

He groans, not knowing why I stopped. "Keep going, slut. I'm not clean yet."

I blink back the thought of him owning me, and stroke his shaft with the soapy bodywash, causing him to grunt with satisfaction. He thrusts his hips a couple of times to fuck my hand before reaching over and brushing my clit with his thumb.

My pussy buzzes as I moan. Fuck, he's good at getting me horny. And I'm all his to use however he pleases. Within seconds, he has me panting in desperation to come, but before I can climax, he orders me to rinse off and get out of the shower. I rush to obey. He's in control of my pleasure.

I scoot out and grab a towel to wrap around myself while he stays in the shower to finish cleaning up. While he's in there, I meander into my bedroom and giggle at the condom wrappers on the floor. I'm going to need to make sure none are hiding under the bed before my parents get home. At least it's just the wrappers, and not the actual used condoms. Mike always made sure those were wrapped in tissue and thrown in the trash. Fuck, I better empty the trash in the bedroom as well.

When Mike joins me in the bedroom, he's naked and toweling off his hair. His enormous erection tells me he's in the mood to use me again. There's a hunger in his eyes that makes me want to lick my lips, but I behave.

"Knees, now," he commands.

Like a good freeuse fucktoy, I drop to the ground. This is our unspoken dynamic, and I adore it. When I'm his toy, I have no decisions to make. I'm just his plaything.

He sits on the edge of the bed and strokes his glorious, massive cock. "Crawl to me."

Mmm, this guy knows how to treat a fucktoy. I ditch my towel and crawl over to him. He strokes my hair, caresses my cheek, then tips my chin up with a firm hand. When his eyes stare into mine, he gives me a soft kiss on the lips, his tender gesture melting my heart and making me crave more kisses and affection from him.

He smiles and positions my head to where he wants it—right in front of his dick. I expect him to put it into my mouth at any moment, and I just stare at it while it twitches inches from my face.

Mike's cock is the finest specimen I've seen in real life—not that I have much to compare it to, but I'm fairly certain it's better than average. I'll have to share notes with Alice someday. Or maybe I won't tell anyone about him. He'll be my wonderful secret.

He finally pushes my head down, and I open my mouth and lick his cock. I want him to fill my throat so badly, but I'll let him take charge, doing whatever he wants to do with me.

When he puts pressure on the top of my head, I know what he wants. I take just the tip into my mouth. I'm not done with the teasing and flick my tongue around, enjoying how his cock responds to the slightest movement. Circling the head, I take just an inch into my mouth and flatten my tongue. I stroke him with it, getting him nice and wet with my spit.

Tilting my head up to look at him, I see the satisfaction in his eyes. He gives a slight nod that indicates he enjoys it. I bob my head while I suck, and I'm rewarded with deep moans of approval.

He keeps his hands on my head, directing my movements, and a haze of lust steals over me. I really *do* feel like a fucktoy. I never knew how much I'd like someone else taking control. Not having to think during sex is pretty fabulous.

When he pulls my head off his cock, I pout. Dammit, why does he have to take away my fun? I was enjoying being mindless and knowing he was getting pleasure from it.

"Get up on the bed, slut. I'm going to make you scream."

Um...well, okay...that seems good too. I jump up and I'm uncertain what position he wants me in, so I crawl on all fours and look behind me to watch what he's doing.

He studies me for a moment as he gets a condom from his discarded pants and puts it on before climbing on the bed and kneeling behind me. "Face down, ass up. I'm going to use you."

Yes, sir. I present myself to him and wiggle my ass, trying to tempt him into a pounding right away. I'm wet and ready for him to fuck me, but I know he likes to tease.

Just as I think he's going to fuck me, the loud ring of my cell phone makes me jump. I try to grab it, and he barks, "Ignore it."

I have the phone on silent, but it's set to ring through if certain people call twice in a row. That means it's Alice or my parents. I'll find out what they need when he's done fucking me.

As soon as the phone stops, he slams into me, sinking in fully.

"Ohhhh, god," I groan as he stretches me out.

Everything about sex with him is amazing, from what he does to me, his cock, his stamina.... just everything. He's going to ruin me for other guys at this rate. I'm going to be comparing every future boyfriend to Mike, and somehow I know they'll come up lacking.

Mike spanks me and my mind clears of everything other than him and his glorious cock as he hammers away at me. Every thrust makes my head spin, and I bury my face in the bedding as my tiny sighs of pleasure turn into one long string of moans.

A tingle spreads deep in my pussy, and I can feel my walls quivering. A low cry bursts out of me, growing louder until I'm begging him to go faster. I lift onto my hands to gain leverage so I can rock back against him. I'm grinding my ass with every thrust, making him go as deep as I can get him.

There's an ache inside me, and it's as if my insides are vibrating, building to some great intensity.

Mike moves his hand to rub my clit, and I scream as my orgasm hits. Wave after wave of exquisite pleasure races through me, and I clutch at the sheets, unable to process the mind-blowing orgasm. My thighs quake uncontrollably, and I collapse face down, barely able to keep my hips in position. It takes all of my remaining strength just to keep my ass up.

Wrapping his hands around my hips, he continues fucking me. When he comes, I shudder again, over-sensitive to every pulse of his cock as he blows his load. I wish we didn't need to use condoms. I want to feel his cum inside me, but that isn't something I'm going to ask for right now.

When he pulls out, he quickly takes care of his condom before flopping next to me on the bed. He rolls to the side and gathers me up into a spooning position—me, the little spoon. Kissing my shoulder, he nuzzles at my neck while I practically purr from delight.

"I screamed."

He chuckles. "Yes, you did. Because you're a good little freeuse slut."

I kiss his hand and snuggle back into him, perfectly content.

A knock on my bedroom door and my mom calling out, "Willow?" makes me yelp, and I grab the sheet.

I get it mostly covering us when my mom opens the door. Holy shit, what're they doing home?

When my mother spots me in bed with Mike, a look of shock crosses over her face before she recovers and returns to her normally placid expression. I can tell she doesn't know what to say and I see her looking at the floor.

Uh-oh, the condom wrappers. My face burns bright red, and she closes the door without saying a word.

Fuck.

Mike kisses my shoulder again. "Is this a problem?"

"I don't know."

Shit, shit, shit. I'm assuming my parents figured I had sex with Oscar-the-Scumbag, but I never outright talked to them about my sex life. But thinking your daughter fucked her long-term boyfriend is a little different from seeing your spare room floor littered with condom wrappers and her in bed with a stranger.

I scramble out of bed, tugging a pair of jeans and a t-shirt on while Mike starts removing the sheets.

"Go talk to them. I'll clean up here. Where should I put the laundry?"

I tell him the washing machine is down the hallway as I brush my hair. I hope my mom isn't furious. I'm 25, I'm allowed to have sex. Wincing, I think of the mess we left of the kitchen. This is their fault for coming home early.

I find my mom in the kitchen cleaning up and I mentally cringe again. Shit. I feel like I'm in high school and about to get in trouble.

When she sees me, she stands and pauses expectantly, as if she wants me to explain myself.

"So, why did you guys come home early?" I don't bother to tell her anything. I'm more curious to find out why they're here.

Mom doesn't look pleased. "If you had checked your text messages or answered your phone, you would have known that your father got food poisoning. We decided to come home." She arches her eyebrow and gives me a pointed stare. "But it looks like you were too busy to check messages."

She's not wrong, and a giggle sneaks out as I think about how 'busy' I was.

She glares at me. "You find this funny? I come home and find my house a mess and my daughter in bed with someone I've never met—do *you* even know him?"

Her condescending tone pisses me off. "I know him."

I decide to keep it simple, not volunteering any information, and leaving my mom to make her assumptions. Mom shakes her head, exasperated, and gestures to the table. "Have a seat. Let's talk about rules when you house sit in the future."

Um, she thinks I'm going to help her again? Not with her bitchy attitude. She can pay the neighbor's kid to get the packages and look after the fish.

"I'm fine standing."

She keeps cleaning the dishes in the sink, and I can only see her back, but I can tell by her jerky movements that she's getting more angry. "Don't be obstinate, young lady, sit."

"DON'T talk to me like a child!" I snap out.

Goddamnit, she was the one who barged into the room without me telling her to come in. It's not like I wanted her to catch me in bed with someone.

There's a clatter in the sink and Mom rounds on me, holding a fork pointed straight at my chest. What the fuck? Is she going to poke me?

I raise my hands up. "Stop, just calm down, Mom. This isn't a big deal. Mike's a nice guy, and if you bothered to talk to me instead of threatening me with a fork, you might actually get to meet him."

My mom pauses with the fork in the air and I get a surreal feeling that I'm watching the scene from above. Suddenly my mom's arm drops and she looks over my shoulder. Mike's touch on my arm doesn't surprise me.

"Willow, I packed our stuff up. Is there anything you need that wasn't in the bedroom? It's time to go."

I smile softly at him, and a stinging in my eyes makes me blink. "No, I'm good. Let's get out of here."

When I move towards him, he opens his empty arm that doesn't have our bags and wraps me up as he walks me to the door. Neither of us say anything to my mother.

I'm quiet for a long time in the car, trying to process everything that happened. Mike drives and stays silent, giving me time to think. I don't know what the hell that was, but something just became clear to me.

"I think my mom has issues."

He makes a noise that sounds suspiciously like a snort. "Maybe."

Oh man, my poor therapist at our next session. My head whirls with the possibility that maybe my mom is more fucked up than I previously thought. I don't want this to ruin my time with Mike.

Wait... "Hey, where are we going?"

He gives me a quick side eye. "Back to my house, if you want to spend the rest of the weekend with me."

Oooh, his house. Fuck, I *do* want to spend more time with him, and I want to erase all memory of my mom walking in on us in bed.

"Can you make me mindless so I forget everything?"

The side of his mouth quirks up. "Yeah, I can do that."

I squeeze his thigh, purposely close to his groin, and reply, "Good," before settling in and trying to set aside my problems.

CHAPTER 6

MIKE

Almost as soon as we walk through the door, she turns around and I see how upset she looks. She's about to launch into an apology or an explanation and before she can, I interrupt. There will be time for that later, but she needs something else right now.

"Down on the left is the bedroom. Go get comfy. I'll be there in a minute."

She gives me a confused look. "What?"

I put my hand on her shoulder and give it a squeeze. "What happened earlier? Forget that for now. The one thing you need to remember is that today you're my freeuse slut. All you need to think about is getting me off."

Her expression changes from confusion to happiness as I continue. "So, like I said, down on the left is the bedroom. I want you to go in there, strip, and get into bed. I'll be along in a few minutes and you had better be ready for me, because I still plan on having my day of freeuse."

She stretches up onto her tiptoes, and when I bend forward, she kisses me on the nose. "Okay."

She starts to turn, but I grab her hand. "No—it's 'okay, Sir.' For the rest of today, you'll call me Sir."

Her eyes go wide and her face flushes a little. "Yes, Sir."

I watch her walking off and smile at her curiosity as she checks out pictures on the wall and glances through doorways. She must be wondering who the woman is in the photographs. I haven't told her about my wife yet.

She's moving slowly, so I give her a stern, "NOW."

She jumps at my voice, but I also hear her giggle as she scampers off to the bedroom. Her ass looks so good in those jeans that I want to go after her and rip them off her.

But I give her a little time to settle in and head into the kitchen. I grab some snacks and a couple of bottles of water. We are going to need them, as I don't plan on leaving the bedroom for a good few hours. Willow needs her mind taken off things with her parents and mindless sex seems to be the best way.

I'm getting the feeling that she doesn't have much of a support network. Most people can go to their family when they have problems, but what do you do when the family is part of the problem? I know that I'm not her boyfriend or anything, but I feel some responsibility to look after her. After all, me being there was what set things off.

Walking to the bedroom, I think how weird this is for both of us. For her, she's in the house of a guy she has slept with twice. Really, we don't know each other that well, but here she is pretty much under my control. And for me, this is the first time that I've had someone stay over who wasn't just a quick fuck before I sent them home.

As I open the bedroom door, I take in the sight of Willow on the bed.

She's naked and on all fours, with an eager look on her face. "Your bedroom's not like how I imagined it, Sir."

I put the snacks and drinks on the nightstand, then sit on the edge of the bed, caressing her ass.

"How so?"

"I think I imagined it with more whips and handcuffs. Maybe a mirror on the ceiling."

Moving forward, I growl in her ear. "You haven't earned the whips and handcuffs yet. Give it time."

I walk over to the dresser and take a condom out of the drawer. Then I come back and stand in front of her.

"Undo my jeans."

She's so excited that she fumbles with the zipper and it takes much longer than it should, but eventually she pulls them down and I step out of them.

"Now my boxers."

She looks up at me. "Yes, Sir. Thank you, Sir."

She tugs at them and almost yelps in surprise when my cock springs up and nearly hits her face.

"Do you know how to put on a condom?" I ask as I unwrap it.

She looks at me and frowns like it's a stupid question. "Of course, Sir."

"With your mouth?"

Her eyes go wide and I place the condom against her lips, then put the tip of my cock against it.

"Put the condom on with your mouth."

She slowly dips her head, taking me between her lips. The condom rolls along until it reaches the base of my shaft and I am fully in her mouth.

"Now, here is what's going to happen. I am going to fuck your throat nice and slow. With every thrust, you're going to get more and more spacey until all you can think of is how good it is to be an obedient fucktoy. And when I have finished using your mouth, I am going to fuck your pussy. Understand?"

She nods her head—at least, as much as she can with my cock so deep.

"I haven't decided if I'm going to let you come yet, but that's not important. What's important is you don't need to think. You don't need to worry. All you need to be is a good slut and make Sir happy."

I rest my hand on the side of her face, gently stroking it, and then slow fuck her mouth.

It doesn't take long for her to start moaning and she gets into a steady rhythm. I keep the pace nice and easy for the moment. I don't want to come for a while yet.

She really is a great cock sucker, and her moans vibrate against me, making me throb. At some point, I need to just have a day of using her mouth.

Wait, 'at some point?'

I seem to think that this is going to be happening again. Is this going to be a regular occurrence? I hadn't realized that I already thought of this as an ongoing thing until the thought was in my mind.

Sliding my cock from her mouth, I lift her head up and smile at her. "How do you feel?"

"Mmm, I love being a fucktoy, Sir. You can use me whenever you want."

I put my hand back on her head and fill her throat again. "You can touch yourself, but no coming."

I've hardly finished speaking and she already has her hand between her legs. The moans and vibrations intensify.

"Mmmm. Good slut."

My movements get faster and she takes every inch, her nose brushing against my stomach with each thrust. Her hand moves so fast it's a blur and I can tell by the sounds she's making that she's close to coming.

"Hand away," I order, and her moan of pleasure turns into a moan of complaint, bringing a smile to my face.

I pull out of her mouth and force her back onto the bed, climbing on top of her and pinning her down. "Who owns you?"

"You do, Sir."

The tip of my cock is brushing against her pussy and it would be so easy just to thrust forward and slide into her. "Say it."

"You own me. You own this slut's body. My mouth, my pussy. Every part of me is yours to use however you want."

"Yes. Yes, it is."

I push my cock into her and her pussy grips around me like it's trying to stop me from leaving. Her hips buck, and I can't stop myself from sliding into her fully.

"Please, Sir. Please, can I come? Please?"

She's panting, and I can see the sweat covering her chest.

"I'll make you a deal. If you can manage not to come before me, I'll let you." I whisper in her ear. "But if I feel you start to come, I'm going to pull out and you won't be allowed to come at all. Understand?"

"Yes. Yes Sir."

Her hands wrap around the bars of the headboard and she stares up at me. "Thank you, Sir."

With a smile, I move inside her, building up the speed. I can see how desperate she is, and it only makes me want to push her even more.

She moans, "I'm so close, Sir. Please, I'm trying."

The bed shakes as our bodies slam together and the sound echoes around the room.

"Sir. Oh no, I don't know if I can stop."

I have no idea if she will last, but right now I'm so close to coming.

"Keep going, slut. Just a little more. Keep going."

And then, with a pulse, I explode, groaning, "Come for me, slut."

Our bodies lock together, frozen for a few seconds. She screams so loud it hurts my ears as her orgasm rips through her. Her entire body shakes and her pussy clenches around me.

"Oh god. Oh god," she cries out as she writhes under me.

It's hard to tell how long it goes on, but when her orgasm finally ends, we're both gasping for breath. I fall back onto the bed, staring at the ceiling.

"Jesus, Sir."

I can feel her looking at me, and I turn my head towards her.

She has a look of complete adoration on her face. "Thank you."

"For what?"

"Everything." She cuddles up next to me and rests her head on my chest. "I think I need to sleep. I'm exhausted."

I give her a kiss on her forehead and wrap her up in a hug. It feels good to have her snuggled against my chest and to have someone looking up at me the way she is.

"What are we doing later?" she asks.

"More of this."

She closes her eyes and I feel her body relax. "Perfect," she says, then drifts off to sleep.

***

We wake up in the evening and shower again, and then fuck some more. Neither of us tries to get the other off. We're just enjoying the intimacy and prolonging the pleasure.

When we come up for air, I put out some of my clothes for her. A pair of shorts and an old t-shirt that are far too big for her.

I'm sitting on the edge of the bed, admiring how incredibly cute she looks when she says, "We're out of snacks, Sir. Do you want me to make us dinner?"

I pull her over to me and kiss her stomach while rubbing her ass. I've noticed whenever I touch her butt, it makes her giggle, and I'm coming to adore that sound.

"Maybe I'll just eat you."

She laughs and spins around, wiggling her ass in my face. "I thought maybe Sir was going to fuck me in the ass this morning after the shower. It seemed like you might want to."

Stepping up behind her, I slip my hands under the t-shirt and squeeze her breasts, growling in her ear as she presses against me.

I have her full attention. "I'm not going to ask for that. You're my freeuse slut, but that's off the table."

She turns around and looks at me, confused and maybe a little sad. "But why?"

"Because at some point, you're going to offer it to me. I won't have to ask." I kiss her nose. "When you trust me and it feels right, you're going to let me be the first person to fuck your ass."

Her eyes widen, and I give her a moment to process what I said. She reacts in a way that I don't expect. She jumps up, wrapping her legs and arms around me, and I slide my hands under her ass to hold her up.

"Okay. Now, where's your kitchen? Can you carry me to it? Or are you too old to do that?"

I growl and show her exactly how easily I can carry her to the kitchen.

***

After dinner, we end up watching a movie. It turns out that she's never seen Bringing Up Baby. We cuddle on the couch while I tell her of my love of classic films. Apparently, she has always wanted to see it but her boyfriend didn't like black and white movies, so she's excited to get the chance.

Her head rests on my lap, and without thinking about it, I stroke her hair. It feels natural for her to be here, not out of place or awkward like I imagined it could be.

About halfway through the film, she looks up at me and I get the sense she's worried about something.

"Sir?"

"Yeah?"

She fidgets a little and rests her hand on my lap. "I know you're in charge, and I have to do whatever you want…"

"Yeah, that's right." I place her hand against my growing hardness under my jeans.

"It's just, um. Can I suck your cock while we watch this? I want you in my mouth."

I open my jeans, taking out my cock. Without speaking, she lowers her head and takes me in her mouth.

Resting back against the sofa, I let my eyes drift shut. The movie in the background, the warmth of our bodies together, and her lips sliding up and down my shaft. It's perfect.

It makes me think of something. "Willow?"

Her lips make a popping noise as she lifts her head. "Yes, Sir?"

"Have you ever 69ed with anyone?"

She blushes. "Oh. No."

I pull her head up and kiss her deeply, growling with need as I remove her t-shirt. Within seconds, I am under her and she is lowering her pussy onto my face, then sucking my cock into her mouth.

Soon, the movie is completely forgotten.

CHAPTER 7

WILLOW

When we wake up Sunday morning, Mike offers to make me breakfast. I can't stop smiling at him. We lounged around all day yesterday, alternating between watching old movies and him fucking me all over his house. I had so many orgasms, my body seems trained to get wet just being around him now. He only has to look at me to turn me into a puddle. Yep, I'm such a slut and it's wonderful. This is the best Thanksgiving weekend I've ever had. Not even the odd moment with my fork-wielding mother could ruin it.

I take a chair at the kitchen bar and watch him make us scrambled eggs and bacon. When he slides a plate in front of me along with a glass of orange juice, my eyes go wide at how perfect it looks. I'm used to Oliver-the-Prick just tossing a box of cereal at me and calling it good.

I hold my fork, ready to dig in. "This looks yummy, thanks."

He smiles. "No, you look yummy. Breakfast looks okay."

He winks at me, and I flush. I think I look silly in his baggy shirt, and yet it also gives me a slutty feeling, like I'm doing a walk of shame, but in the man's clothes instead of mine.

I roll my eyes at him. "I look terrible. I look like a slut."

His lips curve into a smile. "A slut in my bed and my clothes, so it's all good. And you look gorgeous... and fuckable."

My blush deepens. I love how he compliments me so easily. I could get used to this. Hell, I *want* to get used to it, and continue whatever we've got going here beyond this weekend. I need to see him again, and this time I'm going after what I want. I've had a taste of him, and now I'm starving for more.

I pick up a piece of crispy bacon and take a bite. "So, I need to go home today, but when do I get to see you again so you can fuck me mindless?"

He swallows a huge bite of egg and takes a sip of orange juice. "Actually, we need to talk about that. I'm going on a cruise for a few weeks, so we can't see each other, but we can text."

I don't expect that answer, and I blink to hide my surprise. "Oh. Okay. Wow, a cruise."

He watches me closely, and I must look crestfallen because he walks over to me.

He gives me a deep kiss. "I want to see you when I get back."

That makes me feel a little better, so I nod and look into his gray eyes. They sparkle, and I'm so captivated, I almost forget what I was talking about.

Oh right. "And then what? When you get back from your trip, will I still be a freeuse slut to you?"

He laughs. "Cherry is having a freeuse Christmas party. Want to be my date?"

Freeuse Christmas? Now that sounds like fun. I'm tempted to tease him by asking if that means I get to dress up as an elf, but there's a more important question.

"Would I be wearing one of those ribbons that means I'm freeuse at the party?"

The laugh lines around his mouth deepen. "That depends. Do you want to wear one?"

I shrug and try to sound nonchalant. "I don't know…" I take a huge bite of my eggs and make him watch me chew it before I finish answering. "I guess I could think about it while you're on your cruise."

The corners of his eyes crinkle, as if he finds my attempt to tease him funny, but he gives me what I want. "You think about it. And think about whether it will be a red or a green ribbon. They mean the same thing they did at the Halloween party."

The bite of egg in my mouth is suddenly difficult to swallow as I imagine him bending me over a table while I wear a green ribbon around my wrist that allows people to use any hole. Oh fuck. I want that, but I'm also afraid.

He laughs at my expression and kisses my forehead. "Just something for you to think about. Don't worry too much about it. Christmas will be fun."

I nod my head, trying to convince myself of what he's saying. I take a big drink of orange juice to distract myself, and he changes the subject to talking about the cruise and what he'll be doing.

I'm distracted while he talks because my phone is in the pocket of his shirt and it keeps vibrating like I'm getting text messages. It's probably my mom, and I'm not in the mood to talk to her yet. I'm not ready to deal with her until I've had a session with my therapist.

Something Mike says catches my attention. Did he just call the cruise a singles' cruise? I tune into him again.

"...and since it's a singles' cruise, it's usually pretty wild."

Hold up, he's really going on a singles' cruise? I try to keep my tone of voice neutral. "That sounds like fun."

He shrugs. "It was last year."

I'm not done with my eggs, but I've lost my appetite. I stand up with my plate. "I can't eat another bite. Thank you. It was delicious."

"You're welcome. Just leave the plate by the sink. I can take care of it later."

I keep my back to him as a ball of anxiety grows in my stomach. This is not the way I thought the weekend would end. I'm supposed to be happy after all those orgasms, but the thought of him off on some ship full of single women makes me jealous. We don't have an agreement, and we're not committed to each other. He can do whatever he wants.

This is just another thing for my poor therapist to hear about. I need to find out when my next appointment is. Thank heavens I'm still on my parents' health insurance, so I can afford this.

After breakfast, he helps me gather my few things, and he tells me to keep the clothes I'm wearing until he gets back. As he carries my bag out to the car, I realize this is the last time I'll see him until after his trip, and I feel glum.

I can't tell whether he's been enjoying himself. Maybe I'm just a plaything to him, a pleasant distraction during his last week before he gets on board with a bunch of hot older women. I'm not his submissive, or his girlfriend. Hell, he only gave me permission to call him 'Sir' for one day.

Both of us are quiet on the drive to my apartment, and he seems to be thinking, while I'm trying to do anything BUT think.

When he pulls up in front of my run-down apartment, he peers out the window at the building. "You live here?"

I can tell he's surprised and I'm suddenly embarrassed about how low-income it looks. Shit, I should have gotten a ride to come pick me up. That would have been a good idea.

"Yep, this is me."

He studies my building for a moment, and I shift uncomfortably.

Finally, he puts the car back into park. "Let me walk you up. I'd feel better doing that."

"It's just an apartment building," I mumble as I climb out of the car.

Sure, this isn't the best neighborhood, but I'm a barista living on my own. It's the best I can do. I can't even afford to own a car. I'm lucky to have an apartment without a roommate, especially because moving back in with my fork-crazed mother probably isn't an option anymore.

I grab my overnight bag from the trunk, and we head into the building. When he's in the lobby with me, I notice him looking at the stained carpet. Yeah, it's time to end this on a better note. I need to say goodbye to him here without him seeing my actual apartment. I don't want to tarnish the weekend we just had and leave him with thoughts of my pathetic life.

Dropping my bag, I turn towards him and rub my body against his. "Hey."

Surprised, his eyes flick back to mine. "Hi."

I snake my hands around his waist and tilt my head up. "Thanks for everything this weekend."

Giving me a tiny smirk, he teases, "You were the perfect little freeuse slut."

Fuck, that's hot. My face flushes, and I quickly look around. Thank God we're alone. He laughs and brushes his lips against mine. When he deepens the kiss, my knees go weak, and my toes curl while I moan softly.

When he breaks off the kiss, he rests his forehead on mine for a moment. "Until the next time, my slut."

Feeling brave, I whisper, "Thank you, Sir."

He pulls away, winks at me, and heads out the door. Once he's gone, I get my phone and check my texts. I have ten messages, nine of them from my mother—I don't bother opening those.

The last text is from Alice.

Alice

> How did your freeuse Thanksgiving go? I need details! Plus, I've got a crazy story to tell you too. Text me back, bitch.

Oh, she's going to love this story. I snicker as I pick up my bag and take the stairs to my third-floor apartment.

CHAPTER 8

WILLOW

After talking things over with Alice, she convinces me I need to relax about Mike. We're not dating, and we're not exclusive or anything. He's probably had this cruise planned for months, and it's not like he planned to meet me... and more importantly, again, we're not dating. He can fuck whoever he wants, just like I can.

Except... I don't want to fuck anyone else. I only want Mike.

I plop down on my bed and pout at the crack in the ceiling. Fuck, I really do want only him. I've never met anyone like him before, and when I'm around him, I feel like the most important person in the entire world. I know some guys are good at making a woman feel like that, but it doesn't seem like an act. It's who he is.

There's no point wasting time wondering what to do about him. He's going on a cruise and might meet the love of his life who is more his age. I'm probably good to fuck, but it's not like he'd actually want to date me.

Damnit, I really am ruined for any other guy. When I submit to him and he takes control, I crave it. When he praises me for being such a good girl and tells me how much he enjoys fucking me...Jesus. Even the memory of his words is enough to get my heart racing.

I run my hands over my breasts and tease my nipples through his shirt while pleasure swirls in my core. At least I've got his shirt I can wear while he's on the cruise. Maybe I'll put it on, send him naughty pictures and tell him exactly what I'm doing to myself while wearing it.

Oooh, yeah... by the time I'm done with him, he won't even be able to think straight enough to fuck any of those slutty chicks on the cruise. He's going to wish he was home with me.

That settles it. I'm sending him filthy photos of myself while he's gone and I'm going to drive him crazy.

It's the perfect plan.

Chapter 9

MIKE

Back at my house, something seems off. It takes me a while to realize that it's too quiet. Without Willow here, the place is silent and gloomy. Her smile and laughter filled the place up and made it feel like a home again. Here on my own, it's just a house to live in.

Seeing where Willow calls home was a shock. I know she's probably making close to minimum wage, so I don't expect her to be living in a mansion, but I don't want her living in a place like that. If I were her parents, I would do everything I could to help her get out of there. I actually know someone who owns apartment buildings. Would she think it rude of me to talk to them and see if they can get her into somewhere better?

It's been an amazing weekend, even with the weirdness from her mom. In fact, that incident brought us closer together. As soon as she got here, she let her guard down even more and allowed me to fully control her. Maybe at her parents' house, she was still worried about house sitting, but when I took her home, she had nothing to think about except being a good slut. Which she shined at.

And talking about being a freeuse slut, I'm regretting asking her to the Christmas party. Not because it won't be fun. I'd love to see her dressed as a sexy elf and acting like a ho ho hoe. It's more that I'm not sure I want to share her with anyone else. I know that's silly. We're not dating or making any commitment, but when I'm with her, I feel both protective and possessive.

Will she want to fuck other guys at the party?

If she does, maybe I'll just tell her she can be a freeuse cocksucker. She was pretty fucking hot when she was blowing that guy before I found her in the bar at Halloween… and watching her do that while I fuck her? I think I would like her acting all slutty and taking some dude's cock in her mouth while I pound her pussy.

But that's all after the cruise. Not that I really want to go on it, but I don't have a choice since it's for work and too late to ask them to find someone else this year. My company books the entertainment for the cruise line and once a year I get sent as a guest to observe the trip—like a secret shopper, because no one knows I'm there for work.

It might have been my imagination, but she seemed to get a little down when I told her about it. Maybe, like me, she's not looking forward to there being such a long time before we get together again.

We can always sext while I'm away. She seems to enjoy it when I growl in her ear and tell her what to do. Maybe I'll make some sexy videos for her, with me being all dominant and telling her to touch herself. Get her all worked up so that by the time we go to the Christmas party, she'll be so needy for me she won't want to fuck anyone else.

It's the perfect plan.

Freeuse Christmas

Freeuse to Forever After Book 3

April Cross | Matt Lake

CHAPTER 1

WILLOW

Alice and I stomp snow off our feet before entering the lingerie store. It's not even December, so why the heck is it snowing? I hate the cold, and my apartment's windows aren't exactly airtight, so I'm not looking forward to a long winter. But that's not something I need to worry about right now. Today, I'm out with Alice to buy some lingerie that will make Mike think twice about touching another woman on that cruise.

As we enter, the salesperson greets us with a sunny smile. "Welcome! Let me know if there's anything I can help you find."

I beam back, feeling pumped and confident. "Thanks, we will."

Even though I'm feeling good about this, it's a new experience for me. I've never dated a guy who made me actually WANT to shop for lingerie. Oliver-the-Limp-Dick didn't appreciate it. He said it was a waste of time because he just had to take it off to get to the prize. Back then, I thought it was endearing, but now... fuck him.

Alice and I dive into the nearest rack. I hold up a gorgeous white lace babydoll chemise in front of me and quirk an eyebrow at Alice.

She laughs and shakes her head. "Is that really the look you're going for? You don't want to scare him shitless and make him think you're headed down the aisle."

"But I look fantastic in white," I grumble as I put the lacy number back and turn my attention to a nearby section of black lingerie. "Wow, these are pretty." I grab a lace chemise and look at Alice for approval.

Alice's arms are overflowing with a rainbow of silky lingerie and I stare at her until she feels me watching her and glances up.

"What?" she asks defensively.

I shake my head. "How long are you planning on being in the dressing room? I thought this was a quick trip?"

"Oh." She gives me a knowing smile. "We're not trying any of this on. Pick out as much as you want. My treat."

Holy shit. "Seriously? Did you win the lottery or something?"

What the hell is going on with Alice?

Alice rolls her eyes. "Of course, I'm serious! I've got myself a sugar daddy now, you know. He gave me his credit card."

Uh... fine, whatever. "Sounds good to me."

I start picking out whatever I want that's in my size and looks alluring. I hope she doesn't get in trouble when Mr. Moneybags sees the charge on his credit card. Hopefully, he'll be too busy enjoying the result to care.

By the time we make it to the cashier, we're overloaded with lingerie and the cashier peers down at the pile and then looks at us. I elbow Alice and she giggles as another worker comes over to help ring us up. When Alice hands over a credit card, I notice it's her name on the card.

"Hey! You said this was the old geezer's money."

I'm mentally debating what to take back while Alice laughs. "It is. He got a card for me."

My mouth drops open, and she wiggles her eyebrows at me. "Don't worry. I plan to pay him back."

She leans close to me and whispers, "With interest."

Oh God, she's hilarious, but she looks deliriously happy.

Once everything is paid for, we head out with the bags, and I can't resist teasing her. "So, you've been holding out on me. You never said how your Thanksgiving went with Mr. Moneybags. And here I thought you weren't that interested in him."

I watch her expression closely and see her eyes light up and her lips stretch into a slow grin. "It's going... well. I don't want to talk about it yet and jinx it."

I playfully knock into her. "Fine. Keep your secrets for now, but you'll spill sooner or later."

"Deal." Alice holds out her fist, so I bump hers.

***

Alice drops me off at my apartment, and I hurry in from the cold with my new treasures. I won't rip the tags off all of them yet, in case she calls me later and says we have to return them. I still don't trust that her sugar daddy wants her to buy me lingerie.

I shiver as I enter my apartment, and hurry over to the tiny area I call my living room. Dumping my purchases onto my sofa, I switch on the space heater. I need to take the chill off the room if I plan on taking photos.

While the room warms, I step back and eye my purchases. There's so much sexiness in front of me, and it looks like an explosion at a lingerie factory. I do some rearranging, placing everything on the couch, neatly folded by color then type: black silk panties, white chemises, red corsets and so on until the pile is organized to my satisfaction.

It's still too chilly to strip, so I take a hot shower. I lather up and my mind drifts to Mike. Our text messages of 'sweet dreams' have turned into a routine, and my stomach flutters with happiness as I think about him. Since he leaves for his vacation tomorrow, should I send him a naughty photo tonight or wait? Hmm... maybe wait. I don't want him so horny that when he walks onto the ship he starts eyeing the single women.

I take a long shower, making sure to be careful while I shave. By the time I'm finished, the room is heated enough for me to model my lingerie. I pull out the first set I want to try on: a baby blue sheer chemise and a matching garter belt with attached thigh-high stockings. Perfect. Sensual but classy. Well, kind of classy. There's a hint of innocence to it that will hopefully make him remember he took my virginity... and that I'm an obedient fucktoy.

Propping my phone up on my nightstand, I angle it so it's the perfect level to take photos of me on the bed. Before I start, I dig out a length of red yarn from my craft supplies and tie it around my wrist. It's not authentic, but it will get the point across.

I turn on music, and while some rock band sings their hearts out, I snap various poses while smiling, flirting and blowing kisses at the camera. I think about how Mike is going to love these. The longer it goes on, the more I get into it. I sprawl out on the bed, making a variety of expressions ranging from ecstasy to pure adoration. I change outfits several times, each time choosing a sluttier one. This is fun, and I'm feeling sexy and powerful. I'm trying to create naughty pictures for Mike, but I'm also turning myself on imagining how he'll react when I send them. He better darn well appreciate these.

Wait, what if I get him turned on and he runs out and fucks some woman while on vacation because he's got nothing better to do? No. No way, I refuse to let that happen. He's going to get so many pictures and so many flirty messages, his head will be spinning and he won't have time to think of anyone else. I need to stay focused on the plan.

After an hour of taking photos, I'm vibrating with need and I wish I could fuck Mike right now. This has all been to turn him on, but I've succeeded in driving myself crazy in the process. I could try to take care of my problem myself, but I just want Mike.

Heck, what I should have done was drag Alice to a sex toy shop and see if Daddy-Lotta-Bucks would pay for an expensive toy--some big, thick dildo that reminds me of Mike. My body hums and I feel flushed. Yep, I'm making things worse.

I bundle up in a robe, and as I'm reviewing the photos, I giggle when I see that my nipples are standing at attention. I was turned on, but it was also because my damn apartment is way too cold. Ugh, I've got to find somewhere else to live by next winter. I swear I could see my breath this morning. That's not right—and it's only the beginning of the cold season.

I make some tea and snuggle into bed to do some light editing of the photos. I'm fucking hot in most of the shots. Sending them is going to be fun, but I'm still going to make him wait. He doesn't get one tonight.

The tea makes me sleepy, and I text Mike before I zonk out.

Willow

> Good night, Sir. I've got a sexy surprise for you soon. Have a safe trip!

I'm too tired to wait for his reply and I know I'll see it in the morning. I flip off the light and grab my stuffed bear to cuddle, pretending it's Mike as I fall asleep.

CHAPTER 2

MIKE

Staring out over the ocean from my cabin window, I wonder what Willow is doing.

I arrived on the boat this morning after an overnight flight, so I'm still jet lagged, but already I can tell this cruise is going to be a little different from ones I've taken in the past.

Every year, my company sends me on this cruise. It's part work and part reward. We provide the entertainment for the ship—musical acts, comedians, and such—and I'm there to check that everything is going okay from the point of view of an average customer. No one knows I work for the company, so they don't treat me special.

So every December, I go on a three-week singles cruise around the Caribbean, and while I'm there, I enjoy casual hook ups with other like-minded people. I may be getting on in years, but on the ship, there's usually no shortage of women who're looking for an older dom to fool around with.

On previous trips, I've been able to relax and enjoy myself. But this year, I can tell there's going to be a problem.

The problem is Willow.

Within half an hour of getting on the boat, a woman hit on me—long blond hair, tanned body in a tiny bikini, emerald eyes. She's stunning, and she invited me to her cabin to rail her senseless.

But I said no.

I surprised myself, not knowing I was going to say it even as I opened my mouth. But as soon as the word was out, I knew I said the right thing.

As hot as this woman was, she wasn't Willow.

After that, I saw a lot of women that normally I would try to screw, but I knew in my heart of hearts that it would be meaningless fun. Because I would be thinking of Willow the entire time.

I don't know what it is about her that's gotten under my skin. She's gorgeous and sexy, but there's something more than that.

For the first time in a long time, I'm comfortable around someone. It's not just the sex. When we cuddled up on the sofa, I wanted her to rest her head on my chest and feel her hand in mine. Or when we woke in the morning, cuddling up in each other's arms felt like a treat rather than something I should do before sending her on her way. I want to spend time with her rather than going back to my usual self-inflicted isolation.

This is the first time since my wife has died that I want to have a relationship with someone. I'm not saying dating, but something more than fuck buddies.

My phone buzzes, and I glance at the screen. It's a message from Willow. I'd just sent her a picture of the view from my cabin.

Willow

Oh, very nice. But you know the view I want to see.

She signs it with a winking emoji. I'm old-fashioned with my texting and rarely send hearts or funny GIFs. But when she does it, it makes me smile.

I snap a picture of myself, giving her my best dom pose.

She replies almost instantly.

Willow

Are you shirtless?

Mike

Yes. I'm heading to bed.

I climb into bed as I wait for her reply. One of the advantages of an all-expenses-paid trip is that I get a decent-sized cabin with a luxurious bed. It's as soft as a cloud and my eyes are already starting to close.

The ping from my phone brings me back and I check Willow's message.

Willow

So, you're completely naked then?

Mike

Yes.

I wonder where she is while she's messaging me. Probably in that depressing apartment. I hate to think of her there, especially when I'm in such nice surroundings.

Willow

Hmm, how can I believe you? Maybe you need to prove you're naked.

She's certainly less shy than when we first met. I can't imagine that woman asking to see me naked. But just because she's coming out of her shell doesn't mean I won't make her work for it.

Mike

Where are you?

With one hand I type a message to her, while with the other I wrap my fingers around my cock and gently stroke. The dom side of me has woken up and is ready to play.

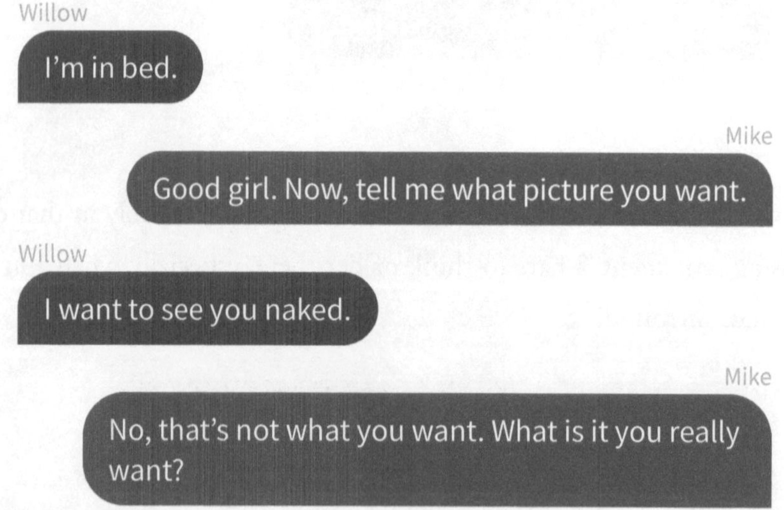

There's no waiting for a reply. She sends an instant, "Yes, Sir."

My cock grows in my grasp as I imagine her rushing to the bedroom and throwing off her clothes. I smile as I think about her tits bouncing as she leaps into the bed and gets under the covers. I bet she's excited and has an adorable grin.

There's a pause and I remember that even though she's becoming bolder, she's still a rather shy sub. But then I get her reply.

Now that's my good girl.

Slip your hand between your legs and touch your-self. I want you fuzzy and wet before I send you anything. Understand?

Whenever she gets turned on, her replies get shorter, either from rushing or because her head gets foggy and she can't form the words. It's how I can tell if she's into what I'm doing.

I pull down the covers and angle the phone at my cock, making sure that the curve is visible. Willow likes the curve; she says that it hits the perfect spot. I believe it based on how it makes her moan.

I make sure the picture is clear and hit send. It's a little strange for me, as I'm not into taking dick pics. When I was with my wife, it wasn't a thing. And now that I'm single, I don't normally stay with anyone long enough to send pictures back and forth. I've only done it a few times, and this one looks impressive.

My phone pings again.

Oh. That's hard, and the tip is so red. Your hand is really wrapped around it.

Red and hard for you. Now I want you to lie back in your bed and rub your pussy. Give your clit atten-tion and imagine it's me rubbing circles against it. I want you to think of me watching you. And you're going to send me a picture to show me how turned on you are.

It takes a few minutes before she replies, and I sit there stroking my cock while I wait. I can picture her, head back and legs wide open. Her fingers inside her pussy as she imagines me watching her from the end of the bed. Maybe when I get back I should do that. Get her to put on a show for me and tell her that if it's good enough, she can have my cum. I'm sure that would be the right incentive for her.

Her reply comes back and I open the picture. She's lying on her back holding her phone camera above her, wearing a gorgeous black lingerie set with her breasts spilling out the top. Her eyes are shut and her mouth is slightly open. I can't see where her other hand is, but I'm pretty sure it's between her legs.

This is the first time I've asked her for a picture, and she sent it without question. Not only is that a sign of a good sub, but also that she trusts me.

As I focus on the picture, I stroke myself harder and some pre-cum leaks out. I wish Willow were here to lick it and swirl her tongue around the tip, then look me in the eyes as she swallows.

Mike

I want you to lift your finger to your mouth and suck it. Taste yourself and imagine how good it'll be when I'm there and eating out your pussy. Now I want you to take that finger and rest it against your clit. Can you do that for me?

Willow

Mike

Rub your clit, round and round. Nice and slow so that it makes your mind all empty. I want you to get soaking wet. And Willow...

All thoughts of sleep are now gone. My sweet submissive is in bed, ready to do whatever I want and fuck herself following my commands. If this is how every night is going to go, maybe this cruise won't be so bad after all.

CHAPTER 3

WILLOW

Mike is driving me insane. I spend my time at work wondering what he's doing and who he's fucking, but then when I get home, he's attentive and toys with me—letting me come only half the time. He's enjoying the lingerie pictures I'm bombarding him with, but am I just fueling the fire for other women?

When I complained to Alice, she told me to stop being a wimp and ask him if he's fucking other people, but she doesn't understand. I like him... a lot... And I'm afraid to scare him off. He didn't sign up to be my boyfriend. I want to be able to enjoy my time with him without becoming too attached... but it might be too late. Just thinking about him sleeping with another woman is eating me up with jealousy.

Between worrying about what he's doing on the cruise and him keeping me a needy, wet mess all the time, I'm distracted and making stupid mistakes at work. I told my boss I haven't been sleeping well, but that's a lie. I'm sleeping like a baby, but Mike's only been giving me just enough orgasms to stop my brain from being total mush 24/7. Every day, he teases me in my texts with promises of how wonderful his cock will feel sliding into me when we see each other again. Dammit, I really should have bought an enormous dildo and named it Mike. It might be enough to soothe this aching need.

***

After two weeks of him being away, I'm ready to burst. If someone told me three months ago how much a dom guy could mentally fuck you up over text messages, I'm not sure I would've believed them. This is seriously crazy and not at all how I imagined submitting to someone would play out. He knows exactly what to say to get me worked up and desperate for his cock... the cock I can't have because he's on a stupid boat in the middle of the stupid ocean for another week!

It's been another long day at work, but when I get off at the bus stop close to my apartment, a shot of adrenaline perks me up. I'm going to go in, put on a comfy pair of pajamas, slip into bed, and tell him I'm ready for him to fuck me.

He knows what time I get home from work, and right as I shove the key in my front door, my phone beeps with a message. I hurry inside and check it as soon as the door is closed.

Mike

> When you get home, I want you to dry hump the corner of your kitchen table or desk for five minutes. Text me when you start. And no coming without permission.

Wet heat pools between my legs, and I glance toward the kitchen nook, where the table is, while fighting down a groan. Why is this hot? I could mess with him and tell him I don't have any suitable hard surfaces, but I want to do what he's telling me to. I live for him calling me "Good girl."

Before I met him, I thought guys in their late 40s didn't have high sex drives anymore. I was wrong. Very, very, VERY wrong, unless Mike is different from most older guys. There's certainly nothing wrong with his libido.

I drop my coat, scarf, and hat on my bed before kicking off my shoes and heading to the kitchen. While I strip out of my work pants and imagine rubbing my pussy against the table, desire stirs in my belly. Once I'm standing next to the table, I text him.

Willow

Starting now.

Mike

Good girl. I'll tell you when to stop.

My brain buzzes at the praise, and I position myself at the corner. I giggle when I have to get on my tippy toes to position it between my legs. There's just the thin fabric of my cotton panties between me and the wood, and with how wet I am, this table is going to need a thorough cleaning when I'm done with it.

I start to rub against it, testing the friction, which feels nicer than I expected. As I rock my hips, I imagine I'm straddling him and riding his cock, feeling it moving in and out of me, hitting every pleasurable nerve ending. Delight spirals in my core from the pressure against my clit. Hell, I might actually orgasm like this.

Within a minute, I'm moaning as the pleasure increases. Fuuuck, it's still a week until I get his cock again at the Christmas party. How am I going to survive until then?

It's been at least three minutes of rocking against the table and every second brings me closer to an orgasm. My hands tremble as I message him.

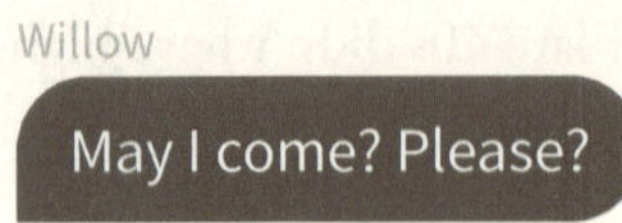

Shit. I grind on the corner. The patch of fabric covering my pussy is soaked and the scent of my sex is in the air. I need to come so badly, and my entire body throbs with lust and need. If he'd let me, I'd bend over the table, rip off my panties and thrust a finger inside myself, searching for that wonderful spot of bliss. But he only said to rub against the table, so that's all I'll do.

As the neediness builds with each passing moment, it becomes impossible to think straight. I'm a mindless fucktoy thrusting against something while waiting for further instructions. I have no idea how long I've been humping this thing, but it feels like forever. He needs to be here using me for real. I imagine him behind me, holding on to my hips and fucking me bareback.

I almost miss my phone beeping with a text message, and I stare down at the screen while my vision blurs.

Oooohhh... I don't think so. I ignore his message and keep rocking against the table, chasing my impending orgasm.

Dammit! His message penetrates the fog and with a frustrated moan, I step back from the table.

Stopped, Sir.

I take several shaky breaths while I rest my ass on the table and try to get my heart rate under control. The heat surging through my veins makes it difficult. I'm a quivering ball of horniness, and he did this to me. I glare down at the text thread and wait for his next command.

Good girl. Now how do you feel?

I want him to tell me I can touch myself until I come.

Frustrated. Desperate. Needy. Ready to be fucked.

I want you to feel this way. Now, get into bed and if you beg like the slut we both know you are, I'll let you come.

Yes, Sir!

I race to get naked and climb into bed. As soon as I settle in, I text him.

In bed, now please, please, please can I touch myself and come? I need to come so badly.

I caress a nipple while I wait for his reply.

First, rub your clit for one minute. Starting now.

Y

In only thirty seconds, I almost peak again, and I writhe on the bed, frantically seeking any bit of relief while my heart races and my pussy clenches on nothing. Fuuuck, if I don't stop, I'm going to come.

Willow

Sir, can I please, please come? Please? I can't keep going or I'll come without permission.

My mind reels as I wait for him.

Mike

Your minute wasn't up, slut. Now it starts over. Get to rubbing.

Willow

Y

Fuuuuck. Within seconds of touching my clit, my hips are bucking against my hand. My body screams for release and wetness leaks down the crack of my ass.

I feel like such a depraved slut to be doing this with a guy over text, and the thought pushes me over the edge. I cry out as my body convulses from pleasure. Waves of delight overwhelm me as I imagine Mike fucking me through my orgasm.

When I come down, I realize he sent a couple of texts.

Mike

Stop.

Mike

You better be stopping, my little slut.

Oops, shit.

Willow

Um, I accidentally came, Sir.

I bite my lip and giggle while I wait to see what he's going to say. That might have been worth any punishment.

Mike

Such a naughty slut. I hope you enjoyed it. Your punishment is not coming until my cock is inside you again.

My body lights up with an aftershock of pleasure. It wasn't a full orgasm, so I'm sure it doesn't count. I had no control over it, but I won't mention it just in case he doesn't agree.

Willow

Yes, Sir. Sorry. I'll be good.

I wrap my comforter around myself and yawn. Now that I've come, I'm euphoric and relaxed.

Mike

I know you will. Now get some sleep and have sweet dreams. You've got a long week ahead of you of not coming.

I giggle, too content to care about my future pain. I wish him sweet dreams and send him a kiss emoji before setting my phone down. As my eyes drift closed, I remember my mom left me a message asking me to call her tonight to discuss Christmas dinner. Since I haven't replied to any of her messages or called her since Thanksgiving, I'm not sure why she thinks I'm coming over. I'll text her tomorrow and tell her I've got plans, even though the freeuse party is technically the weekend before Christmas.

I'm definitely not spending the day with my parents.

CHAPTER 4

MIKE

I pull up outside my house and my whole body relaxes. It's good to be back home at last. The three weeks passed surprisingly quickly, and from the work side of things, everything went well. I'll write the final report tomorrow and send it off to my boss, but I already know he'll be happy with how things are going.

As for things with Willow, my feelings over the last three weeks have been mixed.

Every day she sent me pictures of herself wearing a variety of expensive-looking lingerie. She's never worn anything like that for me, but I suppose she was waiting until she was comfortable with me before breaking out the good stuff. I have to admit, she looks amazing in it, highlighting her already stunning body, and she got me worked up every time she sent me a picture.

And that's the problem. She's been sending two or three pictures every day, so I've been horny as fuck for nearly three weeks solid. We've been sexting all the time and I've been getting off, so that has helped, but it's not the same as fucking. I'm desperate to sink my cock into her and feel her body react to me, hear her delicious moans.

As I get out of the car, I spot my neighbor Nancy leaving her house. She waves over at me and walks up while flashing me a smile.

"Hi, stranger. Back from your cruise? I bet you made a lot of single ladies happy."

She knows I go every year, but not that it's for my job. She thinks it's just me going and having a good time.

"Hey, Nancy. Yeah, it was great, even better than last year."

"I bet it was. Handsome stud like you with your pick of the ladies. I'm quite jealous of them."

I don't know about her being jealous, but she does seem a little sad. Next year I should see if I can send her on the cruise in my place and get another person's viewpoint while letting her have some fun.

"Oh, you know that none of them are half as pretty as you."

She slaps me on the arm and laughs, but looks genuinely pleased.

"You tease. But thank you, that made my day."

She heads towards her car, and I notice she has a little wiggle in her walk. Maybe I did cheer her up. Then I realize I'm still looking at her ass. I laugh to myself about staring at Nancy; I'm so horny I would check out the ass of anyone going by.

Shaking my head, I turn to head into my apartment, grabbing the mail as I go in.

It's mostly junk, but there's one envelope without postage that has my name written on the front. Who would be hand delivering a letter to me?

As I step into my apartment, I throw the rest of the mail on the table and open up the mystery envelope. Inside is a card with the message, "Welcome home. I missed you." The inside says, "Once I noticed you were gone."

It's signed by Willow.

She's such a cutie. Taking a trip all the way across town to drop that off for me when I know she doesn't have a car, just to give me a smile as I got back.

I really want to send her a text to tell her I'm home, but I know that's not a good idea. We've been texting each other goodnight every night, but I know if I do it now, it will end in me inviting her over, and then we'll end up fucking for hours. As much as I want that--no, need that--I've got work to do first. Besides, tomorrow is the Christmas party, and there'll be more than enough opportunity to pound her senseless there. I hope she's not thinking of being with anyone else but me, because I have lots of plans for her.

I'll call her in the morning and let her know I'm back. Yeah, that's what I'll do.

***

In the end, I wake up during the night and send her a text. I thank her for the card and say I'm looking forward to the party. I don't expect a reply, assuming she's asleep. But after a moment I get an, "I can't wait for the party and to be your plaything," message. Then she sends me a GIF of a yawning cat and says she'll see me tomorrow.

I sleep better than I have in weeks.

***

Looking in the mirror, I get a sense of déjà vu. Dressing up to go out to one of Cherry's parties, ready to have some mind-blowing sex. Horny and excited, but holding it in to give off my dom vibes.

Getting ready for the Christmas freeuse party makes me think back nearly two months to the Halloween party. So much has changed in that time.

Last time, I was looking for some no-strings-attached fun. This time, I'm going with someone. And I don't plan to fuck anyone else except her. We haven't talked about it, but I expect I'll be the only cock inside her tonight. I better be. I know we're not exactly dating, but we are... well, something. Thinking about it, why are we even going to the party? I should just bring her back home and use her all night.

Well, it's too late for that now; she'll already be on the way. I'll go and meet her there. Who knows, I might use her in public; she seemed to enjoy being watched last time, so maybe she'll want more of the same. And I know there'll be plenty of people who will want to watch me fuck her.

I put on my suit jacket and straighten out my sleeves. I'm going for a classic suited dom look for tonight. I think Willow will react well to that, and it also fits in with the party.

There's a strange queasiness in my stomach, and I realize that it's excitement at seeing Willow again, mixed with need and lust. I hope she's feeling the same.

I glance at my watch. Plenty of time. Even with finding parking, I should be checking in right as she arrives. I don't want to be late and find her surrounded by hungry guys after her. Not that it should be a problem; I don't expect her to be wearing a red ribbon. This time, she's going to be with me.

Chapter 5

WILLOW

I contemplate my slutty, red velvet dress in the full-length mirror--if you could call it a dress. It ends mid-thigh and has a flared skirt with a tight bodice that makes my boobs pop out. It's short enough that I probably should wear panties, but that seems pointless. Fuck, I better. I might regret it on the car ride to Cherry's house otherwise. Plus, this will make Mike-The-Jerk have to work a little harder to get his cock in me. He's not really a jerk, but after a week of edging me and sexting me every night without letting me come, I'm feeling less charitable towards him.

And let's not forget the pictures.

He started sending pictures of the scenery from the cruise, but I swear there was a curvy woman in the background of each one. The women weren't the focus of the picture and it seemed accidental, but how did he not notice the women spilling out of their bikinis while he was taking the pictures? The very last shot he sent me was him leaning against the railing of the ship while someone else clearly had his phone and was taking the picture for him. Probably someone he just got done fucking for three weeks.

I know my anger towards this unknown woman is irrational, since it's not like he would tell her that he had a side piece waiting at home for him. With my luck, at the end of the night, he'll tell me he's done with me. Maybe I shouldn't have taken the time to put that cute card in his mailbox. Did he deserve it if he was fucking someone else on vacation?

I slide on a pair of red lace panties and some red strappy platform heels. Alice took me shopping again last week and her sugar daddy bought me these shoes that I could never afford in a million years. I tried to protest, but Alice claimed Daddy-Lotta-Bucks told her to buy me a Christmas gift. I'm not one to look a gift horse in the mouth.

The heels make my legs look long and sculpted, and when my ride is almost here, I strut out the door feeling desirable. I'm going to freeze on the way there with this short skirt, but it will be worth it. Luckily the car is toasty warm, and I'm reminded of my first trip to Cherry's house less than two months ago. So much has changed since Halloween, and I feel like a different person. Hell, I can even orgasm now... well, when my asshole dom lets me.

I don't think I'm an edging slut. I'm not cut out for this life. It was okay for two days, and then I wanted to scream every time he told me to stop touching. Yet I also enjoy the pain. It's like some fucked-up mental trickery where I want the pleasure, even though I know I'm going to be cranky at the end. And in my more honest moments, I know I could have come and not told him, but I crave the control of being told what to do—and what not to do as well.

He and I didn't talk about this party other than to agree we'd meet up there. Is he going to fuck other people? Am I? I don't really want to, but what if he assumes we are?

There's just a small line to check in when I get there, and it looks like the party has barely started. If it's anything like Halloween, it'll be wild within an hour. It's been a long time since Thanksgiving, and I'm desperate for Mike to fuck me. I'm buzzing with excitement and every inch of my skin is electrified. Mike will only have to brush up against me and I might combust.

When I finally get to the front, I'm greeted by Bianca, the same woman who was manning the check-in at the previous party, and she smiles when she sees me.

"Hello again! Back for more, I see." She gives me a wink that makes me blush as I hand over my phone and purse.

"It's Willow, right?" she asks, as she puts my stuff in a locker behind her.

Dang, she's good. "Yep, I'm Willow."

She tells me my locker number is 34 while also writing it on her guest list, and then gestures towards two baskets full of ribbons. "So what'll it be this time? Red or green?"

I open my mouth to decline a ribbon and then snap it shut. A strange tingle runs through my body and my nipples harden as I think about sucking on a bunch of cocks like last party. Maybe Mike needs some competition. Except there isn't a ribbon color for the mouth only.

"Red, please."

She gives me the speech about taking it off if I don't want to be used anymore, and as she's tying the ribbon around my wrist, cold air blows in from the door opening behind me. When it closes, a ripple of awareness makes me turn sideways to look at who came in. I'm not surprised to see Mike.

He's so damn handsome in a suit, and all my angst over him possibly fucking other woman drains from me. Whatever he did on the trip doesn't matter tonight.

When his heated gaze meets mine, desire flickers in its depths before he looks down at my wrist. Bianca finishes tying the bow and a visible change comes over Mike. His face hardens and my pulse quickens in response. I shudder when a web of desire unfurls in my core.

My entire focus is on Mike and I barely hear Bianca tell me to have a good night. My brain blips out as animal hunger takes over me. Mike's eyes glitter dangerously, and I know I should say something, but I'm speechless.

I think I'm about to get fucked… hard.

CHAPTER 6

MIKE

As soon as I see the red ribbon at her wrist, my possessive side kicks in. All other thoughts vanish from my mind, and I'm consumed with a burning need for her. Red means she wants to be fucked. Oh, she will be.

Her dress looks amazing on her and clings to her body in all the right places, but even as I have that thought, all I really want to do is rip it off her and show her that she's mine tonight.

Grabbing her by the wrist, I pull her into the house towards the party. We haven't even said anything to each other, but I can see by her expression that she knows exactly what's going to happen to her. There are already a few people gathered in the living room, and I march her up to the sofa.

"Stand at the end, bend over the side."

Her eyes go wide. If she thought she was getting away without being fucked in public, she was very much mistaken.

"Yes, Sir."

She leans and places her palms on the sofa cushions to steady herself. I run my hand down her spine until it reaches her ass and flick up the skirt so that I can see her panties under the dress. She shouldn't have bothered; they're coming off straight away. I pull them down, then off, making sure they don't get tangled on her heels, then leave them on the floor. She doesn't need them tonight.

"Legs wider," I command.

She responds straight away, spreading her legs. From this angle, I can see her ass and pussy, and it's a beautiful sight.

Someone walks by me, and I turn and grab their arm. It's a young guy who I think I saw at the Halloween party.

"What do you think of her pussy?" I ask him.

He grins. "Fuck, she's a wet little slut."

"Yeah. And I am going to pound her senseless."

She already knows this, but I want her to hear it. To hear me talking about her to other people. So she feels even more on show than she already is.

I let the guy go and step up behind her, resting one hand on her butt and gently rubbing it. With my other hand, I pull down the zipper on my pants and take my cock out.

"What do you want?" I ask her, already knowing the answer.

"I want you to use me. Fuck me hard. Make me come."

She leans back against me, her ass pressing against my cock, and I moan.

"Good girl," I tell her as I reach around and grab a handful of her breast, squeezing hard. "But it's me who's in charge here."

I push her forward again and remove a condom from my pocket. Her body shivers in response to the ripping sound as I open it.

Sliding the condom on, I press my cock against her pussy, rubbing against her opening.

"Please," she whimpers. "Put it in."

I love the desperation in her voice. It matches the need inside me. "You want me to fuck you?"

She nods and whines, pushing against me.

"Say it. Beg for my cock."

"Please fuck me. I need it. Oh god, don't make me wait. Please Sir, fuck your slut."

With one thrust, I thrust inside her soaking wet pussy to the base.

She's tight and warm and her moans make my cock pulse inside her. All I want to do is fuck her mindless, all night long. I don't care if people watch, but she is MINE.

"Willow, no coming without permission."

She makes a groaning noise, and I see that her head has dropped forward.

"Do you understand?" I ask.

"Yes. No coming."

I rest my hand on her ass as I set a pace, slow thrusts that fill her up and make her legs shake.

"Tell me when you're right on the edge. Just when you think you can't go anymore without coming."

She nods her head and lets out a gasp as I slam into her. It's not going to take her long, but this will show her who's in charge.

Sure enough, within a few minutes of pounding her, she lets out a cry. "So near. Gonna come!"

I pull all the way out and remove the condom before tucking my cock away. I grab her shoulder, pulling her back up and spinning her around.

She pouts. "I was SO close. Why didn't you let me come?"

"Because of this," I say, lifting her wrist up to show the red ribbon. "And because you needed reminding who's in charge. Now, you're coming with me upstairs and I'm going to use you as much as I want. If you are a very good girl, I might even let you come."

Her eyes sparkle with lust. "Yes, Sir."

***

We get the same private room as last time. It's fitting that we're back in the same place again.

I make her stand next to the bed as I strip. Her eyes are on me as I place my clothes on a chair in a neat pile. I take my time, making her wait for it.

"Come here."

She walks over, stops in front of me and looks at the floor.

"Who decides when you come?" I ask her, tickling her chin as I tip her head to look at me.

"You do."

"And what are you?"

"Your freeuse toy."

I kiss her softly on the lips, and it turns deeper. As we kiss, her hand wraps around my cock and strokes. Somehow it feels even more intimate than fucking her.

"Willow, on your knees."

She nods and smiles. As she sinks down to the floor, she studies my cock swaying in front of her. "Can I suck it, please?"

I laugh and slip my hand into her hair, gently pulling her face close to my cock.

"You can ask better than that."

Her voice is sultry from being turned on. "Oh, please, please, may I suck your cock? Pretty please?"

Rather than answer, I press on the back of her head and feel her lips wrap around the tip and down the shaft.

She lifts one hand and cups my balls, giving them a soft squeeze. They're full and heavy and I bet she's thinking about how much cum I could give her.

"That's a good girl. Take it all the way down. You can touch yourself if you want, but no coming."

She slides her other hand between her legs to play with her pussy. I wish I had my phone at hand. I want a photo of her like this, submissive and loving, trying to give her dom as much pleasure as possible.

She takes me out of her mouth and licks the underside of my cock, sliding it over her lips and sucking on the head. Her happy little noises are making my cock throb. As much as I'm enjoying her mouth, I want more.

"Back up on your feet."

She springs up and gives me a kiss on my chin. The smile on her face makes me want to fuck her so much; she's so adorable and eager.

I climb onto the bed, back against the wall and wrap my hand around my shaft, stroking slowly. Her eyes are locked on my cock, like an animal seeing its prey, as she watches me put a new condom on.

"Come over here. I want you to climb on top of me and guide my cock inside you."

She almost springs onto the bed and straddles me. Her hand moves mine away and she guides me slowly against her pussy. With a moan, she presses the tip into her and sinks down on my cock.

"Oh, fuck," she gasps, and comes almost instantly.

Her whole body shakes, and she falls forward against me. I hold her as she rides it out. Her pussy clenches around my cock, like it's trying to milk it. I wait for her breath to calm down and then tilt her back up again.

"I came without permission," she says, her eyes down. "But I couldn't help it, it felt so good. And I needed it so much, needed you. You're not mad at me, are you?"

I rest my hands on her hips.

"Look at me, Willow."

She raises her eyes to my face.

"I think we can forgive that one; after all, I edged you for a week. But that's only the first orgasm of the night. There are going to be many, many more."

"Yes," she sighs happily.

"But first, put your hands out."

She looks confused but lifts her hands. Then a look of understanding dawns as I take hold of the red ribbon and untie it.

"You won't be needing this. Do you know why?"

She nods and starts grinding against my cock again.

"Because I'm yours. To do with as you want. To fuck me, to use me, to share me. Your toy for the night."

"That's a good girl."

I run my thumb over her lips, but she takes my hand and slips my thumb into her mouth. As she sucks on it, she rides me, lifting herself until I'm almost free of her, then dropping all the way down. Her wet heat makes my head swim, and all I want to do is blow my load inside her.

Her other hand moves to her breast and pinches her nipple. Not gentle - pulling and twisting enough that she moans around my thumb.

This is a woman who wants to be fucked, and fucked hard.

CHAPTER 7

WILLOW

My mind whirls with blissful contentment as I grind down on him and suck on his thumb. The overwhelming relief of finally having Mike's thick shaft inside of me, stretching me with every thrust, is exactly what I needed after the past weeks without him. The moment I saw him earlier, all my worries evaporated, and the only thing I could think about was fucking him.

I writhe against him and the pleasure builds. It feels like I became his possession when he took the ribbon off my wrist, and I've never wanted anything more in my life. I want him to own me and claim me. I'll be his personal fucktoy that he takes care of, and in return, I'll give him my body to use whenever he wants.

Oh god, is this fucked up?

As bliss starts to ripple along every nerve ending, I can't seem to muster up enough concern about it. I'm just too fucking horny to stress about anything right now. Instead, I ride him harder, determined to make him want to keep me, and train me—but most of all, I want to ditch these condoms so I can feel him come inside me.

Just the thought of his cum running out of me tips me over the edge. I moan loudly and whimper around his thumb as the orgasm rips through me. I slam down on him harder as the waves peak again.

With a primal grunt, his cock pulses and he explodes. I refuse to let go, riding him harder and faster until he shakes with the force of his release. I'm lost in the ecstasy, and I shudder with pleasure as I collapse onto him, both of us spent and breathless from the intense climax. When I finally release his thumb, I roll to one side of him and snuggle against his side, putting my head on his chest.

I'm not satisfied. I still ache for more. Is he going to be able to fuck me again tonight?

I giggle, and he rubs my head. "Happy?"

"Maybe," I joke. "But I was thinking you might be too old to keep up with me. I'm ready for more!"

"Insatiable slut," he grumbles, but there's no venom in his voice, and I can tell he's content.

Resting my chin on his chest, I peek up at him. "Is twenty minutes enough recovery time?"

He traces my bottom lip with his thumb and smiles down at me. "Or maybe I should share your mouth with a bunch of guys. That might put me in the mood quicker."

A zing of pleasure heads straight to my clit, and my eyes widen as I imagine sucking on someone else while he watches. Oh god, I want to do it. We've been joking about it since Thanksgiving, but I'm suddenly desperate to suck on all the cocks I can. I want to feel like the ultimate freeuse slut, like I did at the Halloween party.

I keep my tone light so he doesn't guess my real thoughts. "Whatever you want, Sir. I'm yours to share."

"Yes." His eyes glitter. "Mine."

My heart skips a beat as he pushes me onto my back. I love it when he gets possessive. He pins my wrists above my head with one hand as he explores my body with his other. When he pulls my tits out of my top and slaps my breast, I arch my back and cry out.

"Now, slut. I should make you beg to suck another guy's cock."

Oh god, he knows how much I want it.

He moves his hand between my legs and brushes his fingers against my clit. "Tell me, or I'll stop. Do you want me to share your mouth?"

I mewl, "Don't stop. Please don't stop. I want all the cocks I can get."

"Good girl," he murmurs. He lets go of my wrist and removes his hand from my pussy.

Hey, what the hell? He wasn't supposed to stop!

My brain is mush as he climbs off the bed and opens the bedroom door. It's noisy in the hallway, and as someone walks past, he pulls a young guy in by the shirt collar. Oh fuck, he really is going to share me?

"Look at the slut on the bed," he commands the guy. "Do you want to fuck her mouth? She's begging for more cock."

My nipples harden and a bolt of lust makes me gasp.

"Yes," the guy croaks out, and I can tell he doesn't believe this is happening to him.

"Slut, get on your hands and knees. You've got a cock to suck."

Jesus, this is filthy. I scamper onto my hands and knees facing the end of the bed as the young guy approaches me. Mike left the door open, and thinking someone might stop to watch us makes this even dirtier.

He gives me a half smile. "You want this? You don't have a ribbon."

Oh, that's sweet. I appreciate the gesture and I nod eagerly to let him know I do. "Yes, please."

I don't know who I've become, but I love the freedom of doing whatever I want.

Mike moves to the side of the bed and smacks my ass cheek, and then rests a firm hand on my neck while massaging my butt with his other. "Good girl. Now suck his dick."

Joy floods through me at his praise, and I can feel my thighs dampen with my arousal as the guy pulls his cock out. I open my mouth like a hungry slut as he feeds it to me. It's a total power rush to ask to suck someone else's cock and have Mike make it happen. With Mike, there's no fear, and I feel like this is the closest to my true self I've ever been.

When I cup the guy's balls with one hand, Mike growls his approval behind me and lightly slaps my ass. I wiggle my butt and giggle around the guy's cock while he thrusts in and out of my mouth, enjoying this just as much as Mike is.

When the guy grabs my hair, Mike encourages him, "Pull her hair and fuck her mouth. Don't treat her like a lady. She wants to be treated like a cheap little whore."

Mike squeezes my ass while the guy uses my mouth, fucking me fast.

"Whoa," another guy's voice calls from the door. "Can I have a turn?"

The man fucking my mouth gasps and comes. As he's filling me, I swallow everything I can, but some runs down my chin.

When he pulls out, Mike spanks me. "Do you want more cock?"

I feel wonderfully slutty, and I know what I want. "Yes, more."

The second guy walks up to me and unzips his jeans. His cock is thicker than the last man's, and I have to open wide for him to fit. My mind goes numb as he slowly pumps in and out of my mouth while Mike spanks me.

The slaps aren't hard, but it's enough to make me extra fuzzy. I could do this all night long.

When the guy speeds up his thrusts, I see a third man standing to the side watching us. Holy fuck, yes. My insides melt with a wave of delight. I'm going to suck on him next.

He strokes his cock through his pants, as if he's getting ready, and I moan around the cock in my mouth as the guy stiffens and roars. More cum runs down my chin and I try to wipe it off with my hand as he pulls out.

Mike starts finger fucking me as the next guy positions himself in front of me. Pleasure wracks my body and I whine, pressing back against Mike's hand, desperate to come.

The next cock touches my lips and I glide my tongue around it. As the guy sinks into my mouth, the bed dips behind me and Mike thrusts his cock into my pussy. Two cocks? At once?

At some level, I'm aware of my depraved actions, but this is exactly what I've been dreaming about for weeks: being shared, used as nothing more than a cock sleeve, and it gives me the ultimate rush. When Mike spanks me as he fucks me, I moan around the cock in my mouth. My pussy clenches around Mike's shaft. Holy fuck.

The sting of pain heightens the pleasure, and as the rapture builds in layers, I can tell it's going to be a massive orgasm when I finally come. Mike hammers into me relentlessly, grasping my hips as he fucks me hard like this was what I was built for—to service his pleasure. Each whack against my pussy shoves the guy's cock further into my mouth.

As Mike repeatedly hits a pleasurable spot deep inside me, I lose control and a powerful surge of euphoria overtakes me. I scream out in ecstasy, and I can tell from the cum filling my mouth that the guy I'm sucking on is coming, too.

I do my best to swallow it as waves of white-hot bliss turn me into a mindless fucktoy. The pleasure cascades through me, and it's like my body is electrified. I've never had an orgasm this intense, and I'm shaking and crying out as Mike groans and comes. He pounds into me as he chases the last of his pleasure.

Eventually, the bliss recedes, and when Mike pulls out, I collapse onto the bed. Mike leads the last guy out of the room and closes the door before rushing over to me.

He gets on the bed and hauls me against him, brushing away the hair sticking to my cheek. I've never seen such concern on his face before as he asks, "Are you okay?"

He leans against the pillows, and I stare up at him, cum-drunk and happy.

"Mmm, yes," I giggle, and he relaxes and smiles down at me while bubbles of happiness explode in my mind. "Did I come three times tonight?"

A satisfied chuckle rumbles from his throat before he kisses me on my forehead and whispers, "It was plenty. We're done for tonight."

I'm happy as I snuggle against him. Yeah, this was enough.

When my brain starts working again, I get brave and ask, "Did you fuck anyone on the cruise?"

"No," he replies with no hesitation. "Some little minx kept me entertained with sexy photos. I didn't want anyone else."

My heart melts a little as a happy glow builds in my belly. I kiss his chest, inhaling the scent I've come to recognize as him, and I feel the last bit of concern drain from me.

He didn't want anyone else!

I thought the last two holidays were wonderful, but Christmas is shaping up to be even better.

CHAPTER 8

MIKE

We don't stay at the party much longer. We're both exhausted and in need of rest, preferably in each other's arms.

We collect our things and Willow hands in her red ribbon. For a moment, I'm tempted to tell her to keep it so I can tie her up with it later, but before I have time to ask, she turns and kisses me.

"I'm so glad you're back. Tonight's been amazing," she says, pulling back so she can look me in the eye. "I don't want it to end."

An idea pops into my head. "You know, it doesn't have to end. Not yet, anyway."

She snuggles into me to keep warm from the cold air as we walk down the path and away from the house.

"Are you inviting me for a sleepover? I don't think you'll want to stay with me."

We get to my car, and I open the door for her, but turn her around to face me.

"I'm inviting you over for Christmas. I want you to spend the week with me so I can fuck you senseless and then wake up with you cuddled against me. We've hardly seen each other for weeks, so I thought we could spend some time together. And it'll be more comfortable than your apartment."

She pauses for a second and I wonder if she is going to say no, so I add, "If it's work you're worried about, I can give you a lift. You won't be late."

She laughs. "Work is the last thing I'm thinking about. I'd love to stay with you, if you'll have me. But I have one condition."

Oh, what's this now? Someone thinks they get to be in charge and make conditions.

"I'll stay, but only if I can be your freeuse toy for the week."

Now that's something I can happily agree to, but I still tease her. "Hmmm, I'm not sure. Sounds like a lot of work." When she gives me a dirty look, I add, "Okay, okay, you can be my filthy little freeuse toy for the week."

She smiles wider than I've ever seen, and she puts both her fists under her chin and shakes with excitement. She looks just like one of those anime girls she sent me a clip of one night while talking about a show she was watching. I wonder if I could get her to wear a schoolgirl outfit like the girl in the video.

"You're the best. But can we stop at my place so I can pick up some clothes and things? I don't need much and I can come back later in the week if I need to."

***

On the drive to her place, Willow surprises me.

As it's dark and I'm driving in a part of town I don't normally visit, I'm concentrating more than usual. So when Willow stretches over and rubs my lap, it's unexpected and I shoot her an amused look.

She laughs and rubs my cock while trying to kiss my neck.

"Have you not had enough already tonight?" I ask her.

"Mmm, never!"

When we get to her apartment, she makes me wait outside. I don't know if it's because it's messy, or because she's embarrassed by it, but I do know that I'm glad I made the offer for her to stay the week with me.

The building has seen better days. Even from the street, I can see that the windows are old and probably drafty. I wonder how much she's getting charged for renting this place. Whatever it is, it's too much.

Just down the street, I see a group of guys hanging out on the corner, and I'm pretty sure they're dealing drugs. The shop across the road is run down and the light outside her apartment flickers and makes a fizzing sound. I don't like her living here.

Eventually, she appears again and throws a bag into the trunk. As she hops into the passenger seat, she gives me a kiss on the cheek.

"Thanks. I really appreciate this. I promise I'll be the best freeuse Christmas toy ever."

I drive past the dealers at the end of the street, catching them looking as I go by.

"Did you have any other plans?" I ask. "Not going to your parents' for Christmas?"

Willow shakes her head and watches the passing scenery out the window.

"My mom wants me to go over there, but no. I want to spend Christmas with someone that'll make me feel good. That's you, not them."

She turns back to face me and slips her hand into my lap again.

"Besides, if I play my cards right, maybe you'll make Christmas dinner. But NO jokes about stuffing anything."

***

Back at my house, we head for the bedroom, and I show her where she can put her clothes. When she gets her toiletries from her bag, I think how weird it'll be to have another toothbrush next to mine after such a long time. For a moment, my thoughts drift to the past, then I realize Willow is standing in front of me and has her head tilted to the side.

"You okay there? You seem spaced out."

"I was thinking how lucky I am to have a cutie like you in my bedroom."

She giggles, and I know I hit the praise kink she so obviously has. "So, should I put on my pajamas?" she asks.

I step forward and give her a kiss, the kind that goes on so long that you're both breathless but don't want it to end.

"What I want you to do is go sit in the living room and get comfy while I make some hot chocolate. Then we can snuggle up and watch something trashy on TV."

I know she watches reality TV shows; she mentioned it a few times when we were texting goodnight. She uses them to make her sleepy.

"But, I'm your freeuse toy..."

I reach around her and pull her towards me, resting my hands on her ass.

"And a very good freeuse toy. But you've had a busy night and I'm guessing you're tired. So let's just cuddle and talk until we get sleepy and then go to bed."

She is quiet for a second and in a small voice, she says, "Yeah, I'd like that."

She quickly changes into a nightgown and scampers off. I hear her turning on the TV. As I walk down the corridor to the kitchen, a picture of my wife catches my eye. I wonder if I should put it away while Willow is here; it could be weird for her.

Maybe I'll ask her tomorrow.

In the kitchen, I get the drinks ready and call out to Willow. "Do you want marshmallows and whipped cream with yours?"

There's no response, so I walk into the living room to see what she's up to.

The TV is on and something housewife-based is playing on the screen, but Willow's not watching it. She's fallen asleep on the sofa, a cushion under her head.

I switch off the TV and go back to the kitchen, drinking my chocolate in silence.

There's a lot to do. I need to do some grocery shopping; I had been planning to have my usual Christmas dinner for one. But now that Willow is here, I want to make it special for her. I can find the decorations stashed away in the garage. Should I get a tree? We could pick one out tomorrow.

From the living room, I hear Willow call my name.

She's still curled up on the sofa, but her eyes are open.

"I'm sorry. I fell asleep."

"That's okay, kitten," I say, sitting down next to her.

"Oh. I like that. I can be your kitten."

I lean forward and kiss her on the nose.

"My little comfy kitten. And a tired one as well."

She yawns and stretches and my heart aches at how adorable she looks.

She asks, "Will you carry me to bed? Pretty please?"

"Of course."

I stand up and slip my hands under her, lifting her up to my chest. She's warm against me and her sleepiness is setting off my protective dom feelings. When we get to the bedroom, I gently put her into bed and quickly strip and get in beside her.

"Goodnight," she mumbles.

"Goodnight, kitten."

She moves her head and rests it against my chest. Within minutes, she's asleep.

I lay there planning Christmas and what I can do to make it special for her. I'm going to need to get her a present, since I didn't have time to get one while I was away; something kinky and fun—maybe a sex toy? Whatever it is, I want it to be something that will always make her think of me when she sees it.

Before I know it, I'm yawning and I feel my eyes getting heavy. With one last kiss on her head, I drift off to sleep and dream of Willow.

CHAPTER 9

WILLOW

Time flies while I'm with Mike. It probably has something to do with how much he's using me. Literally.

Between work, sex, and then the romantic couple things he keeps suggesting we do, I barely have time to think about my parents and what I'm going to do about them. I'll worry about that after Christmas.

We spent one evening decorating his house while he made ribald Christmas jokes and made me laugh. Then we danced to corny Christmas music and had more hot chocolate than a person should consume in one night. I've never had so much fun decorating a tree before.

Last night, he took me out for Chinese food and insisted he wanted to know everything about me: my childhood, college, the books I liked reading, favorite music artists—the list went on forever. Then we walked off the Chinese food at a local park with a Christmas lights display. It really feels like we're dating, and I like it more than I want to admit.

Now today, I'm at work and it's my last chance to get him a gift, and I told him my shift ends an hour later than it really does so I can sneak out and hit a couple of stores close to work. Luckily, there's a sex toy shop within walking distance. I've been doing some research on what I could get that might be fun for both of us, and I settled on nipple clamps. Hopefully I won't die of embarrassment while buying them.

As soon as I step inside the adult store, I start feeling the blush creeping up my neck and spreading to my face. A store associate asks if she can help, but I tell her I'm fine. She shoots me a friendly smile and I wander the store, feeling weird and out of place. A smart person would have ordered these online, but time is limited.

Finally, I spot a rack with a "BDSM Toys" sign on it in the far back of the store by the bachelorette party items.

There are so many types of clamps. Will the metal ones hurt? I spot a pair with a shiny silver chain and bright pink rubber tips. Oooh, I want those. Rubber shouldn't hurt too much, right? As I look around the store at all the various toys, my body hums alive. I need to make more money if I want a toy collection.

A shelf of high-tech gadgets catches my eye and I pause to look at the sleek, curved, long ones that sync with an app that allows you to change the vibrations.... or play with a partner. Shit, that would've been fun with Mike while he was on vacation. I pick one up and wince at the price tag. Yeah, on second thought, I'm fine being a low-tech girl.

I only have to wait a few minutes in line to pay, and I'm out the door so fast, I've still got 30 minutes before Mike picks me up. When I pass a drugstore, I wander in to kill time and a display of picture frames gives me an idea. I'll give him a racy photo of me along with the clamps.

The store has a self-serve kiosk where I can upload a photo from my phone, and within minutes the picture is printed out on glossy photo paper. It's not until I'm picking out a picture frame that I start questioning whether this is a good idea. Is he even going to want this photo? He's got all those photos of his wife still up, and it's not like he's my boyfriend, so what is he going to do with it? Keep it around to show his friends the woman he's fucking on the weekends? Ugh.

I want more than just nipple clamps for him, and I can't think of anything else that wouldn't be cheesy. Fuck it, I'm going with it. I pick out a sturdy silver frame and a couple of gift boxes. I'm back outside my work a few minutes before Mike pulls into the parking lot.

When I hop into his car, he eyes my shopping bag. I've hidden the nipple clamps inside the drugstore bag, so it looks innocent enough.

"Did you get everything you need?" he asks.

"Yep, and it might be something for you." I give him a sly smile. "Have you been a good boy this year? Do you deserve a gift?"

His eyes narrow as he looks over at me, and he's grinning, but the predatory look on his face has me squeezing my legs together. I get wet thinking about what he's going to do to me when we get home.

"We'll see," he teases, and my heart skips in happiness that he's joking around and not turning dom on me.

I like his softer side, and spending the week with him is letting me see it more. Plus, I've grown accustomed to falling asleep with him every night, and I'm having fun. I try to not worry about the future and just enjoy whatever time we have right now.

When we get to his house, I make an excuse that I want to shower so that I can hide his gifts in my duffle bag in the bedroom. I expect him to join me, so I quickly shove them in the bottom of my bag. I'm barely in the shower two minutes before the glass door opens and he steps into the enclosure with me. Yep, I called it.

Mike moves behind me and pulls me back against him. When he kisses up my neck, it gives me goosebumps. A bolt of arousal zings to my core, and when a low growl rumbles from his chest, it sets my pussy on fire. Warm water pelts down on us as he grinds his cock against my ass and pulls at my nipples. He's wearing a condom so I know I'm about to get fucked.

He bites my ear and whispers, "I've been wanting you all day. It's time to use my freeuse slut."

I moan, "God, yes."

He turns me around and picks me up, pressing my back to the cool tiles. With my legs wrapped around his waist and his cock nestled against my pussy, he stares into my eyes and devours my mouth with a hungry kiss that leaves me panting and needy. I'm a slut for his dominance, and I'm dying for him to take me.

When he buries his face in my neck, nibbling as he licks up the droplets of water on my skin, I'm barely aware that he's positioning his cock until I feel the tip of it pressed against my pussy, poised to thrust into me. I sigh in pleasure as he sinks his length into me all the way to the base in one long movement.

"You have no idea what you do to me," he murmurs into my ear while fucking me so slowly I grow dizzy.

Each stroke is exquisite agony as the pleasure builds inside me in slow layers.

"Faster, please!" I cry out, and he chuckles.

"I decide. You're MY fucktoy."

I claw at his shoulders and arch against him. "Yes, yours."

Water rains down on us as he thrusts in and out of me at a torturous pace. With the ache intensifying between my legs, I dig my heels into his ass and beg for release.

"Willow, look at me," he demands, and I try to focus on him.

When my eyes lock with his, he holds my gaze as he speeds up, pounding into me so fast that all I can do is hold on and moan uncontrollably.

When he moves a hand between us to stroke my clit, it only takes a few moments before my orgasm hits me so hard that stars burst along the corners of my vision. Wave after wave of rapture consumes me. I grip his shoulders and hang on while my cries of ecstasy echo off the tiled walls.

Mike grunts and finds his own release with one last thrust as his cock throbs and his eyes flutter closed. He presses his forehead to mine and murmurs, "Such a good little fucktoy."

Oh, I am. I definitely, most assuredly am a good little fucktoy for him.

***

We decide to have a movie fest for Christmas Eve, and right before we settle down on his couch, his doorbell rings. He looks startled, so I know he wasn't expecting anyone.

"I'll go get that," he says, and instead of waiting for him, I follow him to the door.

When he opens it, a cute blonde woman is standing there—one who is easily around my age.

"Hi!" she says brightly, and then her face falls when she sees me over his shoulder. I'm in my pajamas, so she can tell that I'm an overnight guest.

She's holding a round tin that she quickly offers to Mike.

"I didn't realize you had company. I brought you some fudge I made."

He takes them from her. "Thanks. You didn't have to do that."

Who is this woman? Does he fuck women in their 20s regularly? My stomach churns with jealousy, and I know I'm being irrational. He's not acting like they're lovers.

"Sorry, is this a bad time?" she asks.

Mike starts to answer, but I interject with a polite, "Hey, Mike, I'll be in the living room. No rush."

Mike gives me a side eye look, and I force myself to walk away slowly so it doesn't look like I'm running. I sit on the couch and turn on the TV to check out the options and pretend I'm not trying to listen in. Which I totally am.

I hear their muffled voices, but I can't make out what they're saying. A pit in my stomach opens up and grows until it's a solid ball of anxiety. A couple minutes pass, then I hear the door close.

When he comes into the room, he plops the tin on the coffee table and pulls off the lid. "Do you like fudge?" he asks and holds the tin out to me.

I ignore his question, grab one of the brown squares, and try to keep my voice light. "Who was that?"

I take a bite. Mmm, it's delicious. Figures. I swallow and lick my lips to get all the sugary goodness off my mouth before sucking my fingers clean too because yum, this is divine.

He's watching me with an amused expression as he sits down. "Her name is Nancy and she's my next-door neighbor. She moved in a year ago."

"You bang her?" I ask casually, like it's the least interesting thing in the world, and pop another square of fudge into my mouth as he answers.

"No."

Holy shit, this fudge is orgasmic.

"Do you want to?" I ask while picking through the tin for a different flavor. There are some with pecans and some that are plain but with hazelnut shavings, which sounds heavenly.

Shit, why are my hands shaking? He can want to fuck whoever. I only want him, but that's not how things work. We're not committed to each other.

He takes the tin from my hands and I squeak in complaint. He doesn't give me time to say anything before he hauls me into his lap.

"I have exactly who I want in my arms."

Shit, that's sweet. I relax against him and put my head on his shoulder. I'm not letting him off that easily, though.

I poke his belly. "That isn't a yes or no."

He kisses my forehead and rubs my back. "I only want to fuck you."

I almost protest again, but I hold it in. That'll do for now. To lighten the mood, I try to mess with him. "That's good because, unlike you, I don't share."

Mike tightens his hold on me and nuzzles my hair. "No one is asking you to share."

He always seems to know what to say. I turn my head and kiss him lightly. When he cups the back of my head and deepens the kiss, I relax, enjoying how gentle he is as he explores my mouth with his tongue. I could spend all night exactly like this.

When he pushes me onto my back and peels my pajama pants off, I give a weak grumble. "What about the movie?"

Mike flashes me a wicked grin as he spreads my legs and moves his head right above my pussy. "There'll be plenty of time for a movie after you come."

Who can argue with that logic?

As Mike settles between my legs, his hot mouth trails kisses along the inside of my thigh, sending heat racing down to my pussy and causing my inner muscles to clench. I sink further into the couch, moaning with delight as he holds my pussy lips open and tastes me. As his tongue works magic against my sensitive folds, he glances up at me with heavy-lidded eyes.

I shiver from pleasure when he growls, "You taste delicious, kitten."

Oh god. If he keeps that up, I'm going to purr for him.

I grip the cushions as he slowly licks his way around my clit like he's enjoying this as much as I am. The pleasure increases slowly, starting as a buzz between my legs and spreading up to my lower belly. When he slides two fingers inside me, my toes curl and I arch my back as I cry out, "Ohhh, god!"

My clit throbs against his hungry mouth, and the rapture builds like a tidal wave. I thread my fingers through his hair and press his face against my pussy. When my orgasm hits, I buck my hips to meet his tongue while crying out as ecstasy swirls in my core.

He keeps sucking my clit until I'm nothing but a quivering mess. When I come to my senses, I realize I'm still holding his face to my pussy and I let go of his hair with a giggle.

"Oops, sorry."

"Mmmm, don't be," he murmurs against my skin, then gently kisses my pussy before trailing his mouth up to my chest.

He kisses each breast, and his face is shiny from my wetness. I have a momentary feeling of embarrassment when he wipes it off on his shirt and then licks his lips. "Tasty."

I expect him to fuck me now, so I'm confused when he rolls me to my side and snuggles behind me.

He pulls a blanket over us and pulls me snug against him. "Now we can watch our movie."

Huh. Okay, if he wants to watch a movie, I'm fine with that.

We watch the movie "Elf," which I've seen several times before, and halfway through the movie, I hear the rip of a condom package. After he puts it on, he lifts my leg and sinks his cock inside me.

I moan and he whispers in my ear, "Keep watching and hold still."

Which is easier said than done as he thrusts into me.

"This pussy is mine, understand?"

"Yessss." I feel floaty, like I've melted into a puddle, and my body trembles as I struggle to keep still like he instructed.

He moves his hands to my breasts, and as he tugs on my nipple, it's almost too much pleasure.

Pinching tighter, he hisses, "Tell me your pussy is mine."

Oh god, I love it when he makes me talk dirty like this. "My pussy is yours, all yours."

As soon as I admit it, I cry out with pleasure as an orgasm hits me. At this moment, I'm absolutely and completely his.

As soon as I stop shaking from the climax, I realize he hasn't stopped thrusting. He's still fucking me hard and he's pulled my pajama top up to expose my breasts. One hand goes to my left nipple and tugs on it, sending a wave of pain and pleasure straight to my clit.

"Oh, god," I gasp.

"Mmm, more," he says, biting my shoulder hard enough that it probably leaves a mark.

When he twists my nipple again, the mixture of pleasurable pain shocks me into another orgasm. This time he grunts and pushes hard into me and comes at the same time. He fucks me through both our orgasms, and when he pulls out, he hugs me close to him and caresses my shoulder while planting kisses on the back of my neck.

"Merry Christmas," he whispers, and I realize it's after midnight.

With him, it truly is merry.

CHAPTER 10

MIKE

We wake up early on Christmas day, like giddy schoolkids.

Willow wants to open presents straight away, but I insist that we have breakfast first.

In my family, growing up we always had lox on a bagel with cream cheese. When I suggest that to Willow, she looks at me like I'm weird, but nods her head and goes to get dressed.

It doesn't take long to get the food ready and when I bring it to the living room, she has Christmas music on and is sitting next to the tree.

"I put some old Christmas tunes on. 'Cause, you know, you're old."

When I hand her the bagel, she eyes it suspiciously, but after taking a bite she gobbles it down. I explain that my family came from Sweden and that's where the tradition comes from.

"I never had Christmas breakfast growing up," she says between gulps. "Well, only cereal. Nothing fancy like this."

I clear the plates away and when I get back, she's still on the floor, some wrapped presents next to her that I suspect she may have gotten for me. I search under the tree and pull out the present I have for her and sit down beside her.

"Mine first!" she says, getting overly excited.

She hands me a small wrapped box. I take the paper off carefully, sliding the box out from the wrapping. When I open it up, inside is a silver chain with pink nipple clamps attached to the ends.

She has a wide-eyed look on her face as I pull it from the box and dangle it in front of me.

"What do you think?" she asks.

"I think perhaps you bought this for me, but actually it's for you. Am I right?"

She giggles and her face goes red.

"Um, it's for both of us. I've never used them before, but people online say doms like to put them on their subs. Unless you don't want to?"

She bites her lip as if she's worried, so I lean forward and kiss her gently.

"I love them, thank you. And let's see how much you enjoy them when I'm pulling on the chain."

She looks startled, as if the idea has never occurred to her.

"Oh, yeah. Okay."

I hand her over her present, and she rips the paper off and pulls the box open. When she pulls out what's inside, she comes to a stop.

"Wow."

"You know what it is?" I ask.

"Yeah. It's a sex toy, right? I saw one like it at the store, but it was too expensive. Is this one you can control with an app while I'm using it?"

It wasn't that expensive, but I'm guessing that we have very different ideas of what that is.

"Yeah, that's right. So I can be at work and send you a text to get your toy ready. I can make it buzz and pulse inside you and get you all needy and mindless for me."

She has that faraway look in her eye that she sometimes gets when she's horny, like she's having trouble thinking about anything else.

"Is that something else for me?" I ask, looking at the rectangular package next to her.

"Mmm, what? Oh, yeah." She laughs. "Sorry. You distracted me!"

She picks up the package, but hesitates before giving it to me. Her face is pink, so I ask, "Are you okay?"

She looks up and I can see that she's nervous. For a second she reminds me of the shy girl I first met.

"Yeah, I'm okay. Only... I got this for you, but I don't know..." She starts talking fast like she's trying to explain herself before I even know what the gift is. "You might not like it. You don't have to keep it if you don't. It's stupid. I'm just being silly."

I rub her knee and take the package from her.

"I'm sure I'll love it."

Slipping it from the wrapping, I hold it up to get a good look at it. It's a silver frame with a picture inside it, one of the lingerie shots that she sent me while I was on the cruise.

She's still talking fast. "I remember you said you liked that one. It's dumb because you have it on your phone, but—"

I lean forward and stop her with a kiss.

"I love it. It's going straight up in my bedroom. I might even get you to sign it, or give it a lipstick kiss."

She's obviously surprised but happy, that smile beaming at me.

"You really like it?"

I take her hand and slip it into my lap, letting her feel how hard I am.

"Does that answer your question?"

She gives me a little squeeze and gives me a doe-eyed stare that I'm coming to realize is her innocent act. "Are you going to fuck me on Christmas?"

"Do you think you deserve it, young lady?"

She nods. "Well, I was very good this year… so, yes!"

"Hmmm, I guess we'll have to see about that."

We both laugh and she moves towards me, crawling across the floor. She straddles my lap and starts rocking against me, kissing me and pulling my t-shirt off.

"Please fuck me." She grinds against my cock harder. "I'll even let you make a Christmas stuffing joke, so long as you fuck me."

I roll her over onto her back and pull at her pajama bottoms, taking them off her and revealing her nakedness underneath.

"No panties?"

"No, because fucktoys don't wear panties. You said so."

I pull my bottoms off too and spread her legs, dipping my head down so I can taste her wetness. She tastes delicious and I move my tongue to her clit, swirling it against her as she wriggles underneath me.

"Two or three?" I ask.

I can tell she's confused. "Three?"

I push three fingers into her and smile as she gasps, then relaxes again as she gets used to the motion. Slipping them in and out of her makes her back arch and I suck on her clit and make her moan.

"Whose pussy is this?" I ask her.

"Yours."

"Who gets to fuck it?"

She bucks her hips and gasps, "You do. Only you."

I crawl forward over her, kissing my way up her chest, along her shoulder, and to her lips.

"I need to go get a condom," I say as I stroke her hair.

"In my pocket... brought one with me. Figured you would fuck me. Need your freeuse toy."

She's right, I need her. My cock's throbbing and I want to pound her hard into the carpet.

I fish a condom out of her pajamas and rip it open. I put it on with one hand so that I can hold her down with the other. She has a thing about control, needing to know someone else has it. Just like I need to be the one controlling her.

As soon as it's on, I press the tip of my cock against her and savor her body's reaction to me.

"Do you want it?" I ask.

"I'm your freeuse toy to use."

I growl in her ear. "I want to hear you say it."

"Please fuck me," she cries out, and tries to press up against me to get me to slide in. "I want you to explode and know it's all for me. Please, Sir?"

I thrust into her and watch as her eyes roll back. She wraps her legs around me, as if to make sure I don't go, giving me just enough room that I can thrust into her.

"Ohhh, god. So good," she cries out, and I can feel her pussy tighten around my cock.

I grab her wrists, pinning her down. This is going to be short and sweet. Each thrust into her is hard and deep. No talking is needed. The room fills with the sound of my grunts and her moans, echoing off the walls as we fuck.

Suddenly, Willow is thrashing under me.

"Oh god, I'm going to come. Don't stop. Harder—don't stop!"

I thrust into her hard, my own orgasm building.

"Come for me," she cries out as she tips over the edge.

I explode into her and my body goes rigid. For a second, it's like my brain has been switched off by an overload of pleasure, and then suddenly I'm back again, fucking her as she thrashes in the midst of her orgasm.

She collapses under me, and I let her wrists go, slowing my thrusts until I'm still inside her but not moving, just looking down at her face.

"Merry Christmas," she sighs happily, and closes her eyes.

"Merry Christmas, Willow."

Suddenly her eyes shoot open and she giggles.

"What is it?"

"I just realized something. We fucked on Halloween. We fucked at Thanksgiving. Now we're fucking at Christmas. We should do this every holiday. It's tradition now!"

She bursts out into full-on laughter and I roll over, taking her with me so that she's on top and can finish her laughing fit.

She's right. We've been together all the recent holidays, and each one has been better than the last. We really should make it a tradition to get together on each holiday. Sure seems better than being at home alone.

Although as we cuddle, I realize that the next major holiday is New Year's, so it's not too long to wait.

CHAPTER 11

WILLOW

When Mike drops me off at home, I still don't let him come up to my apartment. After spending the week with him at his cozy house, I don't want him to see my place. We'll have to keep fucking at his house.

I unpack my bag and daydream about the future. We didn't make any plans for New Year's… maybe he's already got something to do. He better not have a date!

I pause with my pajama pants in my hand. Shit, what if he really does have a date? Now that we're doing… whatever this is, are we exclusive? I spend the next hour stewing about Mike.

It's been two months. Shouldn't we talk about where this is heading? My stomach ties itself in knots, but I can hear Alice's voice in my head telling me to fucking ask him and stop being a wimp. She's right. If I want a relationship with him, I need to be able to communicate. Not talking about how I feel about things was part of my problem with Oliver-The-Scumbucket.

Feeling determined, I sit on my bed and compose my message to Mike.

Willow

> Question for you. Are we exclusive? And if so, are you my dom or are you my boyfriend?

I almost stop there, but bite my lip and continue typing.

Willow

> Question for you. Are we exclusive? And if so, are you my dom or are you my boyfriend? I'd like to be exclusive, if you want me.

I hit send before I can change my mind, and then tip over and bury my face in my pillow as my heart races. Part of me wishes I could take the text back because I'm afraid of his answer, but knowing where this is going is better than living with anxiety and wondering. I'm a bundle of nerves and my pulse won't calm down. I want to be his girlfriend, but I'd settle for him as my dom.

Thinking back to how amazing the last week with him was, my heart skips a happy beat as imagine future holidays together.

My brain freezes as a realization hits me. Oh my God, I love him.

Shit, what if he says no to being exclusive?

CHAPTER 12

MIKE

I stare at the screen and try to take it in.

It should be an easy answer. But my mind is frozen and I can't focus on the words. I know that Willow is sitting waiting for me to reply, and that every second that ticks by, she's wondering why I haven't. But I can't just answer something as big as this straight away. It wouldn't be fair to her or to me.

When my wife died, I thought that was it. I was going to be alone for the rest of my life. Not just because I was old, but also because I thought no one could replace my wife.

I saw my life stretching out in front of me as a string of adventures full of meaningless sex and resigned myself to living alone.

But now...

Willow has slowly but surely captured my heart. And while our sexual chemistry is undeniable, it's the small gestures that truly make me fall for her; the way she gazes at me as if I'm her everything, the urge to shield her from life's hardships when it gets too tough for her, and that radiant smile that lights up her face whenever she's happy. I want to be the one responsible for putting that smile on her lips.

I always thought that the age difference would be a problem. We have so many things that we do differently. She talks about things she saw on social media and has accounts on every platform and posts daily. I have an old Facebook account that I've forgotten the password for. Her Spotify is full of Taylor Swift, mine's full of Journey and Chicago.

But we never run out of things to talk about. And when she texts me things that I don't understand, I look them up and usually find it's something interesting. I'm actually learning stuff about the modern world that I would've missed out on without meeting her. It seems the age gap isn't as bad as I thought.

But that's not what's keeping me from answering. All I have to do is glance up from my phone and see a picture of my wife looking back at me. She's been gone a long time now, but she never really left. She's always been around me, in my heart and memories.

Would she have liked Willow? I think she would have. She certainly would have liked her as a sub, but I also think she would've liked her as a person. But that doesn't mean she would want me to date her.

I type a reply and think about it for a few minutes, then I delete it and type something else. I should've seen this coming, but with the cruise and then the party, I've only been focusing on how much I needed to fuck Willow.

My finger hovers above the send button.

Whatever I decide, it'll mean a change for us from now on. Pressing the button will mean no going back.

I breathe in slowly, hold it, and then breathe out.

All I need to do is press the button.

Freeuse Valentine

Freeuse to Forever After Book 4

April Cross | Matt Lake

CHAPTER 1

WILLOW

As I stare at his text, my face flushes and my body hums with desire. Goddamn, he always seems to know what to say to turn me on, but I'm also confused. He didn't answer my question about whether he was my dom or my boyfriend. Did he see it? Maybe my phone didn't send it. Oh wait, does he want to talk in person?

My brain is a kaleidoscope of mixed emotions—turned on, scared, excited, and anxious that he didn't respond to my direct question. I chew on my bottom lip and read his text again.

Fuck it. Let's see what happens. My hands shake as I type.

Mike

> Yep. Looking forward to it, Kitten. Wear something sexy for me.

His pet name melts my heart. I have a small ache in my chest that feels a lot like hopefulness that we're something more than just friends with benefits who get together on special occasions. Deciding to be optimistic, I'm distracted the rest of the day as I daydream about being his girlfriend for real.

***

Work is hectic the week after Christmas, with people coming into the coffee shop in large groups. I swear I blink and then I'm standing in my lobby holding my overnight bag in one hand and my phone in the other, waiting for Mike to get here. I told him to text me when he pulls up so that I can run out and avoid him seeing my tiny apartment.

All day I've been imagining fucking him, and I'm a horny bundle of nerves as I shift from foot to foot, trying to keep my ears open for the sound of a ding from my phone.

I'm wrapped in a blue trench coat I found at a thrift store ages ago. Underneath, I'm wearing blue lacy babydoll lingerie with a matching thong. I paired the outfit with black thigh-high socks and slip-on shoes. With the coat closed, I look totally normal.

When two people who live in the building come into the lobby, I'm glad I took the precaution of the trench coat. I mumble a hello to them, and they nod and greet me as they enter an elevator and disappear. Knowing that I'm waiting for a guy to pick me up for sex, and that I'm wearing only lingerie underneath my coat, gives me a naughty zing of pleasure. I enjoy feeling like a slut.

When my phone vibrates in my hand, my heart rate speeds up. It's Mike and he's outside waiting for me like we agreed. I'm still determined to never let him see my apartment, but it might be impossible if we actually start dating.

It's cold out, and I shiver as I hurry to his car and toss my bag in the backseat. When I sit down in the passenger seat and close the door, he barely gets out a "Hi," before I launch myself at him.

Our mouths lock together and our tongues entwine as we share a hungry kiss. I clutch the front of his shirt with both my fists, not wanting to let him go. He dominates the kiss, his mouth firm while his tongue invades me, and my whole body sings with the promise of an orgasm.

I barely notice that he's unbuttoning my coat, and when a hand slips inside, he groans as he cups my breast through the lace. We're both breathing hard and practically devouring one another's lips.

When he tweaks my nipple, I moan and fumble between us. I'm desperate for him, and when I brush the hardness under his jeans, he breaks off the kiss and pulls both my wrists up between us, holding me captive. "Not yet, my little fucktoy. You have to wait until we get home."

I whimper, frustrated at not being able to touch him like I want, but quickly give in. "Fine, I'll behave."

He laughs and when he lets me go, I sag back against the seat. He reaches across me to get the belt and buckles me in. Mmm, I could get used to being taken care of like this.

The car is still on, and he studies me without making any move to start driving. "I have something for you," he says, and opens the glove box.

When he pulls out the pink nipple clamps with a chain that I bought him for Christmas, my eyes widen and desire pulses in my core. Oh shit, I know I got them for him to use on me, but I assumed we'd do it when we were at his house.

"Now? Right here?" I squeak.

Before I can protest, he turns to face me. There's a playful gleam in his eyes as he grins wickedly. "Yes, now."

He nudges my coat open and pulls my lingerie down, exposing my breasts. He seems to be in no rush, and I peer around outside, hoping no one walks past. Thankfully, the sidewalks are empty.

With one hand, he takes one clamp and begins to stroke my nipple with it, circling the areola while keeping his gaze locked on my face. I moan as my back arches, and I stare at the clamp as he opens it and positions it around my nipple. When he releases the clamp, it shuts around my flesh, and my lips part with a soft sigh. It stings in a pleasant sort of way, and my body warms in anticipation of what it will be like to have both on me at once.

Without saying a word, he repeats the process on my other nipple, taking his time to position the clamp in just the right spot to give me the most sensation. When he closes the clamp, it bites down, and my legs instinctively press together as I cry out and thrust my hips forward. A sharp delight zings straight to my pussy, and when he pulls on the chain connecting the two, it causes the clamps to tug and hold me on the edge between pleasure and pain. I squirm as a wave of lust washes over me while he grins at me in satisfaction. He tugs on the chain, as if testing it, and my pussy throbs, aching to be filled. Oh yeah, this is going to drive me insane.

After closing my coat just enough to hide my nipples, he moves closer and kisses me. It's gentle compared to moments ago, and my lips seem to be ultra sensitive as he delves into my mouth. I relax into his kiss, enjoying the swirls of pleasure building inside me.

When he pulls back into his seat to drive, I glance outside to make sure we still aren't being observed and hold in my giggle when I don't see anyone staring at us. It's not like I know my neighbors, but I still don't want anyone in my building to see how big of a slut I am.

When I imagined the drive to his house, it was always filled with us talking about plans for the night and maybe teasing each other. Instead, my mind is mush and I can't concentrate on anything except the throb between my legs. Every time I fidget, the clamps tug on my breasts and intensify my neediness. It doesn't help that he alternates between tickling the skin of my left thigh above my sock and playing with the chain hanging down between my breasts.

Just when I think I can't handle being teased anymore, he pulls into the driveway of his house, parks, and we both rush out of the car. He fumbles with his keys at the front door, and I want to beg him to hurry. He's usually smoother than this, so I can tell he wants me just as much as I need him.

As soon as he gets the door open, he picks me up and carries me inside to his bedroom. There is no finesse to it—he's all urgent movements and desperate hunger. He sets me on my feet long enough to help me remove my shoes and shrug off my coat before he pushes me onto the bed on my back. I lean on my elbows and watch him toe off his shoes.

We've said very little to each other so far, and I'm expecting him to just climb on top of me and fuck me, so I'm surprised when he starts in with the dirty talk.

"Spread your legs, slut."

With a shudder, I moan, "Yes, Sir."

I part my knees, and he takes off his pants and boxers all in one movement before pulling his shirt off. Normally, I would have enjoyed a slow striptease, but I'm too desperate to get his cock inside me to care right now. Once he's naked, his thick cock juts upwards slightly as he stands at the end of the bed.

I feel a flash of vulnerability as I imagine what I look like, black thigh-high socks with my legs spread, my breasts hanging out with the nipple clamps attached. I still have my thong on, but the hem of my blue babydoll is around my waist, so there isn't much covering me.

His eyes glitter with lust when he asks, "Do you know what time it is?"

Oh, I do. My breath catches in my throat as I shiver in response before whispering, "Time for me to be your freeuse slut."

Instead of a verbal acknowledgement, he crawls onto the bed, spreading my legs even further apart. While maintaining eye contact, he runs a finger over the silk thong covering my pussy before slipping it under the fabric and brushing his finger over my clit. I tilt my hips and moan as he slides two fingers inside me.

My mind spins from pleasure and I close my eyes as he slowly works his fingers inside me.

He growls, "Don't come until I say so, or you won't come again until Valentine's Day."

I force my eyes open to focus on him because fuck if I want to risk that, even if I don't believe that he would actually follow through. With effort, I groan, "Yes, Sir. Whatever you say, Sir."

When he pulls his hand away, he brings his fingers to his mouth and licks them clean.

"Tasty. I want to fuck this pussy, but it's not time for that. First, we have to take off the nipple clamps."

Uh… oh shit. I instantly focus on the tightness of the clamps around my nipples and realize how sensitive the stiff peaks have become. How bad is this going to hurt?

He kneels between my legs and leans forward until one hand is resting on the mattress by my head to steady himself. He tugs on the chain gently, sending shockwaves of delight through me and I almost come. I gasp and fist my hands in the bedsheets while trying to be strong and obey him.

Holding the chain lightly, he continues to toy with it, sending jolts of joy straight to my clit. It's impossible to think of anything other than the delicious pleasure he's giving me.

I'm caught by surprise when he suddenly removes one clamp. My nipple aches with the return of feeling and I cry out from the pleasurable pain. He kisses me deeply, distracting me as he plays with my newly-released nipple, rolling it between his thumb and forefinger until I can feel my clit throbbing in time to the movement of his fingers.

I'm still not prepared when he removes the second clamp, and I'm lost to the pleasure, so absorbed in the new sensation that I'm only dimly aware that his fingers are back between my legs, rubbing circles around my clit.

When he moves his mouth to my breast, my vision swims from a jolt of bliss. My body is on fire, desperate for release. He flicks his tongue around my nipple in the same rhythm as his finger circling my clit. All I can do is moan and beg incoherently as pleasure floods my senses. For a moment, I think for the second time that I'm going to accidentally orgasm, but I'm able to stop myself.

When he releases my nipple, he kisses his way back up my neck and whispers in my ear. "Time to fuck my freeuse slut."

He stops long enough to get a condom from his nightstand, rip it open, and roll it down his hard length. He doesn't bother to remove my thong; he just shoves it aside and plunges into me so hard and deep that I see stars as my pussy clenches around him. This is what I've needed all day.

I wrap my arms around his neck and my legs around his to make sure he stays fully buried to the hilt as he fucks me. Nothing in the world matters, only pleasure.

Our bodies slap together as our moans mingle. The rapture builds deep inside, coiling to unleash. Mike fucks me faster and I cling to him, digging my nails into his back, as I beg, "Oh god, please don't stop. More, Sir. Fuck me harder!"

When he gives a sharp thrust and hits the perfect spot, I explode into an all-consuming pleasure. Waves of pleasure wash over me until it all blends into a glorious sensation.

Mike keeps pumping into me, prolonging my orgasm, and even before I come down from the first one, I can feel the beginnings of another one already forming in my lower belly. I moan as his lips close over mine. Our tongues twirl while our hips slam together and he drives me to another climax.

I cry out as the delight skyrockets me to another plane of existence, one where nothing but Mike matters.

Ripples of pleasure run up and down my body and it's several minutes before I can form thoughts. Once my head clears, I'm totally relaxed, but a part of me wonders how I'm going to live without this if he doesn't want to be my boyfriend.

CHAPTER 2

MIKE

I give her time to calm down before I remind her of her promise.

"I told you not to come without permission. Now you don't get to come till Valentine's Day."

Her eyes widen, but I can tell she's not taking it all in, her orgasms keeping her head fuzzy and thoughtless. She nods, but I figure she's so out of it I could've said anything and she would have nodded in reply.

I slide out of her and enjoy her peep of protest. She wants me to stay inside her, but I have other plans for my little freeuse toy.

It takes a few moments to position her how I want, on her hands and knees with her head lowered to the bed. Moving behind her, I slowly rub my cock against her pussy and try to maintain my calm. No matter how hard I am and how inviting her wet little cunt is, I'm still in charge here.

"Ask for it, slut."

She gives an adorable purr. "Please, fuck me. I want your cock inside me."

She's not begging. It sounds more like a prayer, asking for something she needs.

Tugging on her thong, I pull it down so that it's at her knees. I know that keeping it on her will make her feel even more slutty.

"You don't get to come again," I growl, pressing my cock against her opening. "Not till Valentine's. And I'm going to use you as much as I want."

She nods, and the only sound she makes is a long happy sigh as I sink into her as deep as I can go.

When I pull out slightly, the moan she makes sounds primal, like an animal. She's obviously as worked up for this as I am. I've not come in days, not even stroked. I've been saving myself for her.

"Willow, tell me what you are," I demand as I rock into her, giving her just enough movement to make her want more.

"Your slut. Freeuse toy."

"Good girl."

I place a hand on her hip and trail the other one down her spine. It's taking all my willpower to go slowly rather than fuck her senseless. But each thrust into her is like heaven and I need it to last as long as it can.

"Do whatever you want. I'm yours," she whimpers.

My heart skips a beat. I can tell she doesn't mean only sex.

Without thinking, I go faster, until I'm pounding her so hard that the bed shifts. She claws at the edge of the mattress, trying to hold herself steady. All my convictions to make this last have vanished. I need to fill her and hear her moan.

"Put your hand on your clit. Rub little circles till you can't think."

She lets go of the mattress with one hand and it vanishes between her legs. Almost instantly, she moans louder as she shakes.

"Oh... oh... I'm going to come. Sir, I don't think I can stop. Please, can I come? Please?"

Knowing she's close makes my Dom side roar. "I thought I told you not to come without permission."

"Fuck. Please. I can't stop. Let me come. I'll do anything. Be your freeuse toy all the time. Suck whoever you want at parties. Won't come again unless you tell me. Just please let me come now."

I seize her shoulder, slamming her back on my cock.

"Come for me, NOW."

Her head snaps back as she lets out a howl of pleasure. With a groan, I come, slamming into her hard with each load that I pump inside her.

"Mmmm, my fucktoy's learning. That's how to beg to come."

I withdraw and lie down beside her, pulling her into my arms. She's spaced out, a smile on her face, and her eyes are closed. I'll fuck her more later, but for now, I want her in my arms.

"Sir," she says, her eyes opening. "Am I really not coming till Valentine's?"

I give her a soft kiss and tickle her chin.

Since she sent me the text asking if I was her dom or her boyfriend, I've been thinking a lot about our future. I think I know what I should do, but not how to say it. Now isn't the moment, and what she wants is for me to hold her and comfort her.

"Maybe, little one. It depends on how good you are."

Her eyes are glazed from pleasure when she smiles at me. "That's okay, I can be *really* good."

She's not wrong. She's quickly learned how to be exactly the best toy for me.

I need to tell her my decision soon. But that's for later, after we fuck again.

***

We fall asleep in each other's arms, and I only wake up when I feel her stroking my cock.

"I want you inside me," she whispers in my ear. "Even if I don't get to come, I want you to use me."

I'm already hard and throbbing as her fingers glide up and down my shaft. It only takes a moment to find a condom and put it on. She gives me a squeeze and wraps her leg around me before rubbing the tip of my cock against her pussy.

With a growl, I push her onto her back and climb on top. I grab her legs and bend them up so that her knees are almost touching her face. Her pussy is spread out before me and within seconds, I'm sinking all the way into her. She's so wet, and my body tingles with the sensation of her tight pussy gripping me.

"So my fucktoy wants to be used?"

She nods, her eyes fluttering shut as I press into her. "Use me, Sir. Use me all you want. Fill me with cum."

I love it when she tells me what she wants, even if I have no intention of letting her be in charge.

"Tell me who owns you."

"You do, Sir, you own me completely," she sighs.

"Who decides if you come or not?"

She cries out, "Only you," as I give a sharp thrust.

"And who decides if anyone else can use you?"

"You do– but I only want you. No one else. My Sir is in complete control."

I fuck her so hard that the bedframe rattles. I want to hear her moan my name and make her quiver beneath me.

"Oh god. Mike. Yes, Sir, fuck me. I'm your freeuse toy. Come inside me, please!"

The desperation in her voice drives me into a frenzy. My balls are tight and aching for release. I need to fill her.

"Tell me what a needy fucktoy you are," I gasp.

"Best fucktoy. Need your cock all the time."

I slam into her hard, burrowing deep inside her.

She moans, "Yes. Oh, yes. Like that. Fuck me hard."

I keep pumping into her, bringing her towards her climax. Her body tenses, her breathing becomes shallow and rapid, and her mouth hangs open.

"You're going to come, aren't you?"

She moans and shakes her head. "Not got permission. Not coming till Valentines. Fuck. Your cock is so fucking amazing."

I love her determination not to break my rule. It shows me how much she wants to obey me.

"Don't worry, Kitten, you can come. Do it for your Sir, come NOW!"

As soon as the words are out of my mouth, she howls and her pussy clamps around me. It's enough to tip me over the edge, both of us lost in our orgasms as we slam together.

In the distance, fireworks boom and bells ring. It's a new year.

"Happy New Year, Sir."

Her lips are soft and warm, and her arms wrap around me and pull me closer.

"Happy New Year, Kitten."

It's perfect, the two of us wrapped together at the start of the year. I can't think of any place I'd rather be.

She cuddles against me. "You let me come. I thought you'd make me wait."

"I couldn't make my girlfriend wait all that time," I say without thinking.

And there it is, it's out in the open. I called her what she is, my girlfriend.

I hold my breath while I wait for her reply. What if I've left it too long? What if that's not what she wants?

She kisses me on the nose, then closes her eyes and rests her hand in mine.

"I have a boyfriend. Best New Year's ever."

CHAPTER 3

WILLOW

I stare down at the text and my stomach tightens from anxiety.

Mom

> We need to talk.

Shit, I don't want to talk to her, but we need to clear the air. I've been avoiding her since Thanksgiving, and it's now the middle of January. My therapist suggested I could reduce my stress by at least seeing what my mom has to say. I shouldn't assume that it will be a horrible conversation. But really no matter what kind of conversation it is, I just need to talk to her.

A shiver runs through me, but it's not from knowing I need to call my mom -- my damn apartment is freezing. Rubbing my arms for additional warmth, I consider just getting the talk out of the way. Eh, or not... she can stew for a few more days. I dig myself out of my blanket pile on the couch and bundle up in a second sweater before making a cup of tea.

I really want to move, but on top of this being the only apartment I can afford, I'd also need a deposit for a new apartment. If I had known how cold it would be this winter, I might have tried to move in with Alice. She had to find a new place after Thanksgiving, but it's too late for that now. Alice is settled and seems happy.

While the water heats, I chew on my bottom lip absentmindedly and consider my options. Everything is so new with Mike, so I don't want to assume he's going to invite me to live with him... ever. Right now, I'm spending the weekends with him and sometimes other nights, but I need to grow up and support myself better. Do I want to live in a tiny apartment like this for the rest of my life?

When the water is ready, I take my mug of tea and my laptop to the couch, burrowing under the blankets again. I sip the soothing warmth while looking at the cracks in my ceiling. How secure is this building? When I moved in, I was desperate and didn't care, but the lack of adequate heat makes me wonder what other maintenance items are being ignored. Yeah, I need to get out of here, and that requires more money.

A sense of purpose gives me the resolve needed to job hunt. It's time to not let Oliver-the-Tool derail my life. He was a shitty boyfriend who cheated on me, but I can't throw away my college degree because of him. It's time to find a job in my chosen career field.

I start sifting through the employment sites I used to visit, and I quickly get lost in the search. My resume only takes a little updating, and by the time my stomach rumbles for food two hours later, I've found some jobs I plan to apply for.

I close my laptop and stretch. I wonder what Mike is doing right now. Should I text him and tell him I'm job hunting? Nah, I don't want him to keep asking me how it's going. I'll tell him once I get an interview somewhere.

Knowing I need to eat something, I head to my tiny kitchen and toss my phone on my counter. I dig in my fridge and pull out some sliced cheese and deli meat to make a sandwich. When I grab my loaf of bread, I realize it's got mold on it. Well, shit. Why does life feel so hard today? Nothing is going my way.

As I'm rolling the meat and cheese together to eat them as little protein sticks, my phone buzzes with a text message. Ooooh, maybe it's Mike!

No such luck.

Mom

Please call me. We need to talk. It's important.

Dropping my phone on the counter again, I stick my tongue out at it and grumble under my breath. Why doesn't she text an apology for acting like she was going to shank me with a fork? If she really wanted to talk, she'd apologize first... wouldn't she? Ugh, why is being an adult so complicated?

Tired of my own pity party, I pick up my phone and stare at it for a full minute while I munch on a meat and cheese roll. The more I contemplate talking to her, the more anxiety I feel. There's an annoying nagging question in the back of my head. Maybe my mom or dad is sick. Even though they frustrate the hell out of me, they're still my family.

I swallow the last roll, then wash it down with a glass of water. Talking to my mom is going to take energy and I have to prepare. Once I'm cocooned in my blanket, I call my mom and stare out the window as the phone rings, letting my mind wander. The icicles hanging from the top of my window look deadly. If they broke off and fell on someone below, that could hurt someone.

When my mother answers, I shove the thought out of my mind. *Please, please, don't let this go badly.*

"Hello, mom."

There's a huge sigh as soon as the connection is made and my heart drops. Oh great. I'm on pins and needles to see what this is about, but clearly she's not in a good mood.

"Oh, Willow, finally." She gives another exaggerated sigh. "Your father and I were worried something had happened to you with that old man."

Uh… I don't even know what to say to that. It takes extreme effort to keep a defensive edge out of my tone and I spit out the first thing I can think of. "Old? He's younger than you are."

Shit, did I piss her off? I hold my breath, hoping what I said came across as bland indifference instead of being full of the irritated exasperation that I really feel.

My mom doesn't give an inch of ground. "Well, he was still too old for *you*."

I silently count to four, staying calm before responding in a cheerful but firm tone. "Great to talk to you too, mom. Did you have something you wanted to say?"

There's a slight pause. Did she hear my displeasure? I guess it could have been implied in how I said everything… fuck, this is why I hate talking to my mom. I wish she'd just say whatever she called me for so we can get this over with. At this point it's probably too much to hope that she plans to apologize for the fork incident.

"Do I need a reason to talk to my daughter?" She has a bite to her tone, like my question annoyed her somehow.

Shaking my head while pinching the bridge of my nose, I hold in a sigh, wishing I didn't always get caught in the same emotional landmines with her. Is anything ever going to change?

"You said we needed to talk and that it was important." I let the implication that she does have something to say hang in the air between us for a few beats, hoping it will motivate her to get to the point of this conversation.

When she stays silent, my shoulders droop, and I surrender to the reality that this is just her and she's probably never going to change. "Look, I'm sorry I didn't call or text recently. I didn't mean to avoid you. I've just been busy."

That *should* satisfy her. It's the truth anyway, even if the main things on my list of busy-things-to-do is fucking Mike. Oh, and therapy to help with the messed-up dynamic with my parents, and to deal with some other crap in my life like Oliver-the-Scumbucket cheating on me... and maybe not knowing what I'm doing with my career. So I've got issues, but who doesn't?

"Are you seeing anyone?" My mom's question feels out of the blue, and I'm suspicious.

I keep my voice light. "Actually, I am."

"Oh." Her flat tone tells me she didn't like that answer. "Is it serious?"

A sense of dread overtakes me, and I have a strong impulse to just say no and be done with it. But I really can't bring myself to lie to my mom about it—even when I want to avoid confrontation.

"Yes. It's the guy from Thanksgiving."

My mom pauses and is so quiet that I imagine steam pouring from her ears like she's a cartoon character. Finally, when I'm about to ask her if she's okay, she speaks again. "I didn't like him."

I want to tell her I didn't ask her opinion. This is a weird conversation, but I really should have expected this. Was she going to not ask me about the naked dude in my bed from Thanksgiving?

"Mom, does that matter? Don't I get to choose who I date? You could be excited that I found someone I really like who treats me well."

Why do I sound so upset and defiant? I'm not mad that she doesn't like my new boyfriend—well, actually, she hasn't even met him properly, so how can she know if she likes him? That's irritating—but why do I care?

My mom launches into a lecture. "It does matter. You're far too young to know how men are. He's taking advantage of you, and you can't have a life with this guy."

Every word out of her mouth makes me angry. Fuming, I grit my teeth before managing a neutral tone. "What do you mean? Why can't I?"

There is another drawn-out pause before she speaks. "Because--"

That one word is all I need to hear. A flash of anger makes me cut her off. "You know what? Never mind. I've got to go. It wasn't nice talking to you."

I hang up on her before she can say anything else. It might be immature, but I'm too ticked off to handle any more of the conversation.

I close my eyes and try to relax. As I rub my forehead, I feel myself spiraling down into self-doubt. Shit, what if she has a point?

Pushing that thought away, I refuse to listen to that nasty little inner critic of mine, who I swear sounds just like my mother, but with less of a guilt trip and more pessimism.

Without thinking I find myself texting Mike.

Willow

> Just had a bad conversation with my mom. I need to be mindless.

Dots pop up so I can tell he's responding, but instead of a message, my phone rings. It's him.

I answer it and try to not sound glum. "Hi."

"I'm sorry it went badly, Kitten." His soothing voice helps dissolve the tight knot that is lodged between my shoulder blades. "Why don't you get into bed and we can talk about whatever you want."

Just hearing his offer relaxes me, and I throw myself onto my bed and close my eyes, clutching the phone tightly. "Will you tell me a story about a trip you went on? Something funny."

I pull my comforter over me while he laughs lightly. "Sure. Actually, I do remember something from years ago. Let me see…"

He starts his tale of adventure in Paris when he was about my age and he got lost and then rescued by an older lady who hit on him. By the time he's done, I'm feeling better, but emotionally drained.

When I yawn, he says, "Take a nap, Kitten. I'll be around to talk later if you want."

I end the call and roll over to drift off to sleep, feeling warm and peaceful. He's a great boyfriend.

CHAPTER 4

MIKE

I can't believe that it's almost the end of January already. I've been officially dating Willow for nearly a month.

In practice, I suppose it's not that much different from before. We spend most weekends together. She comes around, we fuck a lot, we cuddle and watch TV.

But it's different. Every time I think of her, there's no guilt. I no longer wonder what my wife would've thought of it. It was always clear that she wanted what was best for me and if that was a freeuse girlfriend who's a lot younger than me, she'd want me to have that.

Willow is coming over for Valentine's Day, and I've been getting the house ready for her. I've taken down the photos of my wife. I don't need them on the wall anymore. She'll always be in my heart and in my memories. What we had was special and amazing, but I think I've come to the point in my life where I'm ready to make new memories. Willow is always snapping pictures of the two of us; I should get her to send me some of them. I'll have them printed out and framed.

In fact, I already have one picture of her up. Her Christmas present is on the wall opposite my bed. When she's not visiting, I can still see her face before I fall asleep. The first time we had sex after I put it up, she said it was weird looking at herself like that, so I put her on all fours facing it while I fucked her. I told her she was my fucktoy and that every night I stroked looking at her gorgeous body and pretty face.

She must have liked that, because she came hard on my cock and slow fucked herself with it, her eyes fixed on the picture until I come inside her and pulled her back onto the bed for kisses.

Since we became boyfriend and girlfriend, my protective side has come out more and I want to keep her away from anything that might upset her or make her sad. Some guy walked by us the other day and eyed her up in a way I didn't like, and I swear I nearly snarled at him. When I'm with someone, I want to shield them from everything, no matter how silly that idea may be.

One thing I want to protect her from is that apartment of hers. I find myself thinking of it all the time. I still haven't been in it, but every time I drop her off, she never invites me in. I'm pretty sure it's because she's ashamed of it. That neighborhood is far too rough for me to ever be happy about her living there. I need to put some thought into what I can do about that. I had originally planned to ask my friend if he had any available apartments, but I'm starting to think that perhaps I should ask her to move in with me. Is it too soon for that? Would that even be something she wants?

As I drink my coffee in the kitchen, my phone buzzes.

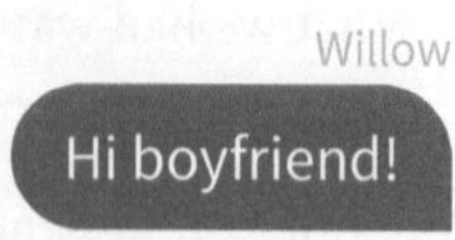

Mike

Hi girlfriend!

She sends a gif of a cartoon dog giggling. It's adorable.

Willow

I still love you calling me that, and I smile every time.

The thought of her smiling makes me happy, and I search the phone for a gif of a beating heart to send her.

Willow

You're so sweet. And your gif game is pretty on point for an old man.

Mike

GRRRRRRRR

She's not wrong. I actually understand all the things on my phone now. I used to look at the apps and think, "That's not for me," but now when she explains them, I can actually see the point. And sometimes that point is to send her a funny picture to make her laugh.

Mike

What are you doing?

Willow

Lying in bed and wishing that my boyfriend was railing me.

Mike

Then I think you need to go find your Christmas present.

Willow

Oh.

She takes a few seconds to reply, presumably because she's getting her toy.

I sit back and move my hand down and pull open my jeans. I'm going to tease her and make her beg to come, and then I'm going to ask if she wants to watch me stroke. I have an idea I already know the answer to that.

It's so good to have someone to share this with. Someone I can be filthy with and have them realize it's not only because I'm horny, but also because I adore them.

I love having a girlfriend.

CHAPTER 5

WILLOW

It's officially February and I'm going to have a boyfriend this year for Valentine's Day. An actual good guy, not some man-child who doesn't know how to please me in bed. I roll onto my back and daydream about a whole weekend of being Mike's fucktoy. I need that again.

Last time I was at his house, I really didn't want to use condoms. Would he agree to ditch them? I'm on birth control, so an accidental pregnancy shouldn't be an issue. My body flushes at the thought, and I decide to text him and ask.

I check the time real quick, making sure it's late enough that he'll be awake.

Willow

Good morning! Last time when we used condoms I felt so empty, I wish you could come without one and fill me up.

I hit send and then re-read it, almost dying inside. I pull my blanket over my head and try to hide. Oh God, was it too much? I was too blunt. Did it sound forced? I wanted to be sexy. Shit, I can't take it back!

My phone dings, and I force myself to read the text, preparing to die from embarrassment.

Mike

> Well that's a delightful message to wake up to. If you were here, I'd do something about that right now.

Ooooh, thank God. I immediately feel like a weight is lifted off me, and I smile while imagining him talking dirty to me and making me beg him to fill me up. Giggling, I text him back, telling myself I shouldn't send this, but I'm feeling too slutty to hold it in.

Willow

> What would you do if I was there with you? Would you spank my bare pussy? Fuck me until I'm screaming from pleasure before filling my pussy full of cum?

Being able to say whatever filthy thought pops into my head is one of the best things about being with Mike. I love that he's encouraging me to be braver with my dirty talk.

MIKE

> Mmmmmm... All that and more, kitten. I think someone is looking to get bred.

Bred? Fuck. Is that taking the dirty talk too far? My nipples harden as I clench my thighs together and let out a tiny moan. The thought of him emptying himself inside me and then me being able to feel his cum drip out of me afterwards is so fucking hot.

I blush, reading back what we both just typed. I was so fucking wanton. I want him to breed me, and it doesn't matter how ridiculous that sounds when we literally just started dating. I close my eyes as I imagine it, but it does nothing to settle the burning desire to have him here right now so we can fuck each other's brains out.

Willow

> Sir, can we ditch the condoms? Please? I'm on birth control.

I don't want him to freak out, thinking that I really want him to breed me. I know it's just dirty talk. But if I was being honest, the idea of accidentally getting pregnant pulls at something primal deep inside me and turns me on, though that's definitely a level of crazy I don't want to admit to anyone.

Mike doesn't respond right away, which makes me squirm in discomfort at the uncertainty. Crap, did I step over a line that is only okay in fantasies, and now he thinks I'm nuts for wanting to ditch the condoms? Maybe I am, but I want to feel him inside me without a barrier between us, and I want him to claim me raw.

Mike

> Kitten, let's get tested and then I can fill you up over and over for Valentine's.

YES! I text him back that I'm in agreement with that plan, and then hurry to get ready for work. In the shower, I spend a little extra time with my hand between my legs, fantasizing about him calling me his breeding fucktoy. I hope he gets super dirty when we're fucking. He always says the most perfect things to make me forget everything but him.

***

The next two weeks feel like the longest weeks of my life, but it's finally Valentine's Day. I have to work and I'm not sure when my shift will end, so I arranged for a coworker to drive me to Mike's once we're done. I've got my duffel bag all packed with a variety of lingerie in reds and pinks to choose from.

Tonight is extra special. We both got tested and we're ditching the condoms. This pussy is getting stuffed with cum, and nothing is going to stop me. I glance at the clock, wishing it was later than it is, as I grab a customer's order off the counter and dash over to them, sliding it onto their table.

"Thanks, hon. This looks awesome." The elderly woman smiles at me, and I recognize her as a regular. I wish her a good day and go back to daydreaming about my future.

Everything in the world is bright and anything seems possible. Soon I'll see my boyfriend for Valentine's Day and give him kisses all over his face. If only I could have switched my schedule so I didn't have to work today. But at least it's busy. That might help make it go faster. Plus, I need the money for a deposit on a new apartment if I want to move out.

Thinking about moving and job hunting creates a pang in my chest. I'll really hate to leave this job: it's low stress, I've gotten to know the regular customers, my coworkers are awesome, and my boss is great, but I'm starting to feel my confidence come back. I don't have to take the first job offered to me, and I can wait until the right position comes along. I just know I want to be out of my apartment by next winter so I don't have a repeat of this fucking arctic situation.

On my break, I see a message from Mike.

Mike

> It's early evening and I'm preparing to have my Kitten with me so I can breed her.

Fuck, that's hot. I quickly message him back.

Willow

> Can't wait to see you tonight. I'm ready to be your fucktoy.

Every time I send dirty messages to him without him prompting me, my face flushes and my body tingles. I get a delicious embarrassment that gives me a slutty feeling. Mike welcomes this naughty side of me, and it's liberating. Is this the difference of dating an older guy instead of someone my own age? I should ask Alice, since she's hooking up with an older guy too.

I look at the time again. Jesus, will this shift ever end? I huff to myself and focus on my tasks. Even though I'd rather be with Mike, I can't wipe the smile from my face. The customers are just going to have to live with me being bubbly and lovestruck. I have a freaking amazing boyfriend who gives me wonderful orgasms and makes me feel safe and appreciated.

My heart beats faster and the swarm of butterflies in my stomach swirls happily as I serve customers. I wonder if Mike has anything special planned for tonight. I don't want to assume he'll greet me at the door with a dozen roses, but I hope he does something to acknowledge the day... though, let's be honest, if he fucks me against the wall as soon as I walk in, I'll think that's special enough.

By the time my shift ends, I'm a horny mess and I'm chatty and hyper while my coworker drives me to Mike's house. She drops me off and every step to his front door feels like it takes an eternity. I'm ready for whatever tonight brings.

CHAPTER 6

MIKE

As soon as I open the door, she lets out a little yelp of delight.

I'm holding a balloon with "Happy Valentine's to the best girlfriend ever" on it.

I offer it to her, and she drops her duffel bag to take it, a huge smile on her face. "Oh wow, thank you! You're the best boyfriend ever."

I grin and hold the door open wider so that she can see past me. The corridor is strewn with rose petals all the way to the end. When she spots them, her eyes go wide and she flings herself at me.

"This is so sweet," she says, peppering little kisses over my face. "I've never had anyone do something like this for me."

For a second, that makes me sad for her. She deserves to be treated right. But now that's for me to make sure it happens in the future.

She lets me go and bounces off down the hall. I close the door behind me and follow her. She stops a few steps in, staring around at everything I've set up. The lights are low. There are candles dotted about and I have a few pictures of her framed and on the wall. She walks over to them and lets out a squeal of delight. I told her I was going to put them up, but this is the first time she's seen them.

When she reaches the end of the corridor, she turns around and tilts her head. "I thought the flowers would lead to the bedroom. Why the living room?"

I walk up to her and take her hand, guiding her to the sofa.

"Because if you lie with your back on the arm of the sofa and your head over the end, your head will be in the right position for me to use your mouth and slap your tits at the same time."

She's such a well-trained slut now that I don't even have to tell her to strip; she does it straight away. The balloon floats to the ceiling as she lets go of it. Pulling off her clothing, she spins around slowly for me to inspect her before hopping onto the sofa and getting in position.

My cock springs free when I open my jeans, and Willow's eyes follow it as it sways and throbs above her face.

"Do you deserve a reward?"

She nods, but doesn't stop watching my dick.

"Do you want it rough?"

That makes her look me in the eyes. "Mmm, yes please. Use me and make me mindless. I don't want to think about anything except how well my boyfriend fucks me."

I push the tip between her lips, groaning as she sucks and teases the head of my cock. As I slide into her throat, she gives a satisfied noise and I pump slowly.

"You have permission to touch," I tell her, and she immediately moves a hand to her clit, teasing herself as I speed up my thrusts.

I slap her right breast, a light tap that's enough to sting a little. Her moan reverberates against my cock, and I stretch out and smack the other one.

"Finger fuck yourself."

She moans and slides her other hand between her legs. Fingering herself and rubbing her clit might not make her come, but it'll make her needy and in the perfect headspace for what's going to happen.

"Do you like me using you?"

"Mmm hmm," is her only reply, the vibration driving me wild.

"You want a throat full of cum, don't you?"

"Mmmmmm."

I pull back and my cock springs from her lips, spraying pre-cum on her face. "Well, you're not going to get it. Can you guess why?"

"Ohhh. I want your cum," she pouts.

I step in front of the couch and lift her up, and over, so that she's kneeling on it and resting her elbows on the other end.

"You don't get a mouthful because I'm going to breed that slutty pussy of yours."

For a second, there's no reaction from her. I think her brain has blipped out with overstimulation, but then she nods her head and I see the gleam in her eyes.

"Mmm, fuck yes. Breed me. I want all of your cum deep in my cunt."

I push her head down and pull her hips up. There is no ceremony, no foreplay. She's soaking already, and as I move behind her, one foot on the floor, the other on the sofa, my cock slides into her easily.

She's babbling, and she trembles. "Fuck me, oh god, fuck me hard."

Her arms are spread out in front of her and she has her head turned to the side. When I reach under her and smack her tit again, her pussy squeezes me.

"If I didn't know better, I would say you're acting like a cum-hungry slut."

I pound into her, each thrust making a wet slapping sound as our bodies collide.

"Please, I need to come, I need to be bred."

I spank her, leaving a nice red mark. "Which one?"

She cries out in distress and sounds confused. "One?"

"Yes, slut. Which do you want first?"

She groans, "Oh god, need to come first. Please?"

"No," I growl. "First you're going to be bred, then you can come."

Her pussy tightens around me as I pound into her. It's so good that I wonder which of us is going to come first.

"Who gets to fill you with cum?" I ask.

"My boyfriend– he gets to use his fucktoy as much as he wants."

"And is his toy allowed to come?"

She moans loudly, "Yes, she can come."

"Oh yeah?" I spank her again.

She squeals. "If I have permission. Need to come."

"Not yet."

She closes her eyes and uses the sofa to steady herself. "Need to. Now. Fuck."

Since her head is turned to the side, I can see that mix of pleasure and frustration on her face. I decide to be kind and give her what she wants.

"Come."

As soon as I say the word, she trembles and lets out a scream. "OH FUCK. COMING. YES. YES... AHHH."

Not that I care, but I'm sure my neighbors heard that. Once she's done coming, she slumps down and her head drops. Her pussy continues to milk me as her body vibrates.

I keep pounding away, slamming my cock deep into her. She rides the aftershocks of her orgasm and gasps for air.

"Now what do you need?" I say as I slow down, letting her catch her breath.

"Cum. Fill me up. Breed your slut."

I love how the more turned on she is, the filthier she talks. "You sure? 'Cause you can't take it back."

"Please. I need it. Want it deep in me and dripping out. Want you to come so hard inside me."

Her pussy seems to tighten around me and I almost tip over the edge.

"Oh fuck," I say. "Can't hold it anymore."

"Fuck yes. Fill me. Give me that cum. Breed me."

It's too much. Her words and the tightness of her pussy are driving me wild. With a few more thrusts, I bury myself deep and unleash a torrent of cum into her.

"Yessss. I need it... breeding me like the slut I am. Oh god."

I hold her hips and with one last slam, I'm sure I've managed to shoot every drop of cum I have inside her.

We stay like that, catching our breath and enjoying the moment, then I slowly pull back.

"Stay still." I withdraw and wait a second. "Tell me what you feel."

I lay my hand on her ass, rubbing it gently, and she lets out a guttural sigh. "Your cum dripping out of me, onto my leg. Fuck. So much cum, all for me."

I move back so I can see her better. Her pussy is bright pink and puffy, and there's a trickle of cum leaking from her. It's one of the sexiest things I've ever seen.

"Look at you, so used and bred. Such a perfect slut."

She lifts her head and glances over her shoulder at me.

"Thank you, Sir. I needed that."

My heart swells with joy. Knowing that I've given her something she needs is as important to me as the sex.

She turns and lies back on the sofa. "You know what else I need?"

"No, what?"

She holds her arms out to me. "I need all the cuddles from my Sir."

I slide over her and kiss her softly as she wraps her arms around me. This is the perfect start to our first Valentine's Day together.

CHAPTER 7

WILLOW

After we cuddle on the couch a bit, he orders dinner while I shower. I had a long day at work and I want to wear something sexy for my boyfriend, so I select a pink lace babydoll dress and panties that make me feel feminine and flirty.

It might be silly, but I can't seem to stop calling him my boyfriend. I'm sure the novelty will wear off eventually, but every time I say it or think about it, I get a little thrill. A tiny voice in my head reminds me that I love him, and wonders how he feels about me, but I push it aside. I'm not going to worry about that tonight. Valentine's Day is for lovers, and I want it to be special as our first holiday as a couple.

When I come down to the dining room, the lighting is turned low, and he's got candles on the table. There's a full plate of Chinese food for each of us, and my mouth waters.

He's smiling, and the corners of his mouth deepen as he takes in my lingerie. "You look good enough to eat."

I bat my eyelashes, feeling flattered, and do a small pirouette for him before sitting down. "Hope I didn't take too long in the shower." I sit and inhale deeply. "This smells delicious."

"You have perfect timing."

I blow him a kiss as we dig in. I'm starving, and I devour half my plate before slowing down. We've got a long night ahead of us and I'm not wearing this lingerie for nothing. I'm hoping to milk a bunch of orgasms out of him… and more cum.

I'm off work tomorrow and I'm staying the next two nights with him. He said he's made plans to entertain us. I'd be fine staying home and fucking for two days, but I won't complain if he wants to take me out on a date.

When we're done with dinner, I get up to clear the table, and he raises his eyebrows. "Where do you think you're going?"

Feeling playful, I sass him and point to the plates and empty containers. "To make room for dessert! You… DID buy dessert, right?"

Shaking his head, he crooks his finger. "Come here."

I change directions and when I'm standing next to him, he pushes his plate aside and pats the table.

"You're going to sit right here."

Following his direction, I perch on the edge, grinning widely. I'm not totally sure where this is going, but it can only lead somewhere good.

"Spread your legs."

Mmm, yes, Sir. I open my legs, giving him a great view of the matching panties under my barely-there babydoll.

He scoots his chair over until he's between my legs and kisses the inside of my thigh. "You're my dessert."

Electricity pulses through me as he runs his fingers along my inner thighs, sending shivers down my spine. He pushes me back with a fierce determination and I willingly surrender to him, lying on the table as he tugs my ass closer to the edge. He stands and swiftly removes my panties before sitting back down, placing my legs over his shoulders to help support me. With each touch, I feel myself unraveling, completely under his spell.

I close my eyes as he explores my pussy with his tongue. Pleasure swirls in my core as I throw my head back and get lost in the sensations. Damn, he's good at this. I moan softly, luxuriating in the feel of him twirling his tongue around my clit. I'm not sure our first Valentine's Day together could get any better than this.

I don't know what to do with my hands, so I press them flat on the table beside me, wishing I had something to hold on to while he ravishes me. Each swipe of his tongue is almost too much and I'm mewling out as I try to hold back my orgasm in an attempt to prolong my pleasure.

Mike toys with me, bringing me to the brink of coming with just his mouth, and then backing off before building the tension again. He pauses long enough to ask, "Do you want to come, my sweet fucktoy?"

I give a strangled moan and nod desperately. "Ohhh, yes."

"How badly do you want it?"

My head spins from pleasure. Oh god, seriously? Why is he torturing me with questions right now? "So bad. Please, can I come, Sir?"

He doesn't answer and dips his head down to taste me again, but this time he slides two fingers inside me as well. I writhe, my entire body alight with desperate need as I buck my hips.

When he makes a noise of approval, the pleasure from the vibration makes me climax and cry out, "Oh fuck, oh god. Mike, fuck."

Rapture burns through me like white-hot energy, and I moan continuously. He doesn't let up, licking me through my orgasm, then keeps going, coaxing a second wave of pleasure, this one deeper, stronger.

"Yes," I hiss through gritted teeth, keeping still as I come undone.

When he pulls back to look at me with a wicked grin, I have trouble processing what he says.

"Now it's my turn."

All I can manage is a nod and a breathy, "Yes." I want to make him come as hard as he just did for me, and then I want to fall asleep in his arms while we're both still humming from pleasure.

Mike helps me up, then carries me to the bedroom. He sets me on my feet just long enough to remove my lingerie and take his clothes off before we tumble onto the bed with him on top. I part my knees for him, and he fits himself between my legs, and we both sigh with happiness as he sinks into me slowly.

Once he's fully inside me, we kiss and I wrap my arms around him to pull him close. I know beyond a shadow of a doubt that I'm head over heels in love with him. I've never felt this way about anyone, and the sensation is powerful. Tears form in my eyes, and I squeeze them shut while I fight to rein my emotions in. I'm not going to be the person who cries during sex.

He continues to fuck me slowly, and I feel every inch of his cock massaging me as pleasure ripples through me. I'm speeding towards another orgasm and it's going to be massive. Wrapping my legs around him, I roll my hips and we surge together in harmony.

"You feel so good," Mike whispers. "You're beautiful and mine."

When he says I'm his, I explode, crying out incoherently as my vision goes white. Joy zings from my fingers to my toes, lighting up every nerve, and I claw at him in desperation. This feels so fucking amazing, it's not just another climax—it's transcendent, a revelation of pure bliss that leaves me unable to speak.

When he comes a few seconds later, pumping hard before driving as far into me as he can, I can feel every pulse and throb of his cock while he unloads ropes of sticky cum deep inside me. He already came once today, but it feels like he's never going to stop.

The world melts away until it's just the two of us coming down from our high together. I feel weightless and I struggle to gather my thoughts again. Everything is floating and heavy simultaneously. I want to ask Mike if I can be his forever, but fear takes hold and it becomes impossible to utter those simple words.

Instead, I cling to him, kissing his cheek and whispering, "I'm so glad I'm spending Valentine's with you."

He buries his face in my neck, nuzzling me, and murmurs, "Me too, Kitten. I'm the luckiest man in the world."

Even though I can't tell him what's really in my heart, I kiss him deeply and try to show him how I feel. He returns my kisses and it's like he's imprinting himself on my soul. I don't know why tonight is different, but I feel changed.

When he moves off me, I snuggle with him, tracing patterns on his chest as I listen to the sound of his heartbeat and wonder if he'll freak out if I tell him I love him. I'm not going to do anything to potentially ruin tonight, but I hope to tell him soon.

In the quiet, post-orgasm stillness, we talk about our favorite board games to play and cartoons we watched as kids until my eyelids get heavy. I think of something and giggle as my eyes are about to close.

"I've never been fucked this thoroughly before."

Mike chuckles, and the last thing I remember is his soft reply. "Kitten, that's because you now belong to me."

Sleep overtakes me and I dream about being with him every single day for the rest of forever.

CHAPTER 8

MIKE

Sometime in the middle of the night, I wake up and can't fall back asleep.

It's weird, like how on Christmas Eve when you're all excited and nervous and there's no way you can just close your eyes and drift off. I have big plans for tomorrow, so it could be that. It's been a long time since I had a girlfriend to impress, and I want it to go absolutely according to plan.

Slowly, I get out of bed and pull on some gray sweatpants. Willow is so out of it that she doesn't even move. I creep out of the room and close the door behind me, not wanting to disturb her.

Her balloon from earlier has floated into the hallway and I give it a tap, sending it back into the living room. Deciding that anything I do in the house might be too noisy, I go out the front door to get some fresh air.

Surprisingly, I'm not the only one who's out at this time of night. Sitting in front of her door is Nancy, smoking what I can only guess from the smell is some kind of weed. I've occasionally smelled it on her, but this is the first time I've actually seen her smoking.

I walk over to her and she gives me a wave as I approach. "Hey stranger, been awhile. Are you not able to sleep?"

I sit down beside her but decline when she offers me the joint. My drug days are way in the past. "Hey, Nancy. Yeah, just woke up and was having trouble dropping off again."

"I would have thought that girl you've been seeing would've worn you out. Especially with it being Valentine's Day. You know, there's a load of gossip in the neighborhood going on about you two, not that it's anyone's business."

She grins and punches me on the arm, but then her smile fades and she stares straight ahead. Apart from Nancy seeing her at Christmas, I wasn't sure if anyone actually noticed Willow coming in and out, but Willow's been over a lot, so it's no surprise.

"You didn't have anyone over for Valentine's?" I ask.

"Nope. Not this year. To tell the truth, I had hopes that you and I would eventually hook up. But that was last year when you were single."

"I'm sorry," I say, and mean it. All that flirting that I did with her seems cruel now, rather than fun.

"It's okay. In fact, it's made me realize something. When I saw you with her at Christmas, it made me realize that it wasn't you I was after, it was the fun and the sex. And I don't need to be in a relationship to have that. I think I'm going to give myself a few years of just fucking around and enjoying myself."

"Yeah, go out and have some carefree fun. You're a gorgeous woman and I'm sure there are plenty of guys out there who would be willing to help you out with that."

"Yeah. I kinda wish I had come to the realization a few days before Valentine's. Perhaps I'd be indoors, getting railed right now."

I nod my head and then have an idea.

"I don't suppose you've met Cherry Thompson? Lives over on Grove."

She shakes her head. "I don't think so."

"You'd like her. She has parties that can get pretty wild and full of sex. The next will be on Saint Patrick's. If you're serious about having some no-strings fun, you should give one a go. I'll drop her contact details off tomorrow. Tell her I recommended you."

She smiles at me and kisses me on the cheek. "You know, I might do that. So, how are things going with you and...?"

"Willow."

"Willow. Pretty name. Are you dating?"

"Yeah. Only recently though. I was worried about the age difference. She's much younger than I am."

Nancy startles me with a laugh. "So am I, but I thought you were worth going after. If she's into you, she's into you no matter your age. And I bet you make a great Daddy dom."

Somehow, hearing her dismiss the last little fragments of my concerns makes me realize how foolish I had been. Why should the number of years between us keep me from being with someone I love?

And then it hits me. I DO love Willow, more than I have loved anyone in a long time. Maybe I should tell her that sometime.

Nancy stands and pats my shoulder. "I'm heading in. You should go back to Willow. Hold her in your arms and don't let her go. It's rare that we have a chance to be with someone who adores us, and from the smile I've seen on her face when she's with you, she adores you."

I glance at her and nod my head. "Thank you."

"I'd like to meet her properly someday, so don't be weird about bringing her around. We can swap stories in the corner while you sit uncomfortably."

And with that, she disappears into the house. I decide it's time for me to head back as well. The bedroom door creaks a little as I go in and I hear a noise from inside the room.

"Mike?"

I slip through the door and to the bed. Willow lifts her head, and I can tell she's' still half asleep.

"Are you okay?" she asks.

I snuggle in next to her and pull her against me, resting her head on my chest. She makes a happy humming sound as I lay my hand on her ass and give it a little rub.

"Yeah, Kitten, I'm okay. I was getting some air. Nothing to worry about. Go back to sleep, you have a busy day tomorrow."

"Okay, Sir," she says and is almost instantly asleep, breathing deeply.

Everything about tonight is perfect. I have the woman I love in my arms, and despite our ages and past baggage, we're happy together. Tomorrow's going to be a big day, because it's the first time that we're going out in public as a couple. And I'll be proud to have her on my arm and for people to see that she's mine.

I plan on asking her to move in soon. Sometime in the next few days, at least. But for now, I'm going to enjoy the warmth of her pressed against me. I stroke her hair and kiss her head until I fall asleep.

CHAPTER 9

MIKE

I'd planned to take Willow out on a fun date for Valentine's Day, but since she couldn't book a day off work, we postponed it until today. It's only a day later, so it still counts.

I had spent a lot of time considering our Valentine plans and ultimately decided that we should venture out in public together. So far, we had only been meeting at my house and hadn't officially gone on any outings as a couple. This seemed like the perfect opportunity for us to hold hands and explore the real world together.

At first, I thought about taking her out to dinner, but that felt too cliche. Maybe a hike or a trip to the theater? However, I realized that my ideas were all based on my own preferences. If I wanted to be a good boyfriend, I needed to consider things she might enjoy.

In the end, I settled on an amusement park. It turned out to be a great choice, because she used to love going to them as a kid.

"I haven't been here for years," she says as we pull into the parking lot at Moose Canyon Park.

It's handy that it's only a half-hour drive away so we don't waste most of the day traveling. And they're doing an exclusive adults day for Valentine's, so there won't be too many kids about.

"Same. The last time I was here was with…" I let the sentence trail away as I realize I'm about to say, "with my wife".

Willow steps closer and kisses my cheek, slipping her hand over mine. "It's okay. You can talk about her around me. It's no secret that you were married before. And all that history makes you the person I adore now. So never think you have to hide that from me."

For someone so young, sometimes she says the wisest things. And I find it amusing that she said adore, just like Nancy did.

It's not too crowded and we pass through the ticket turnstiles quickly and find ourselves outside Moose Mansion, the home of Wilber Moose, the park mascot. There's a shop full of Wilber merchandise and I notice Willow eyeing a cuddly Wilber toy as we walk by. When we leave, I'll buy her one to add to her stuffie collection. If she moves in, she can leave it on our bed all day, standing guard till nighttime.

"So, what do you want to do first? Tipping teacups? The rapids ride? Moose Mayhem? Or do you need to sit down after walking from the parking lot?" she says with a grin.

She spent most of the drive researching all the information about the park and has memorized every ride. I don't even have a clue what Moose Mayhem is.

"What about the Ferris wheel? I mean, it's Valentine's. We can kiss at the top."

"Great idea," she says, taking my hand. "That's good boyfriend thinking."

The queue isn't long, and within a few minutes, we're in one of the little compartments. We have it to ourselves, and we snuggle as the wheel turns slowly until it stops at the top.

"Thank you for taking me out today. Oliver-the-Scumbucket always said that Valentine's is a marketing ploy to sell flowers and cards, but it's nice to be treated like a princess now and again."

I take her pretty face in my hands and kiss her deeply, only breaking it when the compartment jerks as the wheel starts turning.

"I treat you so well because you are worth it," I say. "And you deserve to have someone show you they care."

When the ride ends, we grab some hot dogs and then take a slow walk through the flower gardens. She even surprises me by making blowjob jokes with the hot dog and gets her ass gently bopped for it.

"You were kidding when you said you wouldn't go on any of the scary rides, right?" she asks.

When I told her we were going to the park this morning, she was so excited about the roller coaster and kept talking about us taking a photo on it. It was only then that I had to admit I don't actually like rides. When I used to go to the park, my wife would go on everything and I would sit on a bench and wait for her. I guess I was old before my time; I enjoyed watching her delight at the rides rather than taking part in them myself.

But on the drive over, Willow was so excited about going on everything that I changed my mind. Sure, the idea of riding on a plummeting steel car at a hundred miles an hour is not my go-to idea of fun, but if I'm doing this to give her a fun couples day out, then we should do it together.

"Yeah, I was only kidding. After all, I want to watch your face as we go crashing over the rapids."

So that's what we do. For four or five hours, we go on pretty much every ride in the park. By the end, we're exhausted and happy and have made a whole load of new memories. We bought the official pictures on the rides and Willow has been snapping selfies all day. But we still haven't been on the massive rollercoaster.

"Oooh, cotton candy! Let's get some," she says as we walk past a street vendor. "A good boyfriend would buy me some."

She bats her eyelashes at me and I can't resist her. I order two and tap my credit card against the machine. When did everything change from cash only to digital? Is it another case of me being a grumpy old man and letting the world pass me by?

"Here you go. One for you and one for your daughter," says the vendor and flashes us both a big smile.

I glance at the vendor and then at Willow. I can tell she is trying desperately to hold in a laugh. The vendor looks at her, confused, and then back at me.

"Thanks," I say, taking them and turning away.

It's the first time that something like this has happened. I knew it would at some point, but I hadn't expected it today.

I think a month ago, I would have been furious. Or felt guilty. But now I don't care. I'm with Willow because I love her, and I don't care what others think. Things like this are going to happen, so the best thing to do is find the funny side and go with it. The poor guy made a mistake, and there's no need for me to be upset about it.

"Are you okay?" Willow asks. We've had conversations about our age difference and she's a lot cooler about it than I am.

I hand her the cotton candy, catching her eye, and then burst out laughing. The look of relief from her is clear to see, and she flashes me a wicked smile.

"Does this mean I have to call you Daddy for the rest of the day?" she asks.

"Maybe when we get back home," I whisper in her ear.

We take a quick stroll around the stalls and shops and then decide it's time to do the final ride. The park is closing soon, and we want to go on the biggest roller coaster.

I had thought the other rides were huge, but this is something else. As we stand next to it, I can see the peak of the ride is higher than the top of the Ferris wheel, and then it's a long way down.

"You ready for this, old man?" she asks and squeezes my hand.

"I am, but first, you have to do something for me."

She gives me a quizzical glance as I pull a small box from inside my jacket and give it to her.

"There's a restroom over there. I want you to go into it, open the box, and then you'll figure out what to do with it. Then come back out and we'll go on the ride. Understand?"

The last word makes her suddenly shift and straighten up. The submissive side of her just took notice.

"Yes, Sir."

I watch her head off as I chuckle to myself. Inside the box is a small remote controlled sex toy. I had already gotten her a larger one for playing with at home, but this one is small enough for her to walk around with it in. And that's exactly what I plan to do: make her wear it as we queue for the ride.

By the time she returns, she's flushed and has a slight tremble. I take the box and put it in my jacket.

"How are you doing, Kitten?"

She bites her lip. "It's not even on and my head is fuzzy. Are you going to use it on me here?"

I lift my phone and press a button on it, sending a buzz to her clit.

"Oh, fuck. You are, aren't you?"

The expression on her face is priceless, a mixture of lust and anticipation.

"If you're a good girl, I *might*. Now, let's go ride the roller coaster."

The queue is long, snaking around the base of the ride, but it means that we can stand and chat while we wait.

"Why didn't you bring it out until now?"

"Because if I had done that earlier, I'd have spent all day using it. And it would have distracted you from the rides."

"That's true. I'd have been so wet and turned on, the rides would've been torture. Thank you for waiting, Sir."

There are quite a few people around, and they can't see under her dress, so when the toy starts vibrating inside her, it appears to them that she's just holding the rail, rather than what she's really doing: suppressing a moan and holding herself steady.

"What a perfect little fucktoy you are, being used by your Sir in public," I whisper in her ear.

"Sir. Fuck."

The line keeps moving, and the closer we move to the top, the more I increase the strength of the vibrations.

"Oh fuck, I'm so horny and wet."

"I'm sure I can do something about that later," I reassure her, my cock throbbing at the thought of fucking her. I have an inkling that we won't make it home. Maybe I'll stop somewhere on the way back and fuck her in the car. There's a lovers' lane in town; we could go there like a pair of horny teenagers on a date.

She's clutching my arm. "Please, Sir. Touch me. A little bit. I need you."

I dial down the vibrations so that it keeps her right on the edge. "No."

"Please?" The look on her face is one of pain and frustration.

I turn around and pull her into my arms, resting her head on my shoulder. With one hand I rub her back, but the other one between us gives her breast a little squeeze.

"Mmm, yes."

"Is that what you need, slut?"

"Yeah, I was so fuzzy I needed to be touched by you."

The queue moves and I take her hand and lead her forward. She gives my hand a squeeze and kisses my shoulder.

"This is perfect. A fun day out with my boyfriend and being controlled by my Dom at the same time."

"It's what you deserve," I say, and give her ass a light tap.

As the queue grows shorter and we get closer to the front of the line, I can tell that she's both nervous and excited.

"Are you sure you're going to be okay, Mike? A ride like this is a lot for your old man's body to take."

I nearly hit her with a buzz of the vibrator, but there are more people around us now with the ride staff, so I save it.

"I'll be fine. I've got a hot little fucktoy with me and that makes everything alright."

"Okay. But I have to warn you. This is the scariest one, with the huge drops. I've been waiting to ride this all day, but this is your last chance to back out."

We get to the front of the queue and step into the coaster. The assistant checks that our harnesses are secure and moves to help the people behind us.

"I'm fine. I have the best seat in the house," I say, and stretch across to kiss Willow.

"Why's that?"

"I'm riding with you."

As soon as the bar clamps down, I can see her shaking.

"Besides which, I want to remember what you look like."

She tilts her head at me, confused.

"What I look like when?" she asks.

I put my hand in my pocket and press the button on my phone, setting off the preloaded pattern on the vibrator's app.

I have barely enough time to say, "When you come on a roller coaster," before it zooms forward.

Chapter 10

WILLOW

My head spins and my heart races as the ride twists and turns. I cling desperately to the safety bar, moaning in pleasure as the vibrations increase with every dip. It's like he designed the pattern on the app specifically for this ride. It's a game of pleasure and fear. My screams mix with the others on the ride, but mine are fueled by passion. This is beyond fucking intense.

Turning to face Mike, I catch him staring intently. His expression is of excitement mixed with arousal. He's loving having power over me like this, and I'm half out of my mind as pings of rapture ripple up and down my body. I think I read that the ride is three minutes long, but this seems like the longest three minutes of my life.

As our car climbs the steep incline before the biggest drop, the vibrations from the toy speeds up, each pulse electrifying my sensitive clit. I have to clamp my hand over my mouth to stifle my moans from the waves of pleasure. I'm on the brink of ecstasy as we teeter at the top of the ride, suspended in balance. When the toy switches to a rapid pulse, it pushes me over the edge and into a mind-blowing climax.

As we plunge downwards, the sensation against my clit coupled with the exhilaration of the ride propels me forward and I scream along with everyone else as I'm overcome by delight. One of my hands clutches the bar while my other has a death grip on Mike's arm to anchor me as I float away into complete euphoria. There's a final quick drop towards the end of the ride, and I come again, crying out and trembling with release.

I barely realize when the ride is over and the vibrations have stopped. As soon as the bar rises to let us out, Mike leaps to his feet and leads me away, guiding me to a nearby bench. When he sits down, he tugs me into his lap and cuddles me while I catch my breath.

"How do you feel, Kitten?" he whispers in my ear, his hand rubbing circles on my back.

An aftershock of pleasure makes me shudder and gasp out, "So good. Can't think," before burying my head into his shirt and hugging him tighter.

He laughs. "No need to think when you're being such a good little fucktoy."

Giggling, I kiss his neck. "I came twice."

I shiver from delight when he growls in my ear. "Mmm. Maybe I need to get you off one more time before we get home, for good measure."

***

About halfway home, he pulls off into a secluded parking lot next to an empty baseball field. I assume he's going to fuck me on the hood, but once we're out of the car, he sits down in the backseat so I can ride him.

"Make me fill you full of cum," he orders as soon as he unzips his jeans open, "and come at least one more time for your Sir."

Kissing him deeply, I reach under my dress and tug aside the crotch of my panties before sinking down on his cock slowly, enjoying how deliciously full he makes me feel.

"I can't believe you made me come like that in front of so many people."

"If only they knew what a good little slut you are."

Grinding on his cock, I adjust so I'm getting maximum pleasure while getting him off. I love that we ditched the condoms. The connection between us is intoxicating, and I want him to come as hard as I did on the roller coaster.

As I rock against him, I use his words to remind him how naughty I can be. "I'm such a dirty girl, letting my Sir play with my pussy in the middle of a theme park."

I rotate my hips faster and hold onto the top of seat behind him for leverage.

"Going to make you come so hard," I groan as he slaps my ass. "Then you're going to fill my pussy with cum."

Usually he's the one who talks dirty to me, but I'm enjoying the freedom of saying whatever I feel like in the moment.

As I fuck him hard and fast, my words get dirtier. "Do you like having a naughty slut like me using your cock? Is this what you want?"

For a second, he seems to have been struck silent, but then his moans tell me it's time to ramp things up a notch. I feel emboldened and shameless as I kiss his neck.

"Do you like how wet and tight I am? Does this slut make you feel good?" I purr in his ear, still rotating my hips as I fuck him, impaling myself on his thick length.

I don't know if it's the thrill of knowing anyone could walk by, or maybe he's just as caught up in the pleasure as me, but soon he's thrusting into me hard, panting and gasping as his hands cup my ass cheeks and squeeze. When I start to bounce harder, I can feel how close he is and I'm eager to send him over the edge.

"Come for me, Sir. I want to feel it."

He moans at my words, and when I feel his cock pulsate, I chant, "Come for me," until he erupts.

I feel a swell of satisfaction as he curses and pumps into me a few more times and it's enough to trigger my own release. I cry out as my orgasm hits me and I tremble in his arms. I ram down on his cock one final time and stay still, reveling in the blissful contentment that continues to radiate through me until I slowly come back down to earth.

We stay like that for a long minute, bodies intertwined.

With a sigh of happiness and a satisfied grin, I tease him, "You're such a good little fucktoy."

He chuckles and kisses me. "Don't get too used to it. I can still turn you into a mindless little slut whenever I want."

Mmm, yeah he can. I melt against him, and he holds me until our breathing steadies.

After we snuggle for a few minutes, he gives my ass a love tap. "Let's get home before I end up fucking you again."

Giggling, I steal one more kiss before climbing into the passenger seat while he gets out and walks around to the driver's side. This was the perfect end to a wonderful day, and I hope I get to spend every Valentine's with him for the rest of my life.

Mike takes my hand and kisses my knuckles. I glance over and see the corners of his eyes crinkle, and for a split second, I think he can read my mind and is responding to it.

We don't speak on the drive, but it doesn't matter. It's like we don't have to talk to communicate; all we have to do is connect. This is the closest to pure joy I've ever felt, and I'm determined to make this last as long as I can.

It's late by the time we pull into the driveway of his house. We shower together and it almost ends with another fucking, but we're both yawning, so neither of us try to get the other too worked up. We fall into bed and wrap our arms around each other a few minutes before I zonk out.

Chapter 11

MIKE

I wake up to the smell of bacon and realize that Willow isn't beside me.

Pulling on some boxers, I head to the kitchen and find that she's in the middle of cooking breakfast.

"Hey, handsome. Enjoy your beauty sleep? I suppose people as old as you tire easily."

She's wearing one of my shirts and it's far too large for her, but it actually looks pretty good and shows off her legs nicely.

I walk up to her and kiss her neck while sliding my hand between her legs. "Morning, Kitten."

Her eyes flutter as I stroke her pussy, but then she pulls away and smacks my hand. "Mmm, behave. None of that for now. Here I am, trying to be a sweet girlfriend and make you a lovely breakfast, and you're trying to distract me."

She gives me a fake angry stare, but can't hold it for long before bursting into laughter and kissing me.

"Go sit down. Breakfast is almost done. You need to eat so you'll have plenty of energy to fuck me before I go home."

"Yes, Ma'am," I reply, giving her a salute.

I sit on the couch, and after a few minutes she brings over two plates full of pancakes and bacon. The bacon is nice and crispy, exactly how I like it.

"Oops, I forgot the maple syrup."

She sets her plate on the side table and runs back to the kitchen. She comes back with the bottle, pouring some on her pancakes after she sits down.

When she notices me waiting for the bottle, she puts a dab on her bacon and blinks at me innocently. "Oh, do you want some too?"

I nod and think about taking her back to bed and pouring some syrup on her nipples and sucking it off.

"Oh no, it's that look," she says, giving me a sideways glance as she passes me the bottle. "You're thinking something naughty."

I smirk, but don't reply. The food is delicious, and it takes me almost no time at all to finish it. When we're both done, I take the plates to the kitchen and clean everything up.

"UGH," I hear her mutter to herself.

"What's the matter?" I peek out the kitchen doorway at her, and see she's typing on her phone.

"Surprise, surprise. It's more messages from my mom. Why can't I have a few days of peace without her bugging me?"

I watch her, absorbed in her phone. She curls her legs next to her on the sofa and sinks back, relaxed. She fits in here, and it feels right, so I finally decide to ask her the question that has been buzzing around in my head the last few days.

I walk over and sit down beside her, waiting for her to finish sending her reply. She flashes me a smile. "Can you give me a moment?"

Usually when I have to wait and do nothing I become easily bored, but with her I'm completely happy. It means I get to enjoy having her near. I could sit content like this with her forever.

Eventually she puts down the phone and turns back to me. "Okay, sorry. My mom is being annoying, like usual."

I take her hand and gently stroke it, giving her palm a tickle.

"That's okay Kitten. I don't mind." This is the perfect opportunity to pop the question. "You like it here, don't you?"

She cuddles against me and rubs her cheek on my shoulder. "Of course I do. You have an enormous comfy bed, all the old movies I could ever want to watch... and the house comes with a smoking hot owner. What's not to like?"

I take a deep breath and steady myself. This is a huge step in our relationship.

"So, I was wondering... I'm aware this is a big question and I understand if it's too early to ask, but would you like to move in with me?"

The moment I ask it, my heart starts beating wildly and it seems like an eternity before she replies.

CHAPTER 12

WILLOW

As soon as Mike asks the question, my mouth pops open in surprise and my mind blanks. The ping of a text message of my phone wakes me from my stupor. Panic sets in as I realize the weight of his proposal. Oh shit, what do I say?

A part of me wants to climb into his lap and kiss him, but my practical side takes over. What would I do about work? He doesn't live on a convenient bus line, and he can't chauffeur me around all the time... and I've submitted my resume to several places. I want to move out of my apartment, but not until I have a different job. Do I even have time to think about moving in with him right now? My mind races as I try to come up with an answer that won't disappoint him or myself.

When my phone dings again, I use it to buy myself some time. "Hold on, this is driving me nuts," I mutter as I slide the message open to see what she's written.

Mom

> Are you going to take any responsibility for this sit-
> uation? We should talk.

Wait, is she blaming me for us not speaking much? Yeah, I don't have time to deal with this now. I don't respond and put my phone on silent. When I turn towards Mike, he's got a placid expression on his face and I can't tell what he's thinking.

I'm still trying to sort things out in my head and formulate a response. Is this too fast? Maybe he's only asking me because we've spent a lot of time together and I muddled his brain with sex. How much does he even like me? Am I going to move in and a month later he'll realize it was a mistake?

Fuck. I can't say yes. I don't want to be a burden on him. I need a new job first, and I need to figure out transportation to the new job once I have it.

While I'm still working things out in my head, Mike smiles and reaches over to caress my cheek. His hand is warm, and I wish I didn't feel like I was messing everything up.

"That's okay," he says with a gentle shrug. "Maybe it's too soon. I'm a patient man, Kitten. We can take this slow."

Relief floods my system, but it's followed immediately by a stab of guilt and uncertainty. Maybe it's stupid to turn him down, but I'd feel horrible if he supported me until I could stand on my own two feet.

Trying to mask my inner turmoil, I let out a jovial laugh, hoping it sounds real. "Right? There are a million things to consider."

He kisses my forehead and strokes my hair as he cradles me against his chest. "Sure, let's give it more time."

It's then that I realize why I turned down his offer to move in, and it isn't because it's a bad idea. It's because he doesn't love me. If he did, nothing would stop me from being with him. I'd walk two miles to a bus stop if needed, but right now I can't take the risk of getting hurt. I need to be able to support myself so I don't fall to pieces if Mike and I break up. I can't go through what I did with Oliver-the-Asswipe again.

As if he can sense my thoughts, he pulls me closer to him and rubs my arms. "Kitten, let's just enjoy our time together. Okay?"

I tip my face up towards him. "Sounds good to me."

As we kiss softly, I know it feels right being in his arms, but we don't have to figure everything out today.

FREEUSE ST. PATRICK'S

Freeuse to Forever After Book 5

April Cross | Matt Lake

Chapter 1

MIKE

I turn over in bed, grumble to myself, fluff the pillow up for the hundredth time, and in a fit of anger throw it across the room. I've been in bed for eight hours and have slept for forty minutes at the most. It's time to admit that I'm not getting more sleep.

It's not like I don't realize what's got my head whirring, it's more that I haven't been able to let myself believe it.

Last week I asked Willow to move in with me. I knew it was a big step for us and I understood it might've been too early to suggest it. I weighed up the pros and cons in my head and thought that the good far outweighed any bad side.

So I was surprised when she said no.

Actually, she didn't say no, she stayed quiet. It didn't help that right at that moment her damn mother phoned her and she had to answer. By the time she sorted that out, I could see on her face what the answer was. So I told her it was okay, there was plenty of time for us to discuss it in the future. When I said it, I really meant it.

That was how we left things, but in the last few days it's been really eating at me. I can totally understand her saying no. I'm nearly twice her age. We come from different backgrounds, and we've known each other for less than six months. But I thought that although things were going fast, we were still in sync with each other over our needs and wants. So yeah, she had every reason to say no, but it was her lack of response that really got to me.

And the thing is, I'm not sure she even considered it. She just froze.

Was it such a shock to her that I asked her to move in? She must have known it was at least a possibility. Especially with me making it clear that I didn't like the neighborhood she lives in.

I get up out of bed and head to the shower. For a few moments, the hot water takes away my thoughts, but as I head to the kitchen, the nagging doubts return. Am I too controlling? After all, as a Dom that's my whole thing. Maybe she wants more freedom in her life and moving in with me would take that away. She put up with her mother being controlling all these years; is it so far-fetched that she sees moving in with me as swapping one control freak for another?

As I open the fridge, a wave of depression hits me. This is exactly why I didn't want a girlfriend. No-strings-attached fun was always my thing.

Fuck.

But I love Willow, so we have to work this out. We're dating now and this is what people do, they talk about problems and fix things.

As I make breakfast, I think things through. There's no use dwelling on this. I need to have a conversation with Willow. We are both adults and this is something we can talk about. I don't need her to say yes, but I would like to hear her reasons so we can work through whatever it is. Hopefully, we can find a way past it for the future.

I'm not going to let this come between us. She's the best thing to happen to me in a long time and I'm not giving her up without a fight—even if that fight is between me and my brain.

It's still early so I don't know if Willow is awake yet. I'll leave it until later in the day. A few more hours won't make any difference and I can work out exactly what I'm going to say to her.

My phone buzzes and I glance at it. It's a text from Willow.

Willow

> Hey old man, you awake? I had a filthy dream about you.

Despite my inner turmoil, my cock perks up at the thought of her dreaming about me. I give it a squeeze through my boxers before replying.

Mike

> Oh yeah?

Willow

> I'll tell you about it later and we can reenact it.

She sends an emoji of a face sticking out its tongue.

Mike

> Sounds good to me.

I should leave it at that, but my fingers don't agree and without really thinking about it, I send her another message.

Mike

> Have you got a moment?

Willow

> Yep, what's up? You sound serious.

I breathe in deeply, hold it, and let it out.

Okay, let's do this.

I hit the send button and wait for her reply.

CHAPTER 2

WILLOW

My stomach ties in knots as I stare at the text from Mike. His offer to move in with him has been on my mind all week, and I desperately want to say yes. God, wouldn't it be amazing to come home to Mike every night? The main problem is that I had a job interview yesterday for a case management assistant job at a nursing home and the interview went so great, I'm expecting them to hire me.

The pros and cons have been swirling in my head, and feeling upbeat about the job interview just adds another layer of confusion. Maybe the walk to the nearest bus stop would be worth it. It would only be temporary while I saved up for a car.

The job hunt isn't the only issue. I adore spending my time with him, but I'm terrified I'll make a commitment that ultimately goes badly, like it did with Oliver. If Mike had said he loved me, I would've said yes immediately. What if he only ever feels affection for me? Is loving him going to be enough? This whole situation is beyond confusing, and my anxiety keeps popping up with a laundry list of all the things that could go wrong.

When my phone beeps with another text message, I assume it's Mike asking me if I'm okay since I went silent, but I'm surprised to see it's from Alice.

Alice

> So... you know that guy I've been seeing? I'm going to move in with him. Am I crazy?

I blink at her message and laugh. Talk about timing. As I type my reply to Alice, I know I've already made my decision about Mike.

Willow

> If you love him, you aren't crazy. You deserve to be happy.

Before I lose my nerve, I plop down on the couch and call Mike, waiting anxiously as the phone rings.

"Kitten?" he answers in a puzzled voice.

"Hi," I say, swallowing a lump in my throat. "The only reason I hesitated to move in with you is because I'm job hunting and your house isn't on the bus line."

"Oh, Kitten—"

I cut him off before I change my mind. "But that doesn't matter. I'll walk three miles to the bus stop if I have to. I want to live with you... do you still want me?"

There's a long silence and in that split second, I'm sick and light-headed from the fear that I made a huge mistake telling him I wanted to move in.

Then he says, "I'm always going to want you. How soon can you move in?"

My anxiety immediately dissipates as a lightness fills my chest and makes me giggle. "How about this weekend? I'll get some boxes and start packing."

When he laughs, it sounds relieved, so I know everything will be all right. "I have some broken down boxes in the garage you can use. I'll bring them over after work tomorrow."

After we plan to see each other tomorrow and say goodbye, I set my phone aside. My entire body hums with happiness. I'm actually doing this!

As I jump to my feet, my legs turn to jelly and I'm woozy for a few seconds until the room stops spinning. I feel like I need to pinch myself to make sure I'm not dreaming, but I have so many things to plan. I need to make a list!

I'm tapping out a to-do list on my phone when I think about my parents. Fuck, I should tell them I'm moving in with the guy they don't want me to see. Do I have to tell them? I'm still pissed at my mom about Thanksgiving. Ugh, it's time to act like a responsible adult and talk to my mom. Maybe I'll wait and tell them after I move in, so they'll be nicer about it because it's already happened and they won't be able to try and change my mind. Yeah, that's the way I'll go. In the meantime, I have twenty million things that suddenly need to get done.

After I add two more things to my to-do list, I'm too excited to finish. I get up from the couch and throw myself onto my bed. I scream into a pillow, and then burst out laughing like an idiot. As I release the stress I've been carrying, I kick my feet like I'm in high school again and my crush just smiled at me. Holy fuck, I'm going to be Mike's live-in submissive and I can't think of anything that sounds better than that. I lie there stunned for a few seconds, unable to believe I told Mike I wanted to move in with him, and he said yes. Yes! I'm freaking out a little, but in a good way.

Rolling over, I wrap my arms around my stomach and stare at the ceiling. My nerves are tingling with excitement about this next stage of our relationship. My body relaxes in a way it hasn't in weeks. Everything seems to be working out for me and it's an odd spot to be in after months of unhappiness. I'm going to bask in the contentment and enjoy life for a change.

***

When Mike brings the boxes over after work, I'm waiting downstairs, hoping to cut him off at the pass and bring them up to my apartment myself. He hasn't been in my apartment yet and now that I'm moving out, there's no reason for him to ever see it.

As soon as he walks through the door with boxes under his arms, I give him a big smile and gesture towards the wall. "Hey lover, you can set those right there and I'll ferry them upstairs. There's no need for you to take them up."

He gives me a stern look. "Kitten, if you want these boxes, I'm carrying them upstairs."

Dammit, I think he's on to me. When he continues to the staircase, I skip to catch up with him. "Um, okay. Follow me."

When we reach my door, I open it and lead the way inside, bracing for the worst as he enters my tiny apartment. It's torn apart from my packing, so it looks even worse than usual. After he sets the pile of boxes down, he glances around for a moment before pulling me against him for a long kiss.

He murmurs against my lips, "I'm happy you're moving in with me, Kitten."

When he doesn't say anything negative about my apartment, an unexpected wave of love for him makes me emotional. Blinking away sudden tears, I smile. "Me, too."

As soon as his lips meet mine again, everything else fades away and I get lost in our kiss. There's a new energy between us now that I'm going to be his permanent sub, and I feel closer to him than I did last week. This is definitely what I want.

When he walks me backwards to the bed, I fall on it with him landing on top of me, our mouths still glued to each other's. There's no mistaking his erection pushing against me as we wrestle with our clothing. When his pants are down just enough to get his cock out and my panties are off, he pins my wrists to the bed.

"Have you been a good girl, Kitten?"

"Yes, Sir."

I savor the weight of his body on top of me, and as soon as he presses into my soaking wet entrance, I spread my legs further so he can settle fully on top of me. I groan as he buries his cock into me and begins to thrust, I wrap my legs around him as though I can absorb him into myself and keep him there.

He fucks me hard and fast as he growls, "We're going to have to set limits or else I'm going to be using this freeuse pussy all day, whenever I want."

I moan at how dirty that sounds. A huge part of me wants to be his live-in freeuse slut and give up total control of my body to him. As the waves of bliss build, I arch against him and pant out, "Maybe on set days?"

When he throbs inside me, I can't hold back from the oncoming climax. I come hard, squeezing around him, moaning, "Freeuse Tuesdays!"

Ripples of pleasure run up and down my spine as I ride out the orgasm. He's chasing his climax, and when he shudders and shoots warm cum into me, he shudders and groans, "And Fridays."

In between gasps for air, I agree. "Okay."

He slumps onto me and rolls over, dragging me onto his chest. I melt against him and his breath tickles me when he laughs. "Every day but Thursday?"

I cuddle against his warmth, too content to do anything but giggle. "Ha ha, funny guy. You get two days!"

"Deal," he agrees as his fingers slip under my chin to guide my mouth to his for a lingering kiss that makes my toes curl.

When I settle back down onto his chest, he rubs circles on my back while I drift in a sea of happiness as I plan our future. We're going to Cherry's St. Patrick's Day freeuse party soon and I'll have the option of wearing a red ribbon or a green ribbon. A red one means no anal, but a green means anything goes. Mike doesn't know it yet, but I think it's time to wear a green ribbon and offer him my ass. A live-in freeuse slut might need it in every hole sometimes.

Chapter 3

MIKE

When we park up outside my house, I can tell Willow is confused.

She's moving in this weekend, but when I turned up at her apartment at lunchtime, instead of taking the first few boxes, I told her to get in my car because we had somewhere to go first. She didn't ask questions about where we were going, but when I park next to my house, I can tell she didn't expect me to drive her to my place.

"Mike, if we were coming here, why didn't we bring the boxes?"

"Because I want your full attention on this. Don't worry, we'll grab the boxes later. Can you do me a favor? The garage remote is in the glove compartment. Can you hit the button for me?"

I'm parked along the street facing the garage and it gives her an excellent view of the inside as the door opens.

"Huh," she says. "Do you have another car in there?"

The door opens fully, and we can see the secondhand Honda Fit inside. It's not the newest or the trendiest, but after I spent a few hours cleaning it up, it looks pretty good.

"No, but you have a car in there."

She glances at the garage, then back at me again. "You didn't."

I smile and before I can say anything, she throws herself at me and covers my face with kisses.

"You sweet, silly man."

When she eventually stops kissing me, she settles into her seat and stares out the window at the car.

"I knew you wouldn't let me buy you a new car," I say. "So I got you something that can at least get you to work and back. You can pay me back at the same rate you would've paid for bus trips if you want, but I'd rather you take it as a gift."

She leans over and kisses me softly. "Mike, this is too much. I'm not sure how I can repay you."

"You being here and being happy is enough. Now, let's go look at it."

She nods and climbs out of the car, and together we head to the garage. When she examines it and squeals. "Oh my God, Mike, I love it!"

"Good," I say. "I was worried it was too basic for you. And the paint looks okay. It wasn't very clean."

"I don't care about the paint. I love it! And not just because I have a car, but because you did this for me."

She leans against me, and I wrap my arm around her and kiss her hair. "You're worth it, Kitten."

I watch her as she inspects the car and sits inside, her smile making her face glow as she adjusts the seat. When I pass her the key, she turns it on and listens to the engine roar.

"Mike, this is wonderful. Thank you so much."

She climbs out and throws herself at me again, and I hold her up while she wraps her legs around me.

"You are getting so much 'thank you' sex for this," she laughs.

"I can hardly wait."

I kiss her and gently set her down, taking her hand in mine. "Let's go get some of your stuff and pick up some food on the way back."

I go to walk away, but she stays still and tugs on my hand.

"No."

When I turn around and see her massive smile, I know she's up to something.

She raises her hand and I see the remote flashing in it as she presses the button. The garage door shuts behind us.

"I think I need to give you a little thank-you right now."

She walks over and pushes me back against the car, her hands gliding down to my belt and pulling it open.

"You don't have to, Kitten."

Her mouth is on mine and her hand is inside my pants before I can say anything else. The kiss lasts a few seconds and when she breaks away, she leans in to whisper in my ear.

"I know, but I want to."

Her hand finds my cock and starts to stroke it as she smiles. "See, you're already getting hard. We don't want to waste that. You never know when a man your age is going to get another one.: When she laughs, I decide that it's time to take charge.

"In that case, you better get on your knees and make sure to do a good job."

She immediately kneels, waiting for me to tell her what to do.

"Take my cock out and open your mouth, Kitten."

She does as she is told, taking my cock out of my boxers and stroking it. After kissing the tip, she tilts her head up and opens her mouth wide.

"Yeah, I think you might be able to take it," I say, using my Dom growl. "Now show me what a good cocksucker you are."

She takes my cock into her mouth, slowly sucking me deeper and using her tongue to massage the underside. Her eyes flutter shut as her hand wraps around the base and squeezes me tight.

"Oh, fuck," I moan. "Nice and steady. A little slower, there's no need to rush."

She takes me in deeper, her head bobbing back as she works her mouth, her hand still gripping the base.

"Ah, so good," I sigh, running my fingers through her hair.

She leans back and looks up at me while she continues to rub my shaft. "Mike, I know I'm your freeuse slut and you're in charge, but can I make a request?"

"Of course."

"I want you to fuck me. I need your cock tonight." She strokes me faster and gives me the cutest smile. "Please?"

There's no way I can deny her when she looks at me like that. "Anything for you, Kitten."

I take her hand and help her stand, then open the door of the car.

"Get in, on all fours."

She climbs in with her ass facing me and yelps as I slap it.

"And next..."

I give her stretch pants a tug and yank them down, followed by her panties. They keep her legs together with only a little wiggle room.

"Head down, ass up."

She does as she's told, her legs spread as wide as she can as she grabs the passenger seat. Her pussy is right in front of me and I guide my cock to it, slowly rubbing up and down her wet entrance.

"Ask for it."

"Mike, please, please fuck me. My pussy needs you."

"Good, Kitten."

I squeeze her ass and lean against the car, pushing the tip of my cock into her. She's so warm and wet that I have to stop myself from sliding all the way in.

"Ah, fuck, so tight," I moan.

"Oh god, please Mike, take me."

Her voice is so needy and desperate that it drives me wild. As I thrust forward, her pussy stretches as I sink in. I wanted to take it slow, but she feels too good. I slam into her, desperate to fill her up.

Withdrawing, I slap my cock against her ass and get a satisfying moan from her before thrusting back in. I can't see her face, but I can tell from the sounds she's making that she's just as close to coming as I am. Reaching down, I grab her hip with one hand, while my other hand moves between her legs to rub her clit. Her body tenses and her breath hitches as she gasps, "Oh god. I'm going to come." I know she's on the edge because she doesn't ask permission. Her hips buck, pushing back against my cock as I plunge inside her.

"Ohhh, fuck, yes," she moans, her body starting to shake.

Her pussy tightens around my cock, squeezing me hard and her loud groan echoes as the small space of the car amplifies her cries.

My release comes fast and hard. I bury my cock inside her, filling her with my cum. I bang my hand down on the top of the car as I shoot three loads into her and keep pumping as she takes every single drop.

I slide out and stumble back until I hit the garage wall, and look at her beautiful, wet pussy. She gives a little wiggle as my cum drips out of her and onto the seat.

"My car is going to smell of sex for weeks," she giggles and reverses out to stand next to me.

She's so lovely with her skin glowing and her eyes shining. I can't resist her and I give her a passionate kiss.

"I'm glad you like the car, Kitten. Let's have a shower and then go get your stuff."

She looks at me suspiciously. "I know what you're up to. We're so going to end up fucking in the shower, aren't we?"

I give her a shrug.

It turns out she was right.

CHAPTER 4

WILLOW

On Sunday, I have some final packing to do and I convince Mike to drop me off at my apartment and let me finish alone. If he comes with me, we'll spend all our time fucking because he loves turning me into a mindless mess when we should be doing something else. He agrees to pick me up when I'm ready so we can take another load of boxes back with us.

Before I leave the car, he gives me a deep kiss and fishes something out of his pocket and hands it to me. It's the clit vibrator he used on me at the amusement park.

Wet heat flares between my legs as I remember coming on the roller coaster. Why is he giving me this today? When I give him a confused expression, he winks. "Put that in right now."

Ooooh, he's so bad. I love it. My pulse quickens in anticipation, and I don't argue with him. He smirks when he sees how quickly I obey his command. Shoving my hand down the front of my yoga pants, I adjust it to press against my clit.

Once he knows it's in, he reaches over and zips my jacket up all the way to my neck as if he's making sure I'm going to be warm. "Have fun packing."

I burst out laughing. "Uh huh. You'll be hearing from me."

"I'm sure I will."

The devilish twinkle in his eyes tells me he's going to have a fun time with this today. I better be able to get everything done. Climbing out of the car, I blow him a kiss and roll my hips so my ass shakes as I walk away. Right when I reach the door to the lobby, a strong pulse hits my clit and I gasp as heat streaks through me. As soon as it eases up, I open the door and glance back with narrowed eyes. Mike is beaming and looking extremely pleased with himself as he takes off.

Cocky man. He better be careful while he's driving and not messing with the app. As I head upstairs, the steady, unchanging pulse against my clit proves he's behaving.

An hour later, I decide what he's really doing is driving me insane. The vibrations were a pleasant buzzing earlier, but he's ramped them up to a constantly fluctuating pulse that's making it impossible to concentrate. I need his cock inside me, and now everything in my apartment is beginning to look like a sex toy. I could ride the arm of my sofa and let the toy work its magic on my clit until I explode. Shit, focus. I pack another box and the incessant pleasure distracts me and I find myself rotating my hips and imagining I'm riding his cock. The pulsing has my entire core aching with need.

When there's a knock at my door, I sag with relief. Oh thank God, he's come back to fuck me. The jerkface probably planned this all along.

I yank open the door, intending to launch myself at him but pull up short when I see my mother. Oh, great. This is just what I need.

"What do you want?"

I know I sound unfriendly, but now is NOT a good time for her to visit. And who the fuck let her into the building? It takes a code to get in, but I don't want to argue over that point.

As usual, she gets an offended look, as if I'm the one being unreasonable. "To talk. Are you going to let me in?"

I hesitate for a moment while the oscillations against my clit distract me. I'd like to tell her to get lost. How fast can I get rid of her if I talk to her? Fuck it, let's rip the Band-Aid off and tell her I'm moving in with Mike and then I'll start my new life with a clean slate.

Reluctantly, I open the door all the way to let her in, then shut it and cross my arms before turning to glare at her in a futile attempt to hide my discomfort with the situation.

"Talk," I say while the vibrations have me hot and bothered. I can barely stay still as the torture continues. To distract myself, I get a glass of water while my mother glances around my ugly, bare apartment.

When she doesn't speak for a long moment, I tap my foot impatiently as I sip my water. The pulses of the toy change and I clamp my legs together as my head spins. If she's not gone in five minutes, I'm going to have to excuse myself to remove the toy.

"You're moving?" she asks, finally acknowledging the packed boxes and general disarray.

I'm so turned on, it takes a moment to find my voice and force myself to concentrate on this conversation. "Um, yes, I'm moving in with Mike." I can't stop myself from being snide. "I'm sure you remember him."

She makes a face that immediately makes me bristle. I open my mouth to snap at her, but she interrupts me. "That's a mistake."

Oh hell no, not this shit again. As my irritation builds, I think I'm going to lose my mind, but then the damn buzzing slows down to a stop and I have a moment to collect my thoughts. Suddenly, everything becomes crystal clear in my mind. I don't have to keep her in my life just because she's my parent. I'm done with toxic relationships, and I really can have a fresh start with Mike.

A sense of power wells up inside me, and my voice is firm. "Mom, I'm not a child anymore and I love him. Either you get on board or you're never going to see me for holidays again. It's your choice."

She sputters and I can tell she doesn't know what to say. Good.

I hold up my hand when she tries to protest, and I cut her off. "Mom, I don't want to hear it unless you've got nice things to say about my boyfriend."

Her face turns a blotchy pink color, and I'm disappointed when she fumes. "He's only using you for sex. He'll never marry you and if you stay with him, you'll never have children. Guys his age don't want kids. You're ruining your life."

The 'no kids' comment throws me for a second. I never thought of that, but I won't be swayed from my current path. The fact she's not willing to try for my benefit only solidifies my decision.

Setting my glass down, I walk over to the door and open it. "It's time for you to go. If you ever have an attitude adjustment, I'll be around. Don't bother calling unless you do."

And that's it, we're done. There's no way we can have any sort of healthy relationship while she's this intolerant of my boyfriend. When I give her a look that dares her to say anything else, she huffs and turns to walk out. "This is a mistake," she warns before the door shuts behind her.

Tears sting my eyes as I sink back against the wall, letting my head thump against it. That was hard, but it needed to be done. She doesn't know what she's talking about because she's never taken the chance to get to know Mike. I refuse to listen to her. I love him, and it's time to tell him.

As the thought passes through my mind, my phone beeps with a text message.

Mike

> Is my Kitten going crazy?

Oh, in more ways than one. He has no idea. All I want is to be in his arms right now. I need a big hug and a hard fucking, but I'm not sure in which order yet.

Willow

> I need you. Please come pick me up.

As I wait for his reply, there's a return pulse against my clit. When his next message pops up, I slide my hand down and press the toy firmly against my sensitive bud and rock my hips.

Mike

> I'm on my way. Keep warm for me. I'll be there soon.

Hell, yes!

Willow

> I'm waiting. Hurry.

The steady vibration ramps up, and within a few minutes, I'm trying desperately not to come. Oh fuck. How long of a drive is it to my place? Wait, how long has it been? I'm going to need that hard fucking before the hug.

I leave the door unlocked and text him the code to get in and tell him to just come up before stripping down to my panties. When he walks in the door, I'm bent over the arm of the couch, positioned with my feet flat on the ground and my ass facing him.

Looking over my shoulder, I flutter my eyelashes at him. "I'm yours, Sir."

He gives me a hungry look and stalks over to me with his clothes flying in all directions. Within seconds he's naked and his hard cock is bobbing between his legs like it's waving hello.

He glides his fingers over the fabric of my panties, holding the toy against my clit until I cry out and buck against his hand.

"My freeuse toy is so wet and needy," he says as he drags my underwear down and removes the toy.

He turns the toy off and tosses it on his discarded shirt. When he gathers wetness on his fingers and pulls my ass cheeks apart, I moan as he slowly drags a finger across my puckered hole. Oh god, is today the day he claims my ass?

I whimper and rotate my hips as I mentally plead. Do it. Fuck my ass. A shiver runs down my spine as the pressure from his finger increases.

"Hold on to the couch," he orders.

I grip the edge as his finger slides into my ass. "Ohhhh," I pant as his digit massages me and a whole new world of pleasure awakens inside my core. Fuck, I want this. I want him to claim all of me. My body is in heaven as the overwhelming sensation takes my breath away.

When he removes his finger, I spread my legs and wriggle my ass to entice him to fuck it. He trails the tip of his cock across my buttcheek and down the crack of my ass to my pussy. Wait, what is he doing? He's supposed to fuck my ass!

He gives an experimental thrust that slips the tip inside my pussy, and I whimper, "Please fuck my ass. Please?"

He gives a low and dark chuckle. "Not tonight, my freeuse fucktoy. I need to breed this sweet pussy."

We both moan as he fills me completely. My pussy stretches around him, and every inch of him massages my cave walls. The intense pleasure makes me forget about wanting him in my ass. I just need to come. He wraps my hair around his fist and tugs it gently as he grasps my hip and slams into me. My body is alive with a savage energy and I writhe against him, desperate for more. Every thrust draws me closer to a blissful state. I've been worked up so long that every nerve ending quivers, and thrills run up and down my body. I'm so desperately close that when he slaps my ass and groans, "Come with me, my slut," I explode. A white-hot climax rips through me, and I'm skyrocketed into erotic oblivion. The pleasure short-circuits my brain as he continues to fuck me.

He moves hard and fast, jackhammering into my pussy until he explodes. His body tenses, and he groans in pure animalistic satisfaction while pumping his warm cum as deep as he can go. He shudders and slumps on top of me briefly, keeping us connected with his cock still inside my pussy.

As he strokes my hair and holds me tight against him, my soul melts in contentment. I want to give him everything and I know that he'll do the same for me. He's the guy for me. When he pulls out, he picks me up and carries me to the bed so we can cuddle under the blanket together.

I was riding high for so long that I shiver as I come down. He holds me, whispering sweet nothings until I calm down enough to think rationally again.

"Are you okay?" he asks gently while brushing a damp strand of hair off my cheek.

We're facing each other, so I can easily tip my head and look at him. I smile softly. "Everything is better than okay. I love you."

Mike's eyes shine with emotion. "I love you too."

There's no hiding my happiness at his declaration, and I rest my forehead against his chest, giggling as he kisses my hair and nuzzles my cheek. I'm so relieved to say I love him, and to hear the words in return means everything to me. We stay in bed for a while, wrapped around each other, just enjoying our closeness and not wanting to break the spell of this moment. I'll tell him about my mom later. There's no way I'm going to bring it up tonight, and he'll understand why I waited. I just need to be close to him right now.

CHAPTER 5

MIKE

As I glance in the mirror and straighten my green tie for the St. Patrick's Day freeuse party, I realize this is one of the rare times since Willow moved in that I've been here alone. It's been nearly a month now and we're still in our honeymoon phase. We spend as much time together as we can, and for now, our two-days-a-week freeuse is extended to almost every day. At some point we might do only two days, but so far it's been almost non-stop.

Willow popped out to the store to get a bottle of wine for us to enjoy when we get back from the party. I have a fully stocked red wine cellar, but it turns out she's more of a rosé kind of girl. It's one of many things we're discovering about each other the longer we live together. We have plenty of differences, but nothing that can't be worked out.

As I put my suit jacket on, I think back to Halloween and marvel at how quickly our lives changed. She went from a shy virgin throwing herself into a gathering of experienced perverts—myself included—to now going as my partner and submissive. She's turned into a sexual goddess who has the confidence to ask for what she wants. Last week she blushed and hinted that she'd love it if I let some other guys at the party use her mouth, and I told her I'd think about it. The thought of watching her being a little slut for a bunch of men makes my cock throb, but I haven't told her yet that I'm willing to share her. I even found her red ribbon from the previous party, and it's in my pocket, along with a small bottle of lube. You never know when something like that will come in handy at a freeuse party.

I think part of her newfound confidence is from her showdown with her mother. She's grown so much in the last few weeks from standing up for herself. It was the right thing to do because her mother's attitude has taken a complete U-turn. She sent Willow a text this morning saying that they hadn't given me a chance, and they'd like Willow to bring me to dinner sometime. When Willow got the text, she stared at her phone for about five minutes before laughing and sending back a "we'll see" reply. I guess her parents realized that this time they really could lose their daughter and they want to make up for the past—not that I've even met her father since her mom seems to be speaking for both of them. If Willow wants to mend things with her mom, I'll be there to support her all the way.

I hear the front door open, followed by the sound of Willow in the kitchen putting away the wine. She walks into the bedroom as I'm putting my shoes on. The emerald green dress she's wearing is stunning. It's a short little thing with a cut up the side and it's covered in sparkly gems that draw attention to her curves. She looks radiant, and I'm going to enjoy showing her off at the party.

"Are you ready to go?" she asks.

I stand up and give her a soft kiss on the lips. "Yeah, I'm ready." She slips her hand down and rubs my cock, squeezing as it gets hard under her fingers.

"Naughty Kitten, stop that. You know if you keep doing that, I'll end up fucking you and we'll never make it to the party. Don't you want to suck on all those other cocks?"

She makes a sulky face at me, but in a second it's gone and she squeals. "You're sharing me?"

"Yep." I give her nose one last kiss. "Now let's go."

She laughs and can't seem to stop herself from giving my cock a soft pat before sashaying towards the door. "Come on, slow poke, this pussy needs some attention."

We're taking my car as hers feels too cramped for me. It's like I'm trapped in a sardine can, but it's perfect for her. She got the job she interviewed for, so it's worked out perfectly. Now in the morning, she gives me a kiss before she leaves, and can drive herself to a job she enjoys.

I climb into the car and when she settles into the passenger seat, I slip my hand between her legs to tickle her inner thigh and rub her pussy. She's not wearing any panties, as I commanded, and she's already wet. My fingers sink into her and she spreads her legs to give me more room and rocks her hips in time to my gentle thrusts.

"Fuck. I love you," she moans.

We're both comfortable professing our love now and we actually mean it, so I know she isn't just saying it because I'm fingering her. Sometimes we say it because one of us said something nice, or the other needs to hear it—or, like this, when one of us is doing our best to make the other come.

But we don't have time for that yet. I pull my hand back, and she straightens her dress with only a tiny sigh of frustration. "Soon, Kitten," we leave. It's only a twenty-minute drive to the party, and we'll get there as it starts to liven up.

"Do you miss it?" she asks. "Fucking other women at these parties?"

I think for a moment and shake my head. "You're a loving submissive and partner. Why would I want more than that? And everyone will see what a fantastic little slut you are and be jealous of me and wish they were in my place."

"And you won't change your mind about letting them use me tonight?" she asks with a grin.

I can't resist teasing her. "We'll see."

The rest of the drive goes by quickly, and as soon as we park by Cherry's mansion and get out, Willow walks around to my side and kisses me deeply.

"Coming to the party as your submissive and partner is so much better than that first night. This feels right." She gives me a coy smile. "And whatever happens tonight, I know you'll be looking after me."

"I love you," I say. "I never thought I could say that to anyone again. Thank you for being in my life."

Her eyes sparkle like she's getting teary, so I give her ass a gentle spank. A couple passing by shouts, "Leave it for inside!" and Willow giggles and hugs me. I take her hand. We're ready for another freeuse night.

CHAPTER 6

WILLOW

As we wait in the short line to check in for the party, it feels like an eternity has passed since that first night I came here without Alice. Halloween was only about four and a half months ago, but so much has changed for the better. I'm not even that upset over what happened with Oliver-the-Blessing-in-Disguise anymore because it brought me to Mike. Now I'm ready to have fun, and I have a little surprise planned for Mike. He'll find out in about ten seconds.

As we step to the front of the line, Bianca smiles at us and eyes my dress. "Hey, you're back! Love the dress—very festive."

I give her my thanks as we hand over our phones. This time she puts them both in the same locker together. "You're number 42. That's a lucky number!"

Mike chuckles, "Seems fitting."

While he's amusing himself, I give him the side eye to watch his reaction as I hold out my wrist to Bianca. "I'd like a green ribbon, please."

Mike's eyes take on a wicked glint. "Oh, you think that's how it is tonight, Kitten?"

A tingle of lust runs down my back as I give him my cutest, most innocent smile. "Yep. Whatcha gonna do about it?"

As soon as Bianca ties a bright green ribbon around my wrist, Mike picks me up and tosses me over his shoulder while I shriek with laughter. He immediately heads upstairs and I take the opportunity to fondle his ass.

He spanks me and growls, "Behave."

"What? You put these cute buns in front of me and don't expect me to touch them?"

A man with a naked woman on a leash passes us on the stairs and the woman calls out, "Good luck!" to me. I give her a little wave and giggle. "Thanks!"

Mike enters a bedroom and kicks the door closed and locks it before tossing me on the bed. I expect him to start stripping, but he takes hold of my hand with the green ribbon around my wrist and lifts it up in the air.

"Kitten, do you have something to ask me?"

I blink at him, and he looks pointedly at the green ribbon. A flicker of shyness makes me blush. Shit, is he really going to make me ask?

"I chose the green ribbon for you. Don't you want it?"

Before he responds, he turns my palm face up and kisses each pad of my fingers. When he speaks, his voice is husky with emotion. "I'd love nothing more than to claim your ass, but I told you at Thanksgiving you had to do something first."

Yeah, he told me I was going to have to ask for it. After everything I've done with Mike, it seems silly to be this vulnerable when discussing our sexual needs, but we've been dancing around this for so long, now that the moment is here, my confidence is wavering.

When he can tell I'm struggling to talk, he helps me to my feet for a deep kiss. Our tongues twist together and the longer the kiss goes on, the fuzzier my head gets. This is the man I love. I can do this.

Applying pressure on his chest, I push against him and take a step back. It's time to give him a strip tease. With slow, deliberate movements, I unzip the back of my dress, revealing the emerald lace bra underneath. Mike makes a rough sound and moves towards me as though drawn to me, but stops as I slip the straps of my dress off my shoulders and it slithers to the floor.

"Ask me," he demands and my breath hitches. There's no room to be shy with his intensity.

"Mike, will you fuck my ass?" I ask in a quiet voice. "I want you to be my first."

His expression darkens with lust, and he steps forward and tips my chin up. "I don't want to be your first." What? My lips part in confusion and he continues. "I want to be the only one who ever fucks your ass."

"Yes," I breathe out as a wave of longing engulfs me. "It's yours. Claim my last hole."

As soon as I utter the words, I know it's what I want, more than anything else. And I trust that he's going to make it pleasurable for me. When he lets go of my chin, he waves his hand in invitation, giving me permission to continue stripping. There's something powerful about being asked for it instead of him just taking it, and I suddenly understand why he made it a requirement. It's the last step to owning my sexuality and choosing what I want. I take a deep breath and unhook my bra, letting it fall to the ground. When I slip my shoes off, I'm naked and ready for him.

Before we get to business, I run my hands down his shirt. "Why aren't you naked?"

As he takes off his jacket, I move to stand in front of him and kneel while reaching for his belt to unbuckle it while he takes off his tie. With the belt hanging open, I look up at him as I undo the buttons to free his hard cock. Being on my knees for him always makes me submissive, and I love the slutty feeling I get from surrendering to him. I slowly stroke his shaft and open my mouth, waiting for his instructions.

"Take it deep and if you're a good girl, then this cock is going to be filling up your ass soon."

"Yes, Sir." I lean in and suck his cock into my mouth. Inch by inch, I work down on it until my nose is at the base. My mouth stretches to the limit, and lust simmers low in my belly. Before I met him, I never knew how amazing sex could be. Looking up into his eyes, I hold still as my throat works around his shaft.

When he takes hold of the back of my head, I relax and trust him to stop when the time is right. As he begins to pump his hips, fucking my throat with abandon, I play with my nipples and massage my breasts. My mind starts to empty and I'm just a hole for him to use. He's not gentle and I love every moment of it. Just when I think I can't take anymore, he pulls out. I draw in a huge gasp of air while he rests. Once my breathing is steady, he repeats the process once more.

Again and again, he fucks my mouth, and all I can think about is how I want this. I've given him my total trust and submission, and he's empowered me. I'm such a little slut and it's marvelous.

My pussy throbs and I get wetter the longer he fucks my mouth. If he doesn't fuck my ass soon, I'm going to end up begging him to breed my pussy instead.

When he removes his cock from my mouth again, instead of giving me a moment before starting over, he nods to the bed.

"On your knees. Head down, ass up. It's time to fuck that tight little hole."

Mmm, hell yeah! I scramble onto the bed while he digs something out of his pants pocket. I'm sure it's lube because my man likes to be prepared.

He climbs up behind me, gripping my ass in his hands and spreading my cheeks to examine my waiting holes. As he drips lubrication between my cheeks, I can't hold back my smile. See, I knew it would be lube.

He gets me nice and slippery and I look over my shoulder to watch him stroking some lube onto his cock. When he presses the tip of his cock against my tight ring, I gasp from the illicit pleasure. He applies pressure and then eases up, and I can tell he's teasing me.

"So, my little fucktoy, do you know what's about to happen?"

Uh, duh... "You're going to fuck my ass."

He leans forward and brushes his fingertips lightly over my breasts, then moves lower and rubs my clit before going back to my nipples again. When he rubs the head of his cock back and forth against my tight, hungry ass, pushing in a little more with each pass, I moan loudly.

"That's true," he says in a deep voice that has my body clenching with desire. "But after I've finally claimed all of you, do you know what's going to happen?"

It's difficult to think because all I want is for him to fuck me and ease the growing ache in my core. When I remain silent, he reaches down to rub my clit and chuckles as I cry out in desperation.

"I'll tell you what's going to happen. You..." He pauses and the ring of my ass stretches as he slowly sinks in. "Are going to become an anal slut."

I gasp as he fills me part way and stops again. "Then," he says with a groan as the thickest part of his cock stretches my ass wide and slides home, "you're going to get addicted to having my cock in your greedy little asshole and you're going to beg me for it."

"Ohhh," I moan. He's right. My head spins from the unfamiliar fullness, but it feels so damn good. I can already tell that when I get really submissive in the future, I'm going to beg him to fuck my ass.

When he pulls out slowly and pushes back in, I imagine being his freeuse toy for a day and all he does is fuck my ass without letting me come. I'll be the ultimate cum dumpster, just a hole for him to use. And I love it.

As my daydream consumes me, Mike fucks me steadily. The only sounds in the room are our mingled moans every time he sinks in fully. I don't know why I was so afraid of this; all I want now is to be filled again and again. As the pleasure builds, my moans get louder with every thrust.

"Rub your clit," he demands, and I immediately obey.

My face is smooshed into the bed, and I can easily picture how slutty I look. With him hitting all the right places, combined with being lost in the fantasy of being just a hole for him to use, my ass clenches around him, and I explode with ecstasy.

"I'm coming, oh fuuuuck," I wail into the mattress as my pussy pulsates from my climax. I rub my clit furiously as the pleasure peaks again. This is fucking awesome.

When my shaking stops, Mike holds my hips steady and picks up the pace, chasing his own release. As the powerful sensations take over my body again, I moan and give into the moment with total surrender. I never dreamed I'd like anal sex this much, but Mike is right, I could get addicted to this. I thrash against him, hot and wild. It's filthy and it makes me even more submissive.

Before long, Mike grunts and buries his cock deep as he comes in a rush of hot cream shooting deep into me. As he floods me, it triggers another small orgasm, and I moan in delight as his hips flex while he finishes unloading.

"Goddamn," Mike groans. "You're wonderful."

When he slowly eases his spent cock out of me, I whine at the loss. Instead of collapsing onto the bed next to me, he goes into the adjoining bathroom and I hear the faucet running. He comes back and sits beside me with a damp washcloth and helps me up onto my elbows before gently cleaning me. When I give him a dopey grin, he discards the washcloth in a thoughtfully-provided laundry basket against the wall and leans down for a kiss.

"How was that for you, Kitten?"

He crawls into bed and I nestle close to him. "I loved it, and you are totally right. I'm going to be an insatiable anal slut before long."

"Mmmm, my favorite kind of problem," he growls in a low, sexy tone that makes me shiver. "But now we rest. The night is still young."

And he's right. We have lots to experience tonight, but it's a hell of a good start to a party and I couldn't be happier. I'm already wondering what else is in store for us this evening.

CHAPTER 7

MIKE

Willow falls asleep next to me and I let her rest. I used her pretty hard, and the night is nowhere near finished. She's earned a break.

She sleeps peacefully for an hour, and when she wakes, I tell her to go shower and to come back naked. She can tell from my Dom voice that it's an order, and she has a spring in her step as she rushes off to freshen up.

When she gets back, I'm out of bed and wearing my boxers. As I walk over to the door, she glances at our clothes.

"We're not getting dressed?" I put my hand behind my back and I shake my head. "Come over here. I have the only thing you need to wear."

She looks at me curiously, and as she steps up, I bring my hand out in front of me. I open my fist, showing her the red ribbon from the last party. She'd taken the green one off to shower, and her hand trembles as I tie the red one around her wrist.

Her eyes go round. "This means I'm freeuse."

"Yes, it does."

Her eyes glow with lust. "Are you sure about this?"

She's so adorable. I want to kiss her and fuck her again, but I want her to know that she's free to explore her sexuality with me. She asked for this, and it's something that turns me on as well. "I am, and anyone who wants to use your mouth can do so. But your pussy is mine, and no one gets to use your ass but me."

I open the door and step out into the corridor and Willow follows me. She glances around and I can tell she's self-conscious.

"Don't be ashamed of your nakedness," I growl. "You're beautiful. Let everyone see that."

She straightens her back and stands tall, then tips her face up, clearly wanting a kiss. I brush my lips across hers and she sighs, "Yes, Sir."

As we make our way down the stairs, people start to notice her. So far, no one has approached us, but that might be the don't-touch-her vibe that I'm giving off. She may be freeuse, but I'm still in control.

We walk into the living room and it's basically an orgy. People are fucking on the furniture and on the floor. There's a group of watchers standing around, eager to join in but waiting for an opportunity. I scoop Willow up into my arms and carry her to the center of the room and place her down on the floor.

"Freeuse mouth for anyone who wants to use it," I say. "But ONLY the mouth."

I know how much she wants to be a proper freeuse cock slut for the night. Even though she's trying to look calm as the first guy approaches with his cock in his hand, I see the glee in her eyes. He's muscular and ripped, so I assume he's some type of bodybuilder.

"God damn, you're pretty," he groans as he slides his hand into her hair. "I'm going to love using your throat."

Before he has time to do anything else, she grabs his cock and starts jerking it as she guides it between her lips.

That's my good little cocksucker.

He's setting a quick pace, and I know that if he keeps it up, he's going to blow his load quickly.

"No coming yet. There will be plenty of time for that. Right now, just enjoy using her."

He nods and slows down, making sure that each thrust completely fills her mouth. I look down at Willow to make sure she's okay, and she has the same blissful serenity on her face that I've seen whenever she's blowing me. She's loving it and, as if to reassure me, she rubs my cock through my boxers.

"The lady has a free hand if anyone wants it."

Instantly, a new guy steps up—a nerdy-looking middle-aged guy. His cock is already hard as she wraps her fingers around him and rubs the tip with her thumb. His loud moan says he likes what she's doing. There's a nudge at my side and another guy tries to move me out of the way so that she can use her other hand. I stand behind her and watch as she brings all three of them close to an orgasm, making them pant and moan and fight not to lose control. When it looks like they can't take anymore, I speak up.

"Swap out, three more."

The guys want to come, but none of them argue. They all got pleasure and there's no shortage of other people here who will help finish them off. They all retreat and are replaced instantly.

I'm buzzing from being in control of so many people's pleasure, and while Willow's mouth isn't busy, I ask her a question.

"Why are you sucking all these guys?"

She smiles and wipes some pre-cum and saliva from her chin.

"Because you told me to, and I'm your freeuse toy."

I rub her neck and kiss the top of her head. "Why else?"

She lets out a happy sigh. "Because I'm a cock-hungry slut who wants it."

I don't know if she hears me say 'good girl' before the next guy thrusts between her lips.

Over the next half hour or so, twelve more guys get to enjoy her. She brings each of them to the edge, only for me to stop them. I know she wants their cum, but I have a plan.

"Kitten, stand for me," I command, and she springs to her feet. I lift her up and carry her to a low table, over to the side. We have a small crowd of people watching now and they follow us, wanting to know what's going to happen next.

I lay her down on her back, her head hanging off the end of the table. I run my fingers up her thighs before spreading her legs and stepping away..

"Touch yourself. Show everyone how wet and horny you are."

She slides her fingers over her pussy before rubbing her clit. She moans loudly and her other hand moves up to her breasts and squeezes her nipples. When she pinches them hard, her gasping noises make my cock throb. Her eyes are focused on me, even though there are at least twenty people in various states of nakedness standing close and watching her.

I remove my boxers and my cock springs up. It's been difficult to wait, but I know she's truly ready for me now.

"I'm going to fuck you in front of these people and show them all that you're mine."

She nods, still rubbing herself and still locking eyes with me.

"Ask for it," I demand.

"Will you fuck me, Sir? Please use my holes and make me your freeuse slut."

"Good girl."

I pounce on her, my cock driving deep into her pussy. I pin her arms down so she's completely under my control. Every move I make will drive her wild, and I don't intend to be gentle.

Her eyes roll back in her head as if she's losing focus. I want her to be wonderfully empty-headed and give her the bliss that she craves from not being in control.

"Kitten. Eyes on me." She lifts her head slightly and her eyes flicker open as I continue. "I'm going to fuck you. I am going to make you come. You're going to shout my name as your body shakes and you give yourself to me. But you know what's going to happen after that?"

With each sentence, I ram into her, my cock throbbing as I get close to losing myself in her.

"No, what?" she gasps.

"All these guys watching you are hard and stroking. They're all going to come for you. All over your pretty face."

She lets out a guttural moan.

"Do you want that?" I ask.

"Yes. All that cum. All for me."

She knows I love it when she talks extra filthy.

As happy as I am to share her, there's a possessive part of me wants to fuck her so thoroughly that she can't even think of the other guys.

I let go of one of her arms and give her breast a slap. I know it doesn't have to be hard. The surprise of it will be enough to make her desperate and needy.

"Again," she cries.

"No, I decide what to do. You're not in charge."

She moans, "Please Sir, can I have another?"

I slap her other breast, then pin her down again, furiously hammering into her.

"Oh fuck. OH FUCK. Please, can I come? Please? I'm going to come. Can I come?"

I glance at the onlookers and see that they are all stroking along; even a couple of women are jilling off.

"Come for me, Kitten."

It's like the words set off a chain reaction. Her back arches and her body shakes as she cries out my name. Her pussy clenches around me, and I have to use all my strength to keep her pinned to the table.

Just then, the first onlooker comes. It's the nerdy guy, and he lets out a groan before shooting his load over Willow's lips.

"Oh, fuck yes. More," she whimpers as she licks his cum.

The guy to our right lets out a moan and a spray of cum hits the side of her face. The next guy steps forward and aims at her lips, getting most of it into her mouth and only a little on her forehead. It's like the floodgates are open and within seconds she's getting coated in cum. Guy after guy steps forward and shoots over her face and chest, even into her hair.

I continue to fuck her as I watch, keeping myself on the edge until the pleasure is too much.

"Kitten..."

"Yes?"

"You're mine."

I erupt inside her, slamming into her again and again as I give her every drop of cum that I have. As if from far away, I hear the audience whoop and cheer. But all my attention is on my girl. Releasing her arms, I pound into her and claim her for myself until I'm spent. Pleasure wracks my body, and I sink onto her as the last few spasms ripple down my spine.

"Oh fuck, Mike. Fuck. That was so good. Oh god. So much cum. And my Sir used me in front of everyone."

Wrapping my arms around her, I pick her up as I stand. My mouth claims hers, hungry for her kisses, and I'm not going to stop until I get my fill. Her legs hook behind my waist and she slides her arms around my neck. I can't think of anything except how lucky I am to have this amazing woman.

As the rush of the moment fades, I carry her from the room. Her ribbon falls to the floor, loosened during the fucking. We don't need it now. I'll be the only man with her for the rest of the night. I take her back to the room and we fall into bed, kissing and snuggling.

I expect us to stay here for the night, but after a few minutes she asks to go home.

"I want to fall asleep in your arms, in our bed. And wake up in our house and have you make me breakfast and enjoy how fucking happy I am."

That's all I want too. We get dressed and head downstairs, not caring how disheveled we are. When we stumble out of the house, the cool air revives us a little. I slip my arm around her as we walk to the car.

"Mike. Can you wait a moment?"

She steps away from me and walks over to a woman standing near the end of the driveway, and asks her, "Hey, are you OK?"

The woman is young, about Willow's age. She's staring at the building behind us. She's wearing a green hat and a silver dress, as if she was going to a party.

"This is the..." she lowers her voice to talk to Willow, but I can still hear her. "Freeuse party, right?"

Willow nods. "First time here?" she asks.

The woman grins and glances over at me nervously before looking back at Willow. "That obvious? I was supposed to be here earlier, but I got lost. And now, with all the noise and the people, I'm not sure I can go in. Is it, you know, fun?"

Willow moves closer to her. "Yeah. It's great. It's truly amazing. I was like you and nervous my first time. But luckily I found a great guy, and he made it so special for me." Willow pauses and blows me a kiss. "You might not get that, but everyone in there is having a great time. So I say go in, and don't do anything you don't want to do. Heck, just stand and watch if that's your thing. But it's an incredible experience, and it's changed my life."

The woman looks shocked Willow is talking from the heart about a sex party, but I know Willow means everything she's saying. It's where we met, and it's where she found her kinks and owned her sexuality. The freeuse party changed our lives.

"Wow, that's quite a recommendation. You know what? I think I will go in. Thank you."

Willow watches her as she heads towards the house and disappears inside before joining me again. She wraps her arms around me and rests her head on my chest.

"I hope she finds someone as wonderful as you are," she says, and then laughs. "But hopefully younger, 'cause it's way past your bedtime."

"Oh, yeah?" I chase her to the car, and when I catch her, she laughs and shrieks before I give her a deep kiss. Opening the door for her, I smile as she wiggles her ass at me as she climbs in. By the time I walk around to the driver's side, she's leaning back with her eyes closed.

"Kitten?"

"Yeah?" She cracks her eyes open.

"I love you."

She smiles and sinks into her seat. "I love you too, with all my heart."

She's already asleep before we leave the driveway. While she dozes, I realize that I've made this journey home so many times before and I've always been happy and satisfied. But on all those occasions, it never felt as perfect as this. In the past, sex was always the thing that made me most happy. Now my joy is sitting next to me. And this... this is only the start of our journey.

EPILOGUE

ONE YEAR LATER

WILLOW

I'm lying on my back on my bed in shorts and a T-shirt, staring at the smooth ceiling with no cracks as Alice giggles through the phone. "Wait, wait, are you serious? Your mother actually apologized for being a shitty mother your entire life?"

"Yup." I laugh with her and check the clock on the nightstand again. Mike should be home from work any minute now.

"Holy shit. That's huge."

Her incredulous tone makes me laugh again. "I know, right? She started going to therapy when she realized she was going to lose me. She's even got my dad in couples counseling. When we had Christmas dinner with them, they asked us a ton of questions about how we were doing. It wasn't all about them."

Alice sighs. "Well, at least your baby will have grandparents in their life. The extra support might be nice."

I rub my growing baby bump and smile. This was another thing my mother was wrong about. Mike definitely wants our baby. We didn't try to get pregnant, but we were both tickled when it happened by accident. And every day he reminds me how much he loves me, and the baby growing inside me.

I hear the garage door open and I quickly say goodbye to Alice. "Hey, I'll catch you later. Mike just got home. Next time, we're only talking about you. I need to know what's going on with your man."

Alice laughs, "You got it. We'll catch up later," and ends the call.

"Hi, Kitten."

I put my phone down. Mike is standing in the doorway, unbuttoning his dress shirt, looking completely yummy in his business casual attire. The hunger in his eyes makes me wet, and I desperately want him inside me. I pat the spot on the bed beside me. "Hey, you're home! Come cuddle with me?"

He continues stripping. "Do you know what day it is?"

I shake my head no, playing innocent, because I know exactly what day it is. It's St. Patrick's Day, and we both agreed that I was going to be his freeuse slut all weekend in celebration. "Can't say that I do," I tease. "Remind me again."

In response, he raises his eyebrow at me while undoing the buckle of his belt and slipping it free from the loops of his pants.

"Really?" he says while waving it at me. "I think someone needs to be reminded what a little slut she is. Get on your hands and knees."

Mmm, this is going to be good. I do as I'm told as he finishes removing his clothes. He peels them down to his knees before climbing on the bed behind me.

"Now Kitten," he says as he rubs the tip of his cock up and down my wet pussy. "You better be prepared to beg like you've never begged before if you want to come this weekend. I've got a need to use my pregnant slut until she's dripping with my cum and mindless from not having an orgasm."

Oh fuck! Before I can say anything, he buries his cock deep into my pussy and starts thrusting. I cry out in pleasure and move my head down to the bed, opening myself up wider for him. We both have busy lives, so we don't get to do freeuse as often as we'd like, but we take full advantage of it whenever we both have a weekend with nothing going on.

His fingers dig into the flesh of my hips as he takes me roughly, and his dirty talk makes me dizzy. "Fucking my pregnant slut. I'm going to fill you with so much cum, you'd get knocked up if you weren't already pregnant. Let's see how well you remember to beg while I use this tight pussy."

When he holds my shoulder down, forcing my face all the way into the mattress, it changes the angle of entry and his cock drills in deeper and harder. The friction against my pussy walls plus the tip of his cock hitting deep inside me makes it so damn good, my whole body shakes as the pleasure builds in layers.

"May I please come, Sir?" I pant, unable to get enough air.

I squeak in surprise when he slaps my ass hard. "Nope. I haven't decided if you're coming at all tonight."

Shit, fuck. I try to hold my orgasm back, but he's making it difficult as he continues fucking me and slapping my ass. Each spank is a pleasurable pain that heightens my arousal.

Finally, it gets to be too much and my whole body tenses, but I fight the urge to release, not yet asking to come because I'm certain that he's not going to say yes.

When he reaches under me to brush against my clit, I scream into the bed and curse as I try to hold in my impending climax. "Can I come, please, please, please? Oh god. I'm going to come!"

I writhe under him and right before I come, he pulls out.

"Noooo!" My body spasms from the lack of orgasm, and he continues to rub my clit just enough to keep me desperate.

Mike bends forward, resting his lips next to my ear, still fingering me without mercy. "That was just the appetizer, Kitten." He straightens and slaps my ass one last time. "Now get on your back."

As soon as I roll over, I expect him to fuck me again, but he lies next to me and rubs on my belly. I watch with curiosity as his hand slowly creeps up, pushing at my shirt and exposing my breasts. He plays with one of my sensitive nipples, gently squeezing. "My fertile goddess's body is incredible."

He takes the nipple in his mouth as his hand glides down my body and between my legs. I moan softly as pleasure radiates from my breasts to my clit. He teases the swollen bundle of nerves with a light touch that drives me absolutely mad. Right when I'm at the point of begging him again, he pushes two fingers into my pussy.

The pleasure makes me mewl out, "Oh, fuck, please can I come?"

Saying nothing, he keeps up a steady, delicious rhythm until I can't hold it in any longer, and I beg some more. "P-please? Oh god, I need to come, please?"

In answer, he increases the pace, curling his fingers in a "come hither" motion while rubbing my clit. As pleasure surges through me, he sucks harder on my nipple. I'm so close to coming, I can hardly think straight. Every part of me throbs with need.

Without a word, he pushes deeper, hitting that spot inside me that always makes me lose control. I moan as my hips buck off the bed. His thumb circles my clit, sending waves of pleasure through me. I can't take it anymore. I need to come.

"Fuck, oh god. I'm going to come. Let me come!" I beg him.

He finger fucks me harder and faster. "Come for me," he groans. "Show me how much you want it."

As soon as he gives me permission, I explode. My body shudders and my pussy squeezes his fingers tightly. It's one of the strongest orgasms I've ever experienced. He continues rubbing my clit, refusing to release me until I'm spent and gasping for breath.

"That's it, kitten," he whispers. "You look so fucking beautiful when you come like that."

My head is still spinning from the intensity of my orgasm as he moves between my splayed legs. This time, he enters me slowly, with reverence, as his gaze locks with mine. He kisses me deeply, and I feel drugged with lust. The way I respond to Mike has always been intense, and I love him with all my heart.

His voice is thick as his words echo my thoughts. "I love you so much, Kitten."

I moan and arch against him as we make love. As we kiss, our soft moans fill the air. Our bodies surge together in perfect harmony.

His lips graze my neck, a whisper of a touch that ignites a fire within me. The combination of his tender lovemaking after the raw passion he unleashed in me by calling me his fucktoy and threatening to edge me is exactly what I love about him. He knows how to thrill me and I always feel desired.

As we continue to rock together, the heat builds within me and I'm ready to explode again. He thrusts harder, making me moan, "Oh god, I'm going to come."

"Not yet, Kitten," he says, and I whimper in desperation as I try to hold back my orgasm. He shifts to thrust even deeper, and my entire body quivers from the exquisite pleasure.

I claw at his back, wrapping my legs around him and drawing him further inside me, desperately craving every inch of him. Then, something magical happens. For a split second, I feel as though I leave my body—as if our souls are becoming one. When he sinks deep into me, my entire being lights up, and I'm caught up in wave after wave of bliss. It's unlike anything I've ever experienced before.

I cry out, unable to form words as pure ecstasy rolls over me. Mike follows me over the edge seconds later, emptying himself with a shuddering groan. He fucks his cum back up into me, unloading everything he's got as my body floats in a sea of pleasure.

When he slows down, I unwrap my legs, and he moves to the side. We lie there in each other's arms, neither of us speaking.

I know my man, though; when I look at him, I can tell he's trying to hide a smile.

"Mike?" I ask. "What are you up to?"

When he grins widely, I know I was right as he says, "Yep, you'd definitely be pregnant right now if you weren't already."

I laugh at how silly he is. Our lips find each other's as his fingertips play lightly on the skin of my stomach, tracing the outline of my baby bump.

"For now," he murmurs. "But with how much my Kitten loves to beg me to breed her, I think we're going to have a large family."

I'm not sure he's joking, and my heart skips a beat. "Oh yeah? I don't know, you're kind of old. Won't you be too weak to knock me up again?" I giggle as his eyes widen in mock outrage.

And then my naughty and caring man whispers in my ear. "I'm never going to be too old to breed my slutty fucktoy. You're going to be a pregnant, dripping mess all the time if I have anything to say about it."

His words send a rush of desire through me. Shit, I love that idea. When his cock surges against my side, I can tell he likes the thought as well.

I push on his chest, forcing him onto his back, and lift an eyebrow in challenge. "Well then, Sir. Let's see you prove it."

And with that, I climb on top of him, ready to have the most exciting and sexy St. Patrick's Day ever while I milk him for all his cum. Life doesn't get any better than this.

The End

HOLIDAY HEAT COLLAB SERIES

Matt (Alec) Lake and April (Lacey) Cross have another series together. It's another super spicy romantic erotica. Check out the bundle.

5 Kinky Holiday Stories. A couple finds each other in their dreams, but can it be love?

Magic isn't real...

Noelle and Nick live a continent apart but on the holidays they keep falling asleep and visiting a dream world where they have two hours to do whatever they want to each other.

What starts out as two strangers enjoying each other's bodies turns into a journey of domination, sharing, freeuse, and exhibitionism.

They explore newfound kinks together and the thrills drive a deep connection, but dreams aren't real ... right?

Suspend your sense of reality and enjoy the fantasy in this fun and flirty series set around the holidays.

Includes:

Playing in a Winter Wonderland

Playing in a Lovers' Paradise

Playing in the Shamrock Bar

Playing at the Egg Hunt

Playing for Keeps

Plus a bonus erotic short for the bundle

Note: This story is dual point of view with April Cross writing Noelle and Alec Lake writing Nick. Enjoy the experience of two distinct voices telling the story while both authors bring their own writing style and creativity to give the characters life.

These short stories contains explicit encounters between consenting adults and features elements of BDSM, degradation, freeuse, spanking, sharing, and combines fantasy with real life. Reader discretion advised. And let's be real here, it's just a bunch of sexy fun.

Get all 5 books at:

https://stories.april-cross.com/zonholidayheat

About April Cross and Matt Lake

April Cross (also Lacey Cross)

Writer of spicy stories... okay, I'll be honest, most of my stuff is ghost pepper spicy. I started writing wife sharing stories before branching out to longer romantic erotica series and stories. I write power play stories with guys who demand to be in control.

Website:

https://april-cross.com/

My BDSM Books:

https://books.april-cross.com/

Newsletter signup:

https://books.april-cross.com/freeusesignup

Interested in filthy wife sharing erotic? Check out my Lacey Cross books:

https://author.to/laceycross

Matt Lake (also Alec Lake)

Writer of fact and fiction blended together into Erotica. I write freeuse erotica and love exploring the fantasy.

Website:

https://mattlakewriter.com/

My freeuse books:

https://www.amazon.com/author/mattlakewriter

Newsletter signup:

https://books.aleclake.co.uk/freeusefreebie

Want more than just freeuse? Check out my Alec Lake erotica:

https://author.to/aleclakebooks